HIDING BEHIND ROBES

A Novel by
J.L. Canfield

For information, or to order additional copies, please contact:

Beacon Publishing Group
P.O. Box 41573 Charleston, S.C. 29423
800.817.8480| beaconpublishinggroup.com

Publisher's catalog available by request.

ISBN-13: 978-1-949472-38-7

ISBN-10: 1-949472-38-7

Published in 2021. New York, NY 10001.

First Edition. Printed in the USA.

HIDING BEHIND ROBES

Table of Contents

Chapter One

"Look Samyn, decide. Who's it going to be?" Captain Richard Martin stood behind his desk, patting a pack of cigarettes against his hand.

"Why does it have to be one of them?" Though Samyn was an occasional smoker, it wasn't nicotine he was craving. Philip Samyn had been off the java for five months, but this nonsense stirred up a desire for the fiery liquid. He shifted his gaze to the window. After a week of rain, the sun was shining on Richmond again. *There s a big storm brewing in here. Any second now...* He did a quick glance up, half expecting to see ominous clouds above him.

"Because the higher ups have said, make changes. Cut the budget. Eliminate two people from the investigating section. They didn't say I had to be the rotten guy. So one unlucky detective gets to be picked by you and Rodriguez gets to choose the other from his team."

Samyn adjusted his 6'4 frame in the chair. He needed to stare over Captain Martin's shoulder. If he kept looking at Martin, he would lose control of his building desire to intimidate him with his height and shoulder width. Martin might outrank Samyn, but the Lieutenant had a good eight inches or so on the Captain in size.

He held his emotions in check by stroking his chin with his left hand. His right arm laid across his chest, supporting his left elbow. The outer office normally buzzed with partner chatter, phone calls, and printers printing. Now it was subdued. Everyone working there sensed a dangerous storm was coming.

Samyn's stony eyes focused on the captain's face. "What if I choose to retire?"

"You can't retire." The words exploded into the room. The pack of rolled tobacco sticks fell from Martin's hand. His body shook and his hands moved spastically, as they tried to find anything to punch, choke, or both. Finding nothing to squeeze, he opted to push everything off his desk before glaring at Samyn. He huffed and puffed through tight locked jaws.

"Yes I can, I've got my time in. I can walk." The voice was soft but the lieutenant's face was hard, no emotion showed in his eyes nor did his voice give any away. He seemed devoid of feelings. Even someone who knew him well could not tell if he was bluffing or not.

"You don't get it." Martin shook his head. His undisguised disgust filled all available space. "Reichman suggested you get a goodbye letter. Chief Miller said no. The department can't lose its golden boy, he said."

The Captain picked up the pack, bounced it against his hand and extracted one. His pinpointed glare never strayed from the man sitting in front of his desk. He took a sniff of the rolled tobacco and continued.

"When you solved that missing vase case, you also cleared up some murders that hell, we didn't even know had happened. The officer-in-charge filed those cases as accidental deaths."

Martin dropped the cigarette, picked up some papers, then threw them down on his desk. He hunched over the desk. His gym sneaker breath hung over Samyn's abdomen.

"You're not going anywhere. You're the department's golden goose right now and yes, we will use you to get more funding for the force. I'll be pushing that money comes here."

Martin shrugged with mock sorrow. "Sorry pal. There was a time they wanted you out. Now the muck-mucks want to keep you. But the city accountants say someone has to go. So instead of me choosing, you get too. Who do you want to part with?" Martin drew the battle line.

Deep creases formed on Samyn's face as his eyes narrowed to fine slits. His body tightened. Like a dedicated fighter who has vowed to stay in the ring, he stood up and planted his feet. "I chose Baldwin." He stared at Martin, daring him to argue.

"He's not on your team." Martin slammed his hands down on the desk. The surprised coffee cup spit out some of its contents.

"You stated I get to choose, but you didn't say they had to be on my team." Samyn wanted to grab the mug and drink its contents before more got wasted. He kept his hardened gaze on his boss.

"Damn it Samyn you knew what I meant. Don't make this a pissing contest. Pick one from your group and tell me by Friday morning who to draw up papers on."

Before Samyn said anything, the door to Martin's office opened enough for an eye to peer in. "Sir, there's a phone call."

"I told you not to disturb me." Martin's loud voice increased its volume.

"Yes sir, but this call is kinda urgent, and it's not for you, sir. It's for Lt. Samyn. It's the Bishop of the Diocese, sir. He's asking for Lt. Samyn."

"The bishop? Impressive Samyn. Who else do you know?" Martin's lip curled up at its right corner.

"Never met him." Samyn's brow wrinkled. He gave the cup of coffee a fleeting look before he turned to face the person who stayed hidden behind the door. "What does he want?"

"He didn't say. Only asked for you and said there was an urgent need to speak with you. He's holding on line three."

Martin nodded towards his phone. "Well, don't keep the church waiting. Pick up the phone. Anything else?" He raised his eyebrow at the half face.

"No, sir."

"Then get back to work."

A frantic shutting sound muffled the yes sir Martin expected the intruder to say.

Samyn picked up the cup and took a deep whiff of it. He sat it down, then straightened his tie and stood at attention. The phone's receiver nestled against his ear. He leaned over and took one more sniff from the cup on Martin's desk before hitting the flashing button.

Martin snickered. "Even the church muck-mucks want you. Damn Samyn, you are one much-desired piece of flesh."

"Bite me." Samyn paled. "No sir, I was talking to my boss who thinks he's God. Yes sir, this is Lt. Detective Philip Samyn."

What followed was a few uh's ok's and I see's. Samyn gave no facial signals of what the other party was saying. Martin leaned back in his chair with his feet on the desk and his hands interlaced behind his head. His fingers tapped against his skull.

Samyn knew it was killing his boss not to know what was being said, and he loved it. Savoring this moment was the only way Samyn was able to speak with politeness to a church leader. He didn't know if his animosity was greater for his boss or for Catholic priests.

"Ok, sir. My team and I will be there shortly. Yes, no flashing lights and we'll use the back entrance to the parish." Samyn hung up the phone. He cocked his right eyebrow up and looked down at Martin. His expression was tough to read.

"Well? What does for local highness want from you?"

"Something has happened at St. Stephens. He wouldn't go into much detail. But his eminence has requested my team, you know the one you want to break up, to come over now."

Martin dropped his feet and leaned forward. His demeanor changed. "You better get going then. But don't think this lets you off the hook. You still have to pick one of yours to get axed and I want an answer by Friday morning."

Samyn walked to the door, his right hand raised. "Whatever." His mind was on what the bishop didn't say but had implied.

He headed towards the outer area's entrance door. "Blake, Moore, saddle up. We're going to church."

The words flew over his shoulder. His long legs kept moving him to the exit.

Moore shoved some papers in a file and placed it in the bin on his desk. "Samyn's going to church and it's not Easter. Either something big must be happening there or spring's bringing in some miraculous changes." He whistled, "When The Saints Go Marching In," as he and Blake made their way to the car where Samyn waited.

Chapter Two

"Okay boss, you want to clue us in on why you, a person who avoids religion, decided we need to go to church, on a weekday morning?" Detective Sargent Melvin Moore elbowed their sidekick, Officer Frank Blake, in the ribs. He flashed his most affable grin at Samyn.

"Not just a church, but the large Catholic Church where the bishop resides," Blake informed Moore. "Perhaps we should have dressed in our formal attire for this call." They both broke their solemn, respectful looks with chuckles. They were standing by their car waiting for Samyn to give them any information about this trip to church.

"I like you, Blake. You are proving yourself droll enough to keep company with me." He slapped the younger man on the back. "See Boss, I told you he had a sense of humor, we just had to coax him out of his shell."

Samyn had been studying the outside of the building in front of them and ignoring the chitchat between his partners. "Has either of you been inside this place before?"

Moore responded first. "Nope. I was raised Baptist. My mom wouldn't let me associate with people who didn't shout amen in church." He nodded at Blake. "What about you? You've proven yourself to be a quiet, regimented, and devoted follower of rules." He made a framing square with his fingers, looked through it and continued his commentary. "Yes, I can see you as a good catholic, rote prayers, Hail Mary's and all."

"Hey, you just…" Blake scrunched up his eyes, studied Moores 'face, and laughed. "Ok, Ok, I got it, you're joking. It's not my fault I have a weak sense of humor. I'm Presbyterian. We're not allowed to laugh, especially at Grandma's house."

Moore leaned away from Blake. "Are you serious? You can't be serious?" He studied the fair skinned, lightly freckled Blake who wore his most solemn look and held up the two fingers representing scout's honor. Moore wrinkled up the right side of his face, only the lower white of his eye was visible in his deep brown skin. He cocked his head. His mouth wanted to wear his usual grin. His lips instead puckered and showed their pink insides. "You gotta be joking now." Blake shook his head no.

"Really, I'm Presbyterian and my grandmother said laughter was the work of the devil." He turned his palms skyward.

Moore ran his hand over his close cropped head. "Well, that does explain a lot about you, my friend." His grin came back out.

"So Lieutenant, why are we here?" Blake asked.

"The bishop called and requested our presence. He didn't say much, only arrive with no fanfare and go to the back of the parish. Is this the back of the parish?"

The church bells chimed. They announced the third hour of the afternoon. Doors opened at nearby buildings. Students made their escape from the rooms that confined them during the day. The peaceful quietness lifted, and electric energy replaced it. Students shouldering backpacks headed towards their rides to freedom. Others with sporting equipment made their way towards the gym. As quick as the serene air had left, it returned and resettled itself.

A nun who had observed the men approached them. "You seem lost. Perhaps I can help you." Her face wore a lukewarm smile, her piercing grey eyes reflected nothing.

"Thank you, Sister. I bet you can help. We're looking for the parish." Lt. Samyn kept his face expressionless.

They sized each other up. "Follow me, please. I'll take you to the right building. And for future reference, I am the Mother Superior." She reared her shoulders back and thrust out her chin. It was clear to the men their ignorance of who she was would not be tolerated again.

"So noted ma'am." Samyn cocked his head but kept his eyes on her face. His offering of respect was rejected. She pivoted. Her wimple flared out. The long dark cloth struck Samyn's chest.

"Protestants."

Moore whispered to Blake. "And proud to be one."

Samyn coughed into his hand. He didn't want the nun to hear his chuckle. He knew too many stories about nuns and rulers.

"What building were we at, Mother Superior?" Samyn said.

"The lower school." She turned her head enough to cast a disgusted look on the men behind her. Her tone told them who she thought they were.

Shock blazed all over Blake's face. "She assumes we're child predators," he mouthed to Moore. He reached into his pocket where he carried his ID. Moore placed a hand on his arm and shook his head. He whispered from the side of his mouth there must be a reason why Samyn had not shown his credentials. Blake mouthed okay and pulled out a pack of gum instead.

They walked in silence past two more buildings before stopping at one which looked like an old gothic mansion.

"This is the parish. Whom do you seek here?" The mother superior placed herself in front of the building's entrance. One hand tapped against her leg while she waited for an answer.

Samyn looked around.

"Tell me whom you are here to see and I will direct them this way." The nun raised her voice and patted her foot.

He stood about a foot taller than her, but Samyn wished himself taller. Nuns, no matter how small, had always made him feel little. *More height won t give you more courage. Swallow your fear and go inside.*

"Many thanks ma'am for showing us the right place. We can find the person who we wish to speak with." Samyn maneuvered around the nun and opened the door. He motioned to Moore and Blake to go in. When they had entered, he followed. Before shutting the door, he waved to the nun. "Thanks again, sister. We couldn't have found this place without you." He ducked inside before her icy glare could penetrate his skin.

They were standing in a compact room. On the left wall was a row of old-fashioned coat hooks which held an assortment of umbrellas, sweaters, and scarves with shoes lined up underneath them. The right-hand wall held a framed print of Rembrandt's work called *The Prodigal Son Returns*. Samyn's face registered surprise. "Of all the works…"

"Where to now, boss?" Moore raised an eyebrow.

"Not sure. I thought someone would meet us. I guess we hunt for the person who wants us." Samyn pointed to the doorway in front of them. "No, where to go but forward."

They entered another room. Much larger than the other, where a wooden trestle table with 12 chairs and no obvious exit greeted them. Samyn almost collided with a thin man of average height, dressed in clerical attire whose sudden appearance startled him.

"Lieutenant Detective Samyn?" He said.

"Yes sir, and you are…?"

"Monsignor Talmano, I'm was out front until I remembered you were asked to come to the back." He swiped his hands on his robe before he offered one to shake. "It's good of you to come. Thank you for being discreet. I assume no one saw you come in?" He kept out his hand.

Lt. Samyn looked at it before he took it. "No one, but the mother superior who brought us here."

The monsignor slapped his forehead. "Oh dear God! How did you meet her? She is not near here around this time. She's the school administrator."

"We had no idea where we were going. Your buildings are not marked, and none of us are familiar with this…. campus, church." He waved his hand around. "She found us behind the lower school."

"Forgive me. I'm sorry for my outburst. Yes, I guess if you are on unfamiliar terrain, signs are needed. But of all the ones to find you…" He looked down. "I'm sorry but this a matter we are trying to keep as quiet as possible and the Mother Superior is…"

Out of his mouth came a rush of air "Well let's say demanding, irritating, and presumes her title gives her control of all she purveys." His depleted lungs took in some air.

Moore grinned at the monsignor. "In my church, we call them nosy old busybodies. They would love the title of mother superiors. I'm Detective Sargent Melvin Moore. Pleased to meet you, sir." He offered his meaty palm to the smaller man.

Monsignor Talmano coughed to cover his laugh. "Yes, well, I guess then I should be thankful only one nun is given that name. I couldn't handle more of them." His eyes twinkled as he pumped Moore's hand.

"Amen to that. It's hard work keeping them all happy."

"If you gentlemen will come with me please, I'll take you to his eminence who is waiting for you." He moved to the far wall, laid hands on the center inserts and parted the pocket doors with minor effort. They slid with stealth into the walls. Before them laid fresh territory.

The monsignor led them to what was the receiving parlor back when this place was built. On either side were doors which opened into rooms. The area itself, and the path into it, was adorned with mahogany square panels framed by cherry wood molded edge two by twos. A carpet oriental runner, which had seen better days, covered most of the wood flooring. The hallway ended at the massive oversized front door, which had lead glass inserts on both sides and a lead glass arch above. Sunlight reflected off the glass. It danced on the bare floor and rested on the covered parts. Five feet from the door, on the left-hand side were three steps, and a landing with more stairs above it. All held in place by an ornate handrail also made from cherry.

"This way, if you please." The monsignor proceeded up the first three steps and stopped on the landing. "His eminence rarely receives guests in his private rooms. He uses his office, but this matter that requires discretion. Please, gentlemen, listen and do as he asks. Also, if you see the mother superior again, tell her you were here to discuss the church making a donation to your police fund."

He continued up the stairs with three policemen in tow, too puzzled to remark on his last words.

Chapter Three

Monsignor Talmano stopped at the end of the hall in front of a closed door. He turned to face the men behind him.

"Gentlemen, this is where I was instructed to leave you. Behind that door is The Most Reverend Seamus O'Malley, Bishop of the Diocese of Richmond. You should address him as 'Your Excellency'."

Monsignor passed his hands against his robes. He glanced at the door, lowered his voice and continued with his instructions.

"Please remember sirs, you are here in secret. Nothing spoken to you can be shared with the media and, well… I believe the legal term for this conversation will fall under plausible deniability." The monsignor stared at the door, hesitated, then raised his hand up to knock. "I'll be waiting for you at the end of this hallway." He rapped against the door.

"Please listen with care. We need your help." He whispered the words as he walked away.

Moore bunched up his lips. "I'm not liking all this secrecy, Samyn. Too cloak and dagger for a church. Why are we here?"

"You may enter." An unknown voice gave the command.

Samyn shook his head. "No idea. I guess we'll find out now."

He turned the knob and pushed. The door opened with such determined quietness it shook Samyn. His gut warned him something was wrong. With boldness, he entered the room followed closely by Moore and Blake.

A man standing by the fireplace equaled Samyn in height. He had an aged, but still in shape, athlete's build, covered by a plain black suit with a black shirt, no tie but the white collar worn by clergy. His face suggested he could be no older than forty-five.

The man in the clerical garb extended his hand palm down as they approached. Samyn reached out to shake it. Blake elbowed him. He signaled with his eyes Samyn was to kiss the ring. Samyn placed his hand under the palm of the Bishop, turned it and shook his hand instead. Blake's eye's widened at this action.

The bishop laughed. "I see you be establishing your terms. I'm guessing you, sir, are Lt. Detective Philip Samyn and these are your cronies." His lyrical tone told them his name was not the only Irish thing he carried with him in life. Samyn tilted his head, shrugged his shoulder and let his lips form a half smirk.

"I would like to say it is my pleasure to meet you, but the circumstances requiring us to talk are not ones that brings joy." He pulled his hand away from Samyn's grip and offered it to the other men. "And may I have your names sirs, so I know how to address you?"

Moore took the Bishop's hand. "You may call me Sargent Melvin Moore, sir. Moore, if you're more comfortable with that." They sized each other up. The bishop signaled his approval with a dip of his head.

"Your Excellency, I am Officer Francis Blake." He bowed before taking the Bishop's hand where he placed a kiss on the ring.

"Are you Catholic?"

"No sir. I'm Presbyterian by upbringing, but I have studied most of the world's religions. Besides, my mother taught to show respect to the leaders of all churches." He kept his eyes lowered.

"Well, I guess I can forgive you for being a Presby, it's catholic extra light. As you're not one of us, there's no need to show deference by kissing a ring." He winked at Samyn and chuckled.

Blake flushed and raised his eyes to the bishop's face. "Sorry sir, I did not, I mean it won't…"

Now, why did you call us here?" He stared at the bishop hard. He was looking for any sign that the blank face worn by this man was cracking.

O'Malley leaned back in his chair. "Let's start again, shall we?"

Samyn relaxed a little. "Let's start at the beginning. Why were we called?"

Chapter Four

"Something has happened in our crypt which has puzzled those who know about it." Bishop O'Malley looked at Lt. Samyn. Concern was written in capital letters on his face. "That's why we called you."

"Ok, so tell me what happened. Was it a murder? Did someone disturb or rob a tomb? Or do you think some kids, possibly your monks even, snuck down and had a party?"

"No, nothing like that. Although I have to admit a crypt would make an interesting party room. Wish I had thought of that when I was younger." He laughed.

Samyn grinned. *Good to know he has a sense of humor.* "So if it wasn't used to party in, what would cause you to care about the crypt? Let me guess. An undead person tried escaping?" Lt. Samyn cocked an eyebrow.

"That's close to being right, I think." O'Malley's demeanor broadcast his sincerity.

"Are you saying someone buried there wasn't dead?" Now it was Samyn's turn to look puzzled.

"Perhaps you should see the crypt with no more input from me. You know, go in blind." The bishop rose. The other men stood.

Samyn eyed the bishop and nodded. "Yes, perhaps that would be best. Will you be our escort or will Monsignor Talmano have the pleasure of taking us to your burial lair?"

"I think it would be best if I do it. He made the discovery, though. Maybe he should join us?" The bishop's hands turned up, ready, if needed, to sacrifice another priest.

"Sure, why not?" Samyn looked at Moore and Blake. He expected to hear comments.

Blake shrugged.

Moore agreed. "Why not?" he said. "If life is merrier with more friends, wouldn't the same thing apply in death?" He looked at the bishop. His eyes twinkled, and he winked.

O'Malley who had been donning his clerical robes paused, then chuckled and smiled. "My grandmother would agree."

The bishop moved from behind the desk. "Gentlemen, if you would follow me." He went towards the door. "Oh, and one more thing I should tell you. It is our time of silence. Please reframe from talking until we are in the tombs." He opened the door and headed towards the stairs.

His robes made a soft swishing sound as he moved. It was a quiet rustle of air, almost negligible to hear, but it was there. Samyn would have missed it if it hadn't brought back long-repressed memories from his youth. *What have I done to be punished for now?* His thought startled him. It made his stomach turn and twist. *No, I will not go back to those times. I will not remember those years.* He willed himself to think of only the now, what new agers and psychobabblers call mindfulness, living in the moment. His brow showed a fine line of sweat forming above his eyes. He shook his head, trying to shake it off.

At the foot of the steps, the monsignor stood waiting. The bishop motioned him to follow. He fell instep behind him. No sound, other than the swish of the robes, was made from either Holy Man. The lack of noise made Samyn think they were levitating, not walking. He and his partner's footsteps were loud, echoing, and disturbed the time of solitude now being observed by others.

They went out the backdoor, the same one the officers had used through when they arrived. Outside birds, planes, everything that should make a sound, was silent. The lack of noise was eerie.

Moore whispered to Blake. "Can you train nature to go silent?" The bishop, not looking back, held up his hand for silence.

Blake looked at Moore. His eyes were wide. He shook his head and lipped synced; I don't know.

Samyn kept quiet, but he too wondered how could all sounds cease, as if on command by the head honcho of the Church? His stomach twisted itself into more knots. *What have we gotten into?*

25

Chapter Five

Darkness stood guard inside the gothic stone cathedral. The cool air was motionless. Not even stray bulletins left in racks were moving. Samyn heard not a single sound despite seeing priests moving around prepping the chapel for the next service. Candles, lit by parishioners for prayers, brightened one area near the front section of the building, but even those flames kept quiet now.

Several people, mostly older women and a smattering of aged men, sat scattered about in the pews. A few were using the kneelers. All kept their eyes upon the crucifix above the altar. Rosaries were wrapped around their hands. Some lip-sync ed prayers, but no one spoke aloud.

The bishop had brought the officers in through a heavy wooden door on the right side of the building. He gave everyone time for their eyes to adjust to the inky interior, then motioned for them to follow him down a narrow hall, lit only by low watt electric candles placed on the walls about six feet apart.

This hallway led to an arched opening on the left-hand side of the wall. The hall they walked down ended about two feet later. Inside the arch, sconces on either side of wall revealed stone steps, worn from time and use. The bishop extracted a flashlight from some hidden pocket in his robe. He flashed it down and around the forbidding opening. He whispered his next instructions. "Gentlemen, please proceed with caution. The stones have worn evenly over time, but they can get slick from the dampness here. Use the walls to support you if needed. You'll find some notched places where your fingers can grip." He went down first and projected his flashlight's beam up the stairs.

The monsignor, followed by Samyn, Moore and Blake ascended into a clammy, damp, hidden, room.

"How long has this been here?" Samyn thought he had spoken only to himself. He realized he was wrong when the monsignor answered his question.

"The crypt has been here since the first church. The original entrance under the altar was sealed up when the church celebrated its hundred birthday and this one created. About fifty years ago, the original entrance was found and unsealed by the presiding bishop at that time, but they left this entrance alone. I thought it would be better to bring you in this way. Not all parishioners like to see priests descending in the chamber of death right before a service." He directed a sheepish look towards Blake. "Among my other duties, I'm the church historian. I think I got that job because history is my second passion."

"What's your first one?" Samyn asked. Moore and the bishop laughed. Blake coughed to suppress his chuckles.

Samyn looked at them, confused. *Why had they thought his probing question funny?* Moore tugged at his collar . He gave Samyn a bemused grin, then shifted his eyes towards the priests. Samyn felt his face flush. He was glad Blake and Moore could not see it turn red. He slapped his forehead. "Sorry, I wasn't thinking."

"Don't be." The monsignor made a brushing movement with his hand. "Let's agree you were engaged with the conversation."

"I like that response. Mind if I use it sometime?" Moore asked. He pointed towards Samyn but his laughing eyes were on the monsignor who was chuckling and nodding.

"For the record, my other passion is literature enjoyed with a glass of excellent wine." The bishop injected into the conversation.

The monsignor touched his collar. "This is my calling. It's what I do for a living. I think a passion is what you enjoy when you're not working."

O'Malley looked at the monsignor the way a person studies another when they met for the first time. He directed the conversation back to the crypt.

"I once frightened an old woman when I came up from the crypt at another church. She was kneeling in front of the altar when the trapdoor opened, and I climbed out. Fortunately, her heart attack was mild."

Moore laughed out loud. "Sorry. Forgive me father, but that was funny. I can picture what my grandmother's face would have looked like if she had seen her pastor coming up out of the floor in front of her." He chuckled harder and slapped his leg.

Blake elbowed him in the ribs before placing his finger over his lips.

"Do we need to stay silent down here, sir? If we do, then forgive me." Moore asked. A humbled tone carried his words to the bishop's ears.

"No. We can talk. These stones are thick enough to trap the sounds made down here. No one can hear us even if they are standing at the altar."

The bishop shown his light around the room. "Welcome to our crypt." He gestured with his left hand. The light he held illuminated stone walls, cobwebs in corners, dried up flowers, and the hard closed final homes of those who rested in this dark, unwelcoming place. The bishop spun on the balls of his feet and walked off with the light. The monsignor, in obedience, followed.

Chapter Six

Samyn, Moore and Blake were left in the dark. Ahead they made out the bouncing light, but not well enough to follow in the unfamiliar room. Blake fished his phone from his rear pocket and turned it on. The surrounding area was now lit, thanks to modern technology.

"Good thinking, rookie." Moore nodded his approval and pulled his out.

"Come on, old man. Light yours up."

Samyn said nothing.

"You don't have your phone, do you?" Moore shook his head. "How hard is it to get into the habit of putting it in your pockets?" Air escaped through his puckered lips. He knew he could only get so upset at his boss.

"You know, I almost always have it somewhere near me." Samyn played defense now.

"Well, it ain't near you now and you need it." Moore threw back at him.

"I took it out of my pocket and tossed it back in the car. It's not right taking a phone into a church."

Blake spoke up. "Sir, there's nothing that says you can't. They just want you to turn it off before the service."

Samyn gave Blake a look that shut him down then. "It's not about what you can do or not with the damn noise maker. I'm old school. We didn't have phones to carry into the church, and I can't do it now. It was beat into me this is holy ground and on scared ground you can't do certain things. Can't get it unbeaten out of me now." He huffed. "Now get in front millennial and make it light so I can see where I'm walking. God knows, I don't want to walk into one of these concrete beds and wake up the dead person sleeping in it."

"Yes sir." Blake moved in front of Samyn. He held his phone at an angle that allowed them to see not only the path but also illuminated part of the room.

Moore and Samyn had been partners for almost thirty years. They knew each other's thoughts. They could read each other's body language like a book. Samyn's body was giving off tense vibrations. Moore felt them, but he didn't know why Samyn was uneasy. They were detectives. Death was nothing new to them. He couldn't recall how many dead bodies they had seen. They had seen recently deceased ones and old cold ones, many times in strange places. *So my friend, what s eating you now?*

Moore rubbed his head. He would learn what the problem with Samyn was. Right now his focus needed to be on why they were here. Moore lifted his light to show the tombs and walls along with their shadows. *Why won't they say why we're here?* This crypt and not knowing why they were in it made him uneasy.

Moore was a jokester. It was how he dealt with uncomfortable situations. He figured being in a dark, underground, burial place won the uncomfortable place award for the moment.

"So old friend, let me know if you see a spot you want to spend eternity in. I'll make sure the department puts you there. I'm thinking you might prefer a wall spot." He turned the light towards a wall with a carved opening large enough to hold a body.

They both jumped. Inside the opening laid the skeletal remains of someone put there years ago. From the amount of bones showing, it looked like the one was not alone in its last bed.

"Holy Jesus." Samyn crossed himself.

"Mother of God. Who buries people on a wall shelf?" Moore's deep brown face lost a few shades of color.

"Catholics who have issues." Samyn muttered.

Blake looked at the shelf. He edged closer to it and moved his phone light around.

"There's got to be five or six skeletons here. Must either be the catholic pauper burying place or they may have died from one of the flu epidemics. During the Spanish Flu people died faster than they could be buried, so they were put in mass graves. Maybe these were a family shelved together."

"Do I look like I care? Let's get to the bishop. I want to see this find of his and get out of here," said Samyn.

"Ok. Sorry, I've never been in a crypt before. It's interesting to me. All this history." Blake moved them towards the bishops light.

Moore put his arm around Samyn. "Hey, cut the kid some slack. You know how curious he can get. You also know how much his observations from that curiosity has helped us in the past."

Samyn threw up his hand in acknowledgment. "Sorry, this is just creeping me out. I've got a bad feeling about this."

Moore tapped his chest. "Me too, bro. Me too."

Chapter Seven

"Good, you made it. I'm sorry I got far ahead of you. I'm not used to being down here with strangers. Forgive my rudeness." The bishop laid his right hand over his heart.

"I had the monsignor go over this sight again, to make sure nothing had changed. It's as he found it."

The bishop cast his light over an area to his left. It revealed a marble rectangular box more than large enough to hold a body. This box rested on a wooden platform that raised it one foot above the others in the room. When O'Malley moved his light around, the others could see the top carved with a Chi Roi image and a scripture in Latin and detailed edging around the rim.

Samyn motioned to Moore and Blake to shine their lights around. The wall behind the coffin bore three shelves carved into it. One held seven candles that had been lit in the past. "Can we light those candles?"

The bishop nodded. The monsignor produced a cigarette lighter from an unknown place in his robe and moved to light the candles. When he passed by Samyn, the tobacco essence coming from his robe told his secret. He had a nicotine habit. He also lit the candles placed in sconces on the immediate walls. This section of the room warmed up, but Samyn didn't want to be welcomed by light in a graveyard.

Moore struggled to pick up a candle. Melted wax had dripped down its sides and pooled onto the crypt shelf. "These candles, how old are they?"

"I put fresh ones in those, when we brought the old bishop, I mean his body down here for his service. There's been no reason to change them."

"How long did they burn then?" Blake had pulled out a small measuring tape he carried on his key ring. He laid it against one of the candles.

"Two hours, perhaps three at most. I lit them no more than thirty minutes before the procession began."

"How big are they when they are new?" He wrote the measurement in his phone's note app.

The monsignor nodded. "I see where you're going with this. The candles used down here are typically six inches tall by two inches around, but that's for services of lesser people like me. When it's someone important to the church like a bishop, we use ten inch high three inch around candles."

Blake smiled and noted the sizes. "Would you agree they burn at no more than one inch an hour?" He looked at the monsignor.

After a few minutes doing some mental calculations, Talmano agreed that seemed about right.

Blake started to ask another question, but Samyn interrupted him. "So this is what you brought us down here to view, skeletons on shelves, candles, and a very different looking coffin?"

"Not exactly." The bishop turned to the monsignor. "Please."His upturned palms suggested the monsignor should share his discovery.

"It is my duty to take care of the people who rest down here. Once a week, I come down to check on things and say prayers over the ones whose families have asked. I got lax in my duties and hadn't been here for roughly ten days. When I came down yesterday, I found an altar cloth on the floor by the old bishop's coffin. At first, it puzzled me, but I had other things on my mind, so I dismissed it. I picked it up, intending to take it back upstairs and put it where these linens are kept. When I lifted it from the floor, I saw a stain on it. It looked like blood, but I supposed it was red wine. I found a plastic cup with reddish residue as well. Someone came down here and did the Sacrament of Thanksgiving."

Samyn gave the bishop a contemptuous look. "So you've got a priest who likes to take communion with the dead. Is that a crime?" He shrugged. "I think the church should be happy to have something besides the pedophilic ones." He shook his head. "This is a waste of our time. Come on, boys." He waved to the other officers.

"It's a little more than that. Please let him continue." The bishop's firm tone commanded they obey.

Samyn stopped. That sound awaken another memory. He dismissed it and turned back towards the coffin. "Go ahead."

"I took the cloth and cup upstairs to the bishop and asked him if someone else had been taking care of the crypt. When he said no, not that he was aware, I became suspicious. Priests can develop mental health issues too. Perhaps we had one who was silently struggling and was seeking refuge among the dead. He agreed to speak with each priest and ask if someone had been asked to do my duties. No one had."

He paused for a few minutes, then began again with his tale. "I brought the bishop down here this morning after I discovered this. May I borrow your light father?"

The grim-faced bishop handed it off. Samyn's back tingled from that look. His nasty feeling intensified.

"Eyes perceive this lid to be marble, but it's not. We would never have been able to put it on after we laid the old bishop's body in his tomb." He shined the light close to the top.

Moore whistled. "Looks like real stone to me." He cocked his head. An eyebrow when up.

Blake knocked on the top. "It's hard." He knocked on it again. "Sounds like solid wood."

" It's crafted from a piece of solid mahogany," said Talmano.

" It isn't cold like stone but it can pass for it. Pretty remarkable paint job." Blake ran a hand along the surface. He disguised his admiration, but it showed in how he stroked the top and traced the carved edges.

"We are blessed to have an artist in the church who has done much for us. She can mimic many things with her paint skills. I too thought this was stone." The bishop conceded. "Go on, Talmano. Show, tell them the rest."

Monsignor Talmano bowed his head towards the bishop. He shone the light underneath the lid.

"What are we looking for?" Blake asked the monsignor.

"Follow the beam."

Each man bent down and watched as the monsignor moved the light from one corner to the next. Samyn's knees creaked when he stood. The noise was loud enough Moore flinched.

"Dear God," said Moore.

The bishop chuckled to himself.

" Sorry, Father. Tombs, darkness, dead people, not my cup of tea, if you get what I mean," said Moore.

"It's not my favorite hangout spot either." A weak smile told Moore the bishop shared his dislike of this place. "Did you see what concerned the monsignor this morning?"

"It looked like the top is placed on a slight angle. So did you bring us here to interrogate someone for lack of perfection in death work?" Samyn directed his question to Bishop O'Malley.

"No, stop being so dismissive. Finish monsignor."

"After we finished the service, we lifted the bishop's bier off of the tomb so he could be interned inside. After we placed him in the coffin, then myself and one other priest joined the two holding the lid. We lifted it up over our heads and set it down. We did this so it was even on all sides. It looks like someone tried to open it."

"Tried or did?" said Samyn.

Chapter Eight

Moore whistled. "How many people knew about this fake stone top?"

"Just the priests who lifted it and the artist who painted it. Even the carpenter who crafted it had no idea what we would use it for." Monsignor Talmano's voice expressed his dismay. "It's supposed to have an inset piece attached to the back that will make the lid fit snug and then it will be sealed."

"Why doesn't it have that?" Moore squatted low, examining the underside of the lid.

"The interior board split when the carpenter tried to attach it. He said he would make a new piece when he got the wood in." Talmano glanced at O'Malley. "I forgot about the lid needing to be completed so the tomb could be sealed,"

Samyn and Blake had been busy examining the deceased bishop's resting place from all sides and angles. Samyn rubbed his chin. "Bishop, do you believe your priests told you the truth about being down here?"

Bishop O'Malley drew up in disbelief and stare hard at Samyn. "Why do you dare doubt the word of men of the cloth? They are sworn to the church and can't," he paused and considered his words. "They aren't supposed to break command-ments." The change in tone suggested he too knew that sometimes they did.

Samyn put his hands up in surrender. Arguing with a bishop or anyone in holy orders was not on his to do list. "Just have to ask, father." He pulled his lips down while he pondered about this puzzle. Then he placed his hand under the lid to measure how much overhang existed. "When you came down this morning and noticed the top not right, did you open it up to check on the corpse?"

The bishop and Talmano shook their heads. "No, I didn't think it wise to disturb him unless the police deemed it necessary." The bishop raised his eyebrows at Samyn.

"Good, very smart." Samyn's automatic response mechanism kicked in. His mind was sifting through all possibilities and legalities. *If I have to open this tomb thing without a warrant, will what we find hold up in court? If the bishop gives permission,...* He had never been in a situation like this.

"Your excellency, what does the church say about opening tombs, say in a situation like this?" He crossed his arms and waited.

O'Malley pursed his lips, then stroked his chin. "Well, now if it were in a cemetery, we would need the family's permission to exhume him but as he is only laid to rest above ground not buried that causes some murky waters in the canonical department. He has no family so we have no one to ask for permission." He quit speaking but kept stroking his face. "Do you need to disturb his eternal slumber?"

"Yes, if we are to put this issue, whatever it is, to bed."

"Would you need to remove the body?"

"I would hope not, but I can't make that promise until we see what's under this lid."

"You have my permission."

"Father, is this necessary to disturb the former bishop in his state of rest? It seems, well, it seems unholy and a little sinister to me." Talmano's fingers twitched, the classic sign of someone craving a cigarette. His body seemed poised, but his face could not hide his internal distress.

"Remember , you called us because you think someone already has." Samyn nodded to Blake. "Get some gloves out of the car." He held out the keys. "Monsignor, would you be kind enough to show officer Blake the way out, please?"

Bishop O'Malley bowed his head in assent. "Take this light and hurry. The evening office starts soon."

"Yes, Father."

Blake fell in step with the monsignor and engaged him in conversation. Blake loved his job, but his passion was history, all history, and whenever he had a chance to learn more about something old, he took it. "So tell me more about this cathedral."

Samyn focused on the bishop while Moore scoped out the surrounding walls, floors, and shelves.

"Sir, do you suspect this vault has been opened since the funeral?"

"I am coming to believe it has, though I'm unsure why anyone would. He's buried with little of value. Perhaps a priest desired a keepsake, like a lock of hair."

"Were you here for his mass?"

The bishop eyed Samyn. "Why do you ask?"

"I'm curious."

"No, I was still in Ireland at my church there. Bishop Newman died the night prior to my appointment. I was landing in New York when he was being buried."

"Were you sent here to replace him? I didn't think they moved bishops." Samyn readied himself to throw another gauntlet. *After all this time, why am I still.. let it go old man. You're not catholic anymore.* He changed the topic.

"Do you trust the monsignor?"

O'Malley smiled. "Yes, as much as I trust you." Samyn didn't respond.

"He is a little upset that this will reflect on him, but he is trustworthy. I cannot say that about every priest I know."

His answer did not shock Samyn, who felt few priests can be trusted.

"Is there any in this house you do not trust?"

"I'm still learning them. Right now, I trust them, but I am seeing the usual signs of jealousy, hypocrisy, and the desire to get ahead in the church, if you understand me."

Samyn smirked.

Moore snorted. "I assumed that only existed in beauty pageants and the civil service." He shot Samyn a look. Samyn ignored him.

Sargent Moore kept speaking. "Yes sir. I think we do, but from two different directions. Me, I was raised in a Baptist church, and I came to learn the hard way, ministers are men like me. They have desires, lusts, crutches that they drop at the church door on Sunday and pick back up when they leave. Now, Samyn here, he's not anti-religion, he just doesn't believe in it. Ain't no one holy enough in his book to tell him right from wrong. He's smart enough to figure that out on his own."

"Sometimes I feel the same way. It's hard for me to blindly follow some people." His response was so soft it was hard to tell if he whispered to himself or spoke in quiet acknowledgment of a perceived flaw within a church prince.

"So the monsignor was present at the funeral when the body was put in here?" Samyn looked again at the tomb.

"Yes, he was one of the priests who conducted the funeral mass and definitely the one who adjusted the robes after the body was placed on the bier they used to bring him down, and as he stated one who helped place the lid on the tomb."

"Good then, he'll know better than anyone else if anything got disturbed or removed." Samyn was getting antsy. He wanted to get this done and leave.

Blake and Talmano returned bearing more flashlights, vinyl gloves, and a camera.

"I thought you might want me to get pictures." Blake held up the camera. "And would like more light."

Moore grinned. "Good thinking rookie. We may keep you around. What do you think, Boss?"

Samyn's mind went back to this morning's conversation with his superior. They had no idea what was going on in the department, and what

Samyn was told to do. Now wasn't the time to take their minds off this investigation.

" Maybe. He's still got some learning to do." Samyn's grin was broad and fake. It melted quick. "Let's get to work boys and see what's hiding underneath."

Chapter Nine

"Ok monsignor, is anything different since the last time you saw this body?" Samyn was hoping for a definitive no so they could shut this coffin and leave. The smell of the dead herbs and oils was closing his nostrils.

The monsignor studied the corpse before he answered. "Yes, I'm afraid someone has disturbed him." He crossed himself. "Who would do that? Why would they?" He stood there looking at the body and shaking his head.

The bishop leaned over the coffin. "How can you tell he's been disturbed? Everything looks right to me."

Samyn joined in. "Yes, what's wrong with the body?"

"I am known for being rather particular about my clerical attire. Some have called me, behind my back, a fussy old woman." He smirked.

"Go on."

"I made sure he was immaculate before that we carried his body down and put it in the tomb. I straightened his robe and miter after we brought him down, but before the service began."

"Ok." Samyn struggled to stay patient. He had been lead on a wild goose chase by a crazy cleric and he was ready for this game to end.

The monsignor pointed to the miter first. "It's tilted to the right."

"Perhaps someone came down and snipped a bit of hair as a keepsake, a personal relic?" O'Malley's voice was soft, his words laced with kindness, but his undertone implied he too was bored.

"No. I'm sorry, I mean why would they? We offered everyone an opportunity to snip his hair after his body had been cleansed and readied for burial."

"Could be it was a new priest in training, or whatever you call them, who was too shy to get a piece of hair before?" Blake offered this solution.

"I bet the mother superior came down and snipped some for a voodoo doll." Samyn turned his head so only Moore heard him.

"Can't have been for that. Those dolls are only good for cursing living folks, not dead ones." Moore's kept his face solemn, but his eyes laughed out loud.

The bishop cleared his throat.

"I'm sorry but sir, I don't see what the crime is. Someone opened up the tomb, moved his hat a tad and took nothing of importance or value."

Samyn saw no reason to apologize for his banter. No crime had taken place here. It was obvious a hysterical priest had blown an event out of proportion and was wasting their time.

The monsignor pointed at the body. "His ring is missing. He never took it off. None of the priests who helped me prepare his body for the service removed it either. It was on his ring finger when we closed his coffin." He looked at the bishop. "It didn't seem right to take it off. It was his standard engraved on it. No one could use it."

Samyn donned a pair of gloves. He lifted the dead bishop's hand. On his left forefinger, a wide white circle gave evidence of the monsignor's words. A ring had been on that hand for some time, now it was gone.

"So someone snipped some hair and took a memento? That doesn't seem like much of a crime. The beat boys should have been called, not me." Samyn dropped the dead man's hand.

"Perhaps, but considering his ring was platinum covered in 18k gold, maybe we made the right decision to call you." O'Malley stood with his hands clasped in front of his body, waiting for Samyn's answer.

Those words perked Samyn's interests."That's sounds a little pricey for church bling. Do all the higher ups get the good stuff?" *If he didn't arrive until after the burial how did he know anything about this deadman's ring?* Samyn studied the bishop from his feet to his head. *What aren't you telling us?*

"I knew Newman. He never cared what it cost, and he always expected to have the best. Like the devil, he too wore Prada."

Chapter Ten

Blake dug his camera out of the equipment bag. He got busy photographing everything that could be important for this nonofficial investigation. Samyn asked questions and Moore jotted down the answers along with the person's expressions. Most investigators never detailed interviews this way, but Moore knew what helped him to recall a conversation precisely. Several times these insignificant details had proven vital in solving a case. They came in handy when the evidence suggested one suspect, but facts pointed to someone different.

He glanced over at Samyn, who had grown silent. His head was down, but Moore had worked with him long enough to recognize the wrinkles which formed on the top of his cheeks under his eyes as signs that Samyn was baffled and searching for a direction. The lieutenant raised his head. His mind was busy sorting through things. He gave a slight nod to Moore. The sergeant nodded back. He would take over the questioning for now.

"Excuse me, monsignor. I need to clarify a few things for my notes, please." He waited but got no response.

"Monsignor Talmano, I need you to help me get a few points straight please." He increased his vocal volume somewhat but added an authoritarian tone to his words. This got the monsignors attention.

"Yes, I'm sorry, yes. What can I do?" His hands twisted his robes sleeves. Was it a sign of his discomfort or desire for a smoke stick? Moore made a note. He also adjusted his tone back to conversational.

"Let me make sure I got things right. Bear with me, please. I may ask you to repeat some of your answers."

The priest's head bobbled up and down. His feet tapped left, then right.

"Son, it is ok. I trust you did nothing wrong." The bishops' words worked. The monsignor relaxed.

"Yes, Father." He bowed at him.

"Do I understand correctly, you were here when this," he indicated the deceased bishop with his thumb, "this bishop arrived?"

"Yes, I welcomed him to our monastery and church, but he was not the bishop then."

"What was his title when he arrived?"

"Parish priest, then when the vicar general passed," he indicated a tomb by the left wall, "he was chosen to replace him."

"How long was he here before his promotion? I'm assuming it was a promotion."

"Yes, a rather large jump up the hierarchal ladder. I was disappointed by Bishop Adolphus picking him. Several priests had served this church longer, including me. Father Newman proved himself to be the better choice. He is, was, more inclined towards administrational duties than me."

Moore made a joke about Samyn being better at those things than him before he continued with his questions. "How long was he here before becoming a vicar general? How many are given that title in a church this size?"

"About 6 months, but I'm not sure. I can look up the dates for you if you need the exact length of time."

Moore shook his head. "I don't suspect we will. Now for the other part of the question." He prodded the monsignor, but the bishop spoke up.

"I should answer that part." He paused. "In a church situation this size, which is quite large as we have the school, a cathedral, a monastery and a convent to govern with the 11 other parishes in our diocese, there can be one or two vicar generals. Bishop Adolphus appointed only one. The bishop prior to him had two. I will appoint two."

Samyn asked, "Is there a reason why you haven't done so as yet?"

"I seek first to get familiar with my priests and learn on my own their strengths and weaknesses."

Samyn inclined his head in deference towards the bishop, then retreated to silence.

"Very wise of you, sir. Why promote people to higher positions of authority than they can handle? It's best to put the right person in place, I say." Moore looked at Blake. "See rookie, other people think like me." He clapped Blake's back.

"I learned it's best to know who you are trusting to work so closely beside you." Bishop O'Malley's face showed nothing. His eyes, however, reflected there was more to his words than their literal meaning. He stared at Samyn.

"How did Bishop Adolphus die?" asked Samyn.

"In his sleep. He was eighty-six years old," said Monsignor Talmano.

" How long did it take the diocese to move Newman from vicar general to bishop?" said Samyn.

"Surprisingly quick. Four weeks is all. He was here and had done a wonderful job of keeping the church and school running smoothly," said Talmano. His voice was devoid of emotions. Moore noted that.

"And Bishop Newman, how did he meet his maker?" Samyn returned Bishop O'Malley's gaze.

"Also in his sleep," said Talmano. The monsignor's face was still a blank canvas.

"How old was Bishop Newman?" Moore took over again.

"Only fifty-seven, not old at all." The Monsignor locked eyes on the officers. "He went to bed early with a headache and uneasy stomach. He never woke up after retiring for the evening. The prior bishop had done something similar."

Moore stopped writing, cocked his head at Samyn. They agreed. If this were a different investigation, they would bring in a forensics unit. With hints of potential crimes, but no actual evidence of foul play in either death, besides it not being logged with the force as a case, neither knew what procedural path to follow and no clue to where any of information would lead. They were in over their heads and stumped.

Chapter Eleven

Lieutenant Detective Samyn's stone face hid his agonizing feeling. Something was very wrong in this deceptive spot of eternal peace. He turned to face Bishop Seamus O'Malley full on.

"Were you aware of this?" It wasn't so much a question as a demand for the truth.

"No." There was no hesitancy in his response. "I was told about the circumstances regarding Bishop Newmans'passing, but I was told nothing about Bishop Adolphus and the striking similarities until now." His pitch was even, but a slight tremble after he spoke hinted that he wasn't telling everything yet.

"Was an autopsy performed on either bishop?"

O'Malley shrugged and looked at Monsignor Talmano.

"Well, was it?" Samyn's new tone implied he had tired of this game.

Talmano folded his hands into his robe sleeves. His arms rested across his chest.

"On Bishop Adolphus, no. The examining doctor attributed his death to old age. It seemed plausible, so no one questioned it." He looked at the ground, shifted his weight before his hands appeared again. This time they held a pack of cigarettes and his lighter. He tapped the pack against his palm while he talked.

"I, we, I… it was hard to accept Bishop Newmans death, at least for me. The similarities in the deaths were, well, it seemed strange two bishops died in like manners. The older one, I could accept as a natural death, but one close to my age, no. I begged for an autopsy but the archbishop, the prior, the abbot, all agreed, this was hysteria talking." He pulled a cigarette from the pack, lit it, then inhaled deeply. When he had released the smoke, he inhaled, exhaled, inhaled again. Longer and slower this time. His head tilted up and he let out everything in his lungs. "Each told me he passed because it was the Lord's will."

This time he took a quick puff before dropping what remained of the tobacco-filled paper roll. He placed his foot over it and twisted. All of his motions were deliberate, made with thought but with no wasted motions. He bent over and retrieved the butt.

"Sorry, but I needed that. I don't smoke in the church buildings."

His eyes connected with the bishops. He dropped to his knees before him. "I'm sorry, your Grace. I couldn't accept that answer. I acted against the church. I ignored the archbishop's warning to drop the matter. I..I.. please forgive me, your excellency, please." He lowered his head before the bishops knees. "I understand you can have me defrocked for my disobedience. I beg you to hear me out first. This time I had to follow my heart and my head, not the church."

"What did you do my child?" O'Malley laid his hands upon Talmano's shoulders.

They all waited for the monsignor to answer. Silence was all they got.

Bishop O'Malley pulled Talmano up. "Tell us everything you did. If your confession before us proves you were right in choosing to disobey the elders, then I will absolve you in front of these men."

Talmano gave a slow nod of agreement. "Your grace, sirs, when I washed the body, I saw marks, scratches on places which bothered me. They were not ones made by a priest who practices Opus Dei ways. You know, litigated stripes on his back from self-whipping or pierced places showing he wore a cilice but were ones that suggested Bishop Newman may have engaged in…." Talmano stopped.

Samyn waited for several minutes before giving him a verbal nudge. "Finish your story, monsignor." His impatience hid behind his vocal inflections.

Talmano breathed hard. He choked back the bile raising in his stomach. His right hand found his midsection and rested.

"Son, it must be said. Surely though how bad can it be? He was a cloth wearing man of God, serving in a position of authority in a prominent church. Tell us what you saw and what you assumed it meant."

Talmano shook his head no. "I can't… I would be making an accusation based on a gut instinct, not on hard proof."

Now the bishop spoke firmer, but still gentle. "My brother, please. At the time you saw his body, he had recently passed. You were still in shock. I am sure what you saw you mistook for something else. Perhaps they were bruises from bumping into a table, or marks from some new form of exercise he tried. He was a resident gym rat, I understand." O'Malley's raised eyebrow invited Talmano to agree his suggestions were right.

"No, my Grace, no." His agony filled the room.

Sargent Moore put in his thoughts. "Sir, listen, I'm not a catholic so I'm clueless about vows you take, or why you say you are disobeying the church but I know something went wrong here. It seems to me something else is going on now that's not exactly, excuse my Yiddish, but kosher in a church. Am I right?"

He stood next to the monsignor. His body posture relaxed, his head cocked. He gave the impression of a man verbalizing a math word problem while he worked to solve it mentally.

Talmano clutched Moore's jacket. "Yes, yes, you are right. Something is wrong in this church, very wrong or was wrong. Perhaps it is better now that Bishop Newman has passed. Maybe I shouldn't have pressed Bishop O'Malley to call you, perchance, perchance….." He tapered off his sentence. His sigh suggested he had control again of his emotions.

Samyn spoke, but Moore raised his hand. "If I am right, then it's only fitting we figure out if the previous bishop died naturally or got helped into the afterlife?"

Talmano's hands flexed spastically as they longed for his pack of smokes again.

"Now if you have some secret proof, he died any way but in his sleep, like the previous bishop, then it would be good to share that with us." The hidden demand in Moore's tone was hard to miss.

The priest laid his hand on the crypt. His heightened state of mental turmoil hid from no one. "I admit I didn't really like him, But he stood above me in the church, and I am no one to judge him."

The bishop with a few discrete hand motions suggested the others step away from him while the monsignor sorted out his feelings.

Seconds turned into minutes, it seemed to the officers. Patience might be a virtue and expected to be practiced by those who do church work, but it wasn't a trait Samyn practiced often. He was done practicing it now. Right when he decided to leave this creepy dwelling, the monsignor showed he had decided about his next actions.

Monsignor Talmano dropped to his knees and assumed the usual position of a priest praying. He clasped his hands together. His gaze looked down then heavenward, back down, then up again. Silence ruled the crypt. After a short eternity, Father Talmano lifted his eyes heavenward, crossed himself and kissed his crucifix. He stood. His posture resembled a beaten old man who has been forced to bear a heavyweight long enough he aged prematurely.

"Your grace, forgive what I say. I will explain how I know I am right.' He faced the officers who had gathered in a clump. They leaned against the wall. 'Gentleman, there were, I guess still are slight marks, scratches, on the Bishops Newman's chest, around his hips, and back, close to his shoulders. They look.. they appear to have… It's my guess that someone trying to protect themselves from him made them,' Samyn suppressed his surprise by coughing. Blake's eyes widen. Moore took notes.

"They surprised me, but I served in another church where the parish priest felt corporal punishment to be better than Hail Mary's and Our Father's for the absolution of certain sins." Father Talmano lost himself in reflection. "At first, I thought he too did this, but that wouldn't be in his character. He was an arrogant jackass. Sorry your grace."

"Is there anything else you wish to share?" Bishop O'Malley gave him a gentle verbal nudge.

"Yes Father." Talmano shook off his lapse. "There was bruising, not deep, but below surface level, on the tops of his thighs and on his chest. My sisters made ones like those on me when I held them down to tickle them." He lit another cigarette. This one served more as a security blanket though. It stayed out of his mouth but rested between his fingers. Unconsciously, he stroked the filter.

"When I found several unused pregnancy tests in his room, I suspected I was right. Someone had been trying to defend themselves. He viewed everything on these grounds as his. Did he think that included the women as well? I suspect he did and decided to fight back."

The three officers looked at each other. Shock expressed itself in distinct ways on their faces. Blake's jaw muscle had slackened its hold on his mouth. Moore drew himself up to his full height. His shoulders grew stiff and his eye whites were now large and glowed. Samyn's right hand reached for an invisible cup of coffee. His left patted his pockets for a cigarette pack.

Bishop O'Malley tilted his head down a fraction and placed his right arm over his midsection. His left arm, bent at the elbow, rested on the right one and his left hand formed a fist which now tapped against his mouth. He offered a solemn gaze to the monsignor before he turned and walked away.

It was clear this news had affected each one differently, but the officers could all agree; it was not anything they expected to hear.

Chapter Twelve

Samyn regained his composure first. "Are you convinced you saw bruising and scratching?"

"Yes."

Samyn readied himself for another round of shock. He thought priests were supposed to be celibate. *How does he know about things?*

"Pardon me for ignorance, but would there be a reason for him have a pregnancy test? I've been told Catholics don't believe in premarital sex, but you do have a high school here and hormones run wild in the teen years. I got the impression from the mother superior she would love to humiliate a teen thought to be in trouble. Could he have insisted on keeping these tests as a way to take away some of her power?"

The monsignor shrugged. "No girl would turn to her for help when they could get a test from a drugstore without condemnation raining on them."

Samyn and the others agreed he was right. Each had tried to find an explanation for what Talmano had said. Nothing seemed plausible. Samyn pushed away mental images from his youth. Ones of his sister crying, ones of a priest keeping his hand too long on his mother's arm.

Inside all humans live an area of innate curiosity. That area grows larger inside a detective. This information seeking sense pushed him to do his investigative work and ask questions. At the same time, the areas he had to explore sicken him. They caused bile to churn in his stomach and long forgotten memories to return.

Father Talmano blushed. "I wasn't always a man of the cloth. There's only one reason why."

Sargent Moore nodded his head. "Sir, you're the first person, excuse me minister, I ever heard admit to that." Moore had a deep respect for honesty. That respect showed on his face.

The monsignor's underlying message registered now with Samyn. He crossed his arms and leaned against the shelf in the wall. "Father, are you suggesting to us, you know from personal experience why a man would have marks like the ones you described on his body?" He stared at the priest, but it wasn't a stare of intimidation. It was one that combined with wonder and trepidation.

Father Talmano dipped his head at Samyn. "That would be a correct conclusion." Moore slapped his pen against his leg. His eyes narrowed and the newfound respect was withdrawn. The monsignor glanced at Moore. "I'm an Italian male who was at one time a hot-blooded teenager." He shrugged his shoulders and opened his hands. "I never raped a girl, didn't have too. There were plenty who were willing, but I kissed one or two forcefully, hoping to ignite their passion. They let me know physically my affection was not wanted. My sisters also taught me girls do fight back, sometimes."

"You can't say though, based on what you saw, he had broken his celibacy vow?" said Samyn.

"No sir. I can't. I can say I am certain those bruises, the scratches, he didn't get them from working out in a gym and the tests were there for someone to take."

Samyn cleared his throat. "That my friend is true."

Talmano continued without regard for Samyn's remark. "Because I was concerned by what I saw, and couldn't get support from the church, I rented a post office box, called the morgue and pretended to be the archbishop. I requested an autopsy and asked that all test results be sent to my box along with the death certificate."

Talmano raised his voice. "Forgive me, Father. I admit I broke my vows, a commandment, and yes probably the law for impersonating someone of such authority. He lowered his head.

"I wish I could say, I'm sorry, but I am not. I followed the nudging of my soul and isn't that what we should all do when we feel prompted by the Holy Spirit?" He looked at O'Malley, not defiantly but as one seeking an answer to a complex question.

"My son, in this circumstance, I believe you did right. I see no reason to ask forgiveness. However, when I got here, you should have come to me."

"Yes, I suppose I should have. But we were told you were only coming here to help to increase growth and finances, not here as an active parish or diocesan priest."

O'Malley pursed his lips. His brow knit itself into a tight formation. His head gave a slow long nod. "Yes, yes, that is what you were told."

" What about the bruises? Any thoughts you care to share?" Samyn had heard enough but there was more he needed to learn.

"The bruises were on his upper abdomen and chest areas, a few on his upper thighs. I don't know how they got there. I suspect someone applying pressure with their hands could have placed there them, say pushing away from him or by someone using their fists."

Samyn shot a look towards Moore. Moore didn't see it. He looked at Blake next, but he was too busy processing all he had heard. *I think the rookie has lost his innocence.*

Samyn leaned on the crypt. "Father, I thought all you priests took a vow of celibacy."

"We do."

"I thought it meant you gave up all sexual activity. Am I wrong?"

"No. You are right."

Samyn thought hard. This next question had to be phrased so that no loophole, no wiggle room existed. "Sir, did you tell the archbishop or anyone else what you saw on his body?"

"Yes. I begged him to do an autopsy because of what I had found and because it seemed odd to have two bishops die in their sleep, at the same church, one after another."

"What about the others you mentioned? Wasn't an abbot or prior involved?"

"I followed church procedure. I talked first to the abbot, then the prior, and to the archbishop last. The abbot told me I was mistaken, what I saw was because of hysteria. The prior said to forget what I saw. He said we did not need to put ideas into other's heads regarding the bishop and his faithfulness to his vows. The archbishop stated it was not his place to cast assertions upon other church princes. An autopsy would only bring about information that may hurt the church more. After all, the bishop was dead and that fact could not change."

Blake, at last, spoke. "Nothing like this has ever happened in the Presbyterian church, at least as far as I'm aware.. Wow. I'm happy I practice Catholic extra light."

Bishop O'Malley let his head rest on his right shoulder while he answered Blake. His arms crossed behind him. He sighed. "Son, I can't tell you what happens behind the doors at Presbyterian minister's home. All I know for sure is this one little fact: no robe, no vestment, no clerical collar, or habit, erases, changes, removes humanity from a person who's called to serve the church. We are still human with innate desires and senses and emotions still active. Attire doesn't suppress those, nor does it make us holy, no matter what religion you practice. People often forget that. I'm not justifying what others have done. I only ask for people to forgive instead of condemn."

O'Malley's hand extended towards the crypt's entrance. He suggested they follow the path out.

Samyn crossed his arms. He wasn't done talking. "I still have questions."

"And you may ask them later and I will answer them, if I can, but it is close to Vespers and my presence will missed if I am not there and re-marked on if I am late."

Samyn extended his hand. "Here's my card. Call me when it's convenient to talk."

The Bishop took it. "Thank you, I will." He pointed his light towards the exit. Moore and Blake shook his hand and followed Samyn out. They hadn't gone far when the monsignor called out. "Don't forget, if asked by anyone, you came here seeking a donation."

Samyn kept walking. "Got it." He waved.

Moore tapped his shoulder. He lowered his voice. "So boss, what are we going to do?"

Samyn uttered back. "We lie to everyone. Can't be a sin if you told to do it by a priest, right?"

Blake chimed in with his thoughts. "Am I wrong, or is something off? And what are we to investigate, the missing ring from a dead man, the strange deaths of two church princes, how a bishop got bruised or why he has a stash of preg-nancy tests?"

Neither Samyn nor Moore spoke until they got closer to the stairs leading out. "You're right rookie, something's off. There's some strange juju here and it ain't because we're surrounded by dead people." Moore rubbed his upper arms. It was a habit he adopted long ago from his Cajun grandmother.

They headed down the hall in silence. It got lighter as they approached the end. Candlelight from the chapel flowed into the bleak areas near the edges of the room. Brothers and sisters from the churches monastery and convent were filing into the building. The officers were going against the flow. They made it out after some bumping and sideways shuffling. Samyn walked to where he had a good view of this building. The wooden doors decorated with ironwork caught his attention and his imagination.

"Definitely some bad juju happening behind those innocent-looking doors." He shivered. So did Moore as he rubbed his arms again. The air wasn't cold, but the atmosphere had changed.

Close to where they were standing, two nuns stopped walking to the chapel. They stared at the officers, then each other. One put her head down and continued to the chapel. The other older one watched until the officers left for their car. She stood there until they were out of sight, then she too hung her head and entered for the office.

Chapter Thirteen

"What did the bishop want?"

Samyn did not make it into the precinct before his boss accosted him. "I'm not sure." He told himself he had answered honestly. He didn't know what the church wanted from him.

"Well, he must have told you something about why he asked for you?"

"I think it was more to calm the nerves of a priest who tends the crypt. He thought something had disturbed one of the tombs, but we saw no evidence of it." Samyn looked his boss in the eye as he spoke his white lie. He liked this freedom of lying without guilt.

"You were there for a long time for nothing." The Captain raised an eyebrow and his cup of coffee.

"We did our best to be thorough, sir. That meant we asked lots of questions and looked around in a dark hidden hole in the ground with only phones and candles to light the area. It took a while to discover nothing."

"Did you decide who you want to part with?"

"You said I had until Friday. Today's not Friday." Ice cold steel wrapped around Samyn. He stood his ground. He rarely caved to anyone, but never to someone he didn't respect.

"You do. But sooner would be better. So get busy and make your choice." Martin exaggerated, inhaling his coffee. He had heard Samyn was fighting to stay clean from his legal addiction. After he swallowed some, he grinned at Samyn, his yellow teeth in full display. Samyn looked at him, nonplused, serene on the outside. Inside he craved a black hot cup the same way a junkie needs a fix or an alcoholic, a drink. Martin waited but when he didn't get his desired response, he turned away and entered the building.

Samyn watched Martin walked in and away down the hall. Bile crept up his throat. He spit it out. Martin had a way of irritating him without trying. Few people had ever caused Samyn to have this grating sense of annoyance and disgust. At first, he blamed this feeling on how Martin got his job, but over time he realized no; it was just Martin's personality or lack of it that caused his stomach to churn up more than the usual acid life created there. *What a jackass.*

Martin held the undeserved title of Captain because he had kissed the right butts in the department. When the former Captain retired, Martin got what he had worked politically hard for, a higher paying position which also put him more in the public eye. Samyn saw it like this: Martin had gotten what he wanted, not what he deserved.

Samyn had no problem with authority when the person over him was one he respected. He could not accuse Martin of that.

He walked up the steps toward the doors with dread. He was growing to dislike this building. Friday was not a day he wanted to come. It would be hard to enter this building that day. He wanted less to go in now. "Oh God, I need a cup of coffee." He closed his eyes and sniffed the imaginary cup in his head. He smiled. The coffee was Irish with no whipped cream, heavy on the Jameson's no Baileys allowed.

Chapter Fourteen

"Yo boss, why are we meeting at the coffee shop?" Sargent Moore lowered himself into the bench seat across from Samyn. He motioned for Blake to pull up a chair.

"Martin wants information about our meeting with the bishop. I gave him an answer, but you guys need to give the same story, original words."

"Shoot then." Moore signaled a waitress for his usual iced tea order. He air tapped his finger in Blake's direction so she would bring him water with lemon at the same time.

"I told him it was to calm down a hysterical priest who thought someone had disturbed something in the crypt. I said we looked for hours and asked lots of questions but found nothing amiss."

"But we found something wrong," said Blake.

The waitress arrived with a tray bearing a pitcher of southern sweet tea, a pitcher of water, a small container of lemons and limes, and two glasses full of ice. She placed everything on the table in front of Moore. "Will this do you for now, cousin?" She stood with her weight resting on her left leg and the tray held by her fingers dangled behind her.

Moore grinned. "Man, do you know how to make a person feel special or what? I'm being treated like a king getting my own pitcher of cousin Lizzie's world famous sweet tea."

She waved aside his compliment. "It ain't world famous, just Moore family famous."

"It gets my vote for world renown. Best tea I've ever had." Samyn smiled at the girl who he had known since her birth twenty-five years ago. Back then, neither he nor Moore thought she would co-own a local coffee shop, which prided itself on being more than a millennial hangout. Lizzie had told them, when she planned this adventure, she envisioned one of the old time shops where her parents had met up with friends, older people went for lunch, and folks, no matter their age, or income, felt comfortable. Samyn believed her hard work paid off. The noise level and ambience made it the perfect place for him and his partners to discuss cases without being overheard.

"Carl's making his special tuna salad now and he's mixed the coating for chicken breast to fry up for sandwiches. Aunt Betty's bringing coconut cakes and apple pies for our desserts today, so if you gentlemen stick around you can order early before we sell out." She flashed her teeth before flouncing away.

"She's a good kid, Melvin."

"Yep. Good girl who found and married the right man. They're doing ok with this place. I'm proud of her." Melvin's grin took up his entire face. "She turned out smart and pretty. Must have taken after her uncle."

Samyn deadpanned. "Which uncle was that?"

Blake choked on his laughter.

Moore looked at Blake. "This has been my life for almost thirty years." He shook his head at Samyn. "Cut me some slack, man. I could use an ego boost from the golden boy."

Startled, Samyn dropped his glass. "You know about that."

Moore pulled napkins from the dispenser and called out, "Hey Lizzie, need some paper towels please."

"How?"

"Word gets around." His eyes twinkled.

"Talk." Samyn grabbed some napkins. He tried to catch the flowing liquid as it made its way towards him.

"One of the muck-mucks involved with the meeting last week hit the intercom button on the phone while they were talking. I heard from someone in our precinct you were called a golden boy and now considered to be untouchable. It's no wonder Martin questioned what's going on with the bishop." He gave Samyn an unreadable expression while he sipped his tea.

Lizzie came over with a roll of paper towels and a fresh drink for Samyn.

"I'm sorry for the mess, Lizzie. It's Melvin's fault. He said you were smart and pretty like him."

She shook her head. "Every family has a crazy person and well he's ours. We just humor him. You should too. I read that keeps them calm and passive." She cut her big brown eyes at her uncle. Her face tried to wear a solemn look, but it gave up and she burst into laughter. "Now you boys behave over here. I've got other people to take care of. I can't keep cleaning up your messes." She waved her finger at them, then headed towards the kitchen counter where two breakfast plates waited.

"Did you hear what else they said?"

Moore shook his head no.

"Golden boy and untouchable." Blake leaned back and arced his head towards his left shoulder and looked at Samyn. "Does that mean you're like a reverse Midas? If we touch you then we turn into gold statues?" Blake's boyish face had this air of innocence and solemnity, as if he had asked an important question regarding jet propulsion. His eyes however betrayed him.

Samyn's gut halfway assured him neither of them were aware of what he had been told to do, but the irony of Blake's statement hit him hard. He thought about King Midas and the myth surrounding him. *By God, he's right. Their value lies with me now.* He would have to point out to the higher ranking officers why cases would not have been solved without the help of Blake and Moore.

"Hey GB. Come back out of your fog." Moore snapped his fingers. "What are we supposed to do about the bishop and what's happened at the cathedral if we can't tell Martin?"

"Are we supposed to investigate? I didn't get the feeling they wanted us to. In fact, it seemed to me it upset the bishop when Talmano spotted the ring missing." Blake shrugged. "Did you guys not get that impression?"

"My gut says there's more wrong than a missing ring, an opened tomb, and an out-of-place altar cloth. I suspect the bishop is hiding something. I also don't like that no official autopsies were done." Samyn glanced at each man, wanting their comments.

Neither said anything.

"Blake, you're our resident history buff. Dig into the cathedral's past. Find out if funny things were going on before."

"I'll dig deep, sir."

"Good." Samyn raised his glass. He looked over the rim at Moore. Moore's lips sunk down on the right side. He gave a slight nod to Samyn. They agreed. This investigation would be off the books for now. If they found something criminal, then they would tell Martin.

The phone in Samyn's pants buzzed. He pulled it out. One glance at the screen told him their guts and suspicions were right. He showed it to Moore, whose lips drooped further. Blake leaned over. His eyes grew larger.

The ringing phone displayed the private number given to Samyn by Bishop O'Malley.

"Good Morning, sir. Is there something I can do for you today?"

Chapter Fifteen

This time they knew where to go. Samyn parked in the lot closest to the Parish and they entered by the rear door again. Unlike before, this time as they walked through the building, it was more alive. Several monks were busy in the kitchen, two were preparing the dining room for the mid-day meal, and, in one room off the hallway, an intense discussion was taking place regarding a Greek to Latin translation of a biblical scripture and its interpretation by Jerome.

Father Talmano was waiting for them by the front stairs. "Thank you for agreeing to see us to-day. I hope we can be of help to you." He spoke a little louder than usual, and his words were more formal. Blake opened his mouth, but Moore spoke first. He understood what the Father was trying to convey.

"It's our privilege, sir. We're thankful you could meet with us on such short notice." He grinned at the monsignor and offered his hand.

Samyn caught what was happening. He too offered his hand to the priest before speaking. "Yes. We're pleased you could accommodate us today, especially since we're here for a donation."

Blake, his face pink, shut his mouth, nodded and shook the monsignor's hand. "Happy to meet you, sir." He stammered.

"If you'll follow me, gentlemen." Talmano mounted the steps as he spoke again. "I must remind you the bishop is a very busy man so please do not plan to stay long. State your request and either myself or he will get back to you in a few days."

The officers followed behind him. Nobody spoke. The sounds below faded and the only noise made was by the officer's heavy shoes.

Outside the bishop's door, Talmano thanked them for playing along with him downstairs. "I was praying you would understand. I'm sorry, but the bishop and I believe we must act in secret regarding this matter." He knocked, waited for an acknowledgement, counted to ten, then opened the door.

"Your Grace." He bowed after entering.

Moore elbowed Blake. "Hey smarty, do we have to bow too?"

Blake shrugged. "I'm not a full-bodied catholic, just an extra light one."

Moore chuckled. "You're all right, kid."

The bishop was standing by his desk. He opened his arms in welcome and suggested they gather in the sitting area, which was in the turret of his private space. Semi-sheer ivory linen shielded its long windows. Medium weight raw silk fabric dyed in a deep rich blue finished their look. Tone on tone sage striped wallpaper covered the walls, and overstuffed chairs done in soft sage velvet invited them to sit. A low table in the center held a pot of coffee, one of tea, condiments, and a plate of delicacies.

"We may be awhile." The bishop offered this explanation for his hospitality. "Please, would you care for a cup of coffee or tea? I can get you another beverage if you prefer."

Moore looked at Samyn, then Blake. "I'll have a cup of coffee, sir." He nodded at Blake, "and a glass of milk for the kid, please."

O'Malley let loose a loud, deep belly laugh. "Aye, I can make that happen. Talmano, pour please, then fetch some milk for the young man."

Blake, red faced, fighting to keep his tone and words polite, said he was old enough to drink coffee but would like to have tea if it was Irish Black.

His request surprised the bishop."You're familiar with Irish tea?"

"Yes, my maternal grandmother was of Scot-Irish descent. She liked Irish Breakfast tea best."

"A lady with good breeding and taste." He picked up the teapot. "This is one of the finest blends of Irish Afternoon tea. I think you'll like it." He poured a cup and held it under Blake's nose before handing it to him.

Blake balanced the saucer on his leg, then took a sip from the cup. "That's strong but has a mellow after taste. Thank you, your grace."

"Would you care for a cup?" He pointed the pot in Samyn's direction. "I'm old world Irish catholic and we drink tea instead of coffee, Guinness not IPA and Jameson's not Bushmills. As we are in the land of Starbucks, would you prefer coffee?"

"I'll pass. Thank you," Samyn held a hand up. "Now sir, why did you want us back today?"

The bishop motioned for Monsignor Talmano to check outside the door, then waved him over to the turret. He leaned close to the men. "Talmano did his rounds again in the crypt. I think he should tell you what he found. When the fathers gather for their meal, we'll go to the tombs to show you. I don't want anyone to see us."

Father Talmano looked first at the bishop who nodded then at Samyn. "Do you remember the top of old bishop's tomb? How it was carved?" He paused, waiting for an answer.

"Go on." Samyn pushed with his words.

"That carving was defaced, and a cloth was on it."

Moore leaned back. "What do you mean, defaced?"

"Was the cloth covering it or the whole grave area?" Blake asked.

"Just the area where the head rests and by defaced I mean someone marred the carving that is on there."

"Anything else different, with the body or its resting space?" Samyn eyed the coffee pot.

"I didn't open it, but I checked to see if the top was crooked again. It wasn't. It looked to be straight, the same as we made it. Then I left everything as I found it."

"Good. Best not to disturb things until you have too." Moore spoke. He was watching Samyn's face. It told him Samyn's body was with them, but his mind had left the room.

"So bishop, tell me, why did you leave Ireland? Do you get to choose places to live or are you just sent to wherever they need you?" Moore didn't care. He was trying to fill in the dead conversation space.

The bishop sloshed some of his tea. "Is that important?"

Moore's detecting skills warned him the bishop was guarding something. "Just curious. I'm Baptist. We do things another way. If we want a preacher to leave a church, we call a church meeting and fire him or we complain to his council who fire him or suggest he look for another place to preach so we'll shut up. I was wondering how and why Catholic priests get placed at other spots."

"I see. Well, there're deaths like the one that keeps me here. There're priests who decide they prefer to do mission work or ones who enjoy educational life instead so they leave parish priesthood for work in other fields."

"And you came here because of the other bishop dying?"

Bishop O'Malley looked at Moore. Shutters covered his eyes. "I stayed for that reason, took over his position for that reason, but I came for another." He said nothing else.

Moore glanced at Samyn, then at Blake. He sensed there was something else going on that hadn't been discussed yet. Did his companions see it that way? He guessed Samyn did, even if he was mentally absent now. Blake was working something out in his head too, so his face was not commenting on this odd ending to the bishop's sentence either.

They sat in silence for a minute or two before Blake began idle questions on the books and things having to do with the different orders. The bishop and monsignor answered and commented on Blake's religious knowledge. Every few minutes the monsignor glanced at his watch. After his last look down, he tugged on the bishop's sleeve and pointed to the door. The bishop nodded and stood in tandem with the monsignor.

"Gentlemen, it's time to take you back down into our sacred resting place for the deceased. There you'll see why you were called back. I had Father Talmano do a little shopping this morning. He secured everything you should need to take photos and fingerprints and collect any evidence."

The monsignor waited by the office door. "Everything I purchased is in the crypt."

A sheepish smile creeped up on the bishop's face. "I've always enjoyed solving puzzles and riddles. Come on lads, let's sort this out." This time he half danced, not glided down the hall.

Chapter Sixteen

The officers followed the bishop less enthusiastically out the door and down the hall. Each face wore a different attitude. Samyn looked like a junkie in desperate need of a fix. Moore struggled to not whistle away his uneasiness, while Blake showed blatant signs of worry and distress.

Blake couldn't stand it any longer. There were things he had to say. "Sirs, he wants us to collect evidence with tools he bought."

"That seems to be his desire." Moore said.

"But how can we do that? Isn't that against, I'm not sure, protocol?"

Samyn nodded. "Could be. Depends I guess on how protocol is defined."

"And who's doing the defining." Moore winked.

"Ok. Suppose we collect evidence that makes a case against someone, can they use it in court since we didn't get it in an orthodox manner?" Blake wasn't sure his superiors saw the problems this could cause.

"If it were something that would be used in court, probably not if the prosecutor was good. But kid, there's more than one justice system in the world."

Blake stopped walking. "What?"

Moore chuckled. "You want me to tell him?"

Samyn shook his head. "The kid's smart, he'll figure it out."

"Guys, there is just one legal system in the US. Remember we took an oath to uphold its laws."

Samyn turned to gaze at him. "Hey Moore, give the boy a clue."

Moore took a step back towards Blake. He laid one of his large arms on Blake's shoulders and drew him close. "Hey rookie, look around you. What denomination church are you in?"

"Catholic."

"Right kid. How often do Catholic priests go on trial in the court system?"

"Never, well, hardly ever. But priests don't break the laws." Blake looked at him. His puzzlement was obvious.

"Let's say Catholics deal with their own. They have a court system for priests and nuns to be tried in for breaking canonical laws."

"They do? Where? I've never heard of that."

Samyn's face mirrored his thoughts. "The Vatican where the high holy one rules all. Come on kid, you studied history, still do. Think."

Blake didn't speak for several minutes."So you're saying anything we collect will be used by their own legal system?"

"By Jove, I think he's got it" Moore smacked Blake on the back.

Samyn held back his laughter. "Good impression. Listen kid, you still have the innocence of youth and I envy you for that. But the world isn't black and white and rosy."

"Ok, so who will process it? Do they have a secret lab somewhere?"

"God works in mysterious ways." Moore spoke with in his most solemn voice.

"So they say." Samyn walked again.

Moore elbowed Blake. "Hey rookie, I respect you have deep faith values. I do too, even if it sometimes seems I walk close to the edge of our legal system. I was raised to believe in God, Jesus, and the Holy Ghost like a good southern Baptist boy should. Samyn, well, I suspect he went to church as a kid, not sure of the denomination, but he follows his own spiritual theology now. The only time he'll break a law is when he sees no other way to bring a person to justice." He nodded at Blake before moving away. He took a few steps, stopped, then looked over his shoulder.

"Whatever you do, don't ask him his theories on the Catholic church and the mafia."

Blake picked up his feet and followed. He kept his eyes on the ground. He wasn't liking this situation at all. It wasn't the way a church or police should operate. He tried to reason he was only doing what his superiors said to do, and that they were outstanding officers who did their jobs well and right. His heart wasn't buying what his head was selling, though.

Chapter Seventeen

Bishop O'Malley was waiting by the steps leading to the crypt. When the officers caught up to him, he had flashlights in his hands, turned on and ready to give them. They each took one and thanked him. He looks like a kid ready to break rules, thought Samyn. O'Malley's eyes showed his eagerness. His fidgety body, which hide under his clerical robes, gave away his excitement.

"Shall we head down, gentlemen?" He pointed his light towards the steps.

"Lead on." Samyn said.

The officers followed O'Malley down the steps. Their lights combined to expose more of what lurked in the church tomb. Even though now it was better lit than before, the same eeriness lingered in the stale air.

The bishop led the way to the grave he wanted them to violate. Samyn wasn't eager to do this, but he stayed with the bishop. With all he had on his shoulders regarding his elite group and his order to fire one, he cared nothing about police procedure, or breaking laws. He was curious about this dead man. His suspicions said more happened here than the passing of a man who had lived a devout and holy life.

***

Moore held back. His body language said he was unsure if this holy man was in his right mind or not. Moore accepted whatever happened here could affect his remaining time with the police force. Everybody knew the Catholic church has a long reach. He kept his thoughts to himself.

***

Blake moved slow. His face showed all scenarios regarding what they were getting ready to do. It had flashed puzzlement when he asked about the legality of this adventure. Now it showed worry when he thought about being fired for following the orders of a man who, in Blake's mind, held a higher rank than his commander. He, too was certain something happened to that man, the deceased bishop, that wasn't natural, but did suspicion give the reigning bishop the right to open a coffin, call in policemen for some underhanded sleuthing, and possible violation of their oath to uphold the laws? Blake let all his thoughts swim in his head but not climb out of his mouth.

***

"Don't worry about us, Officer Blake. We're happy to stand here and wait for you." The rest of the group noticed Samyn's irritation.

Moore jerked his head towards the bishop but kept his mouth shut. Blake picked up his pace, arrived, but refused to apologize for his slowness.

The bishop extended his hand to Father Talmano, who leaned over and lifted two navy bags from the floor. He set them on the tomb's lid and opened them.

"Gentleman, I suspect our amazing padre has secured everything needed to collect any evidence. I did a little internet research and not much info exists on collecting body samples from an embalmed corpse," he grinned. "But the church has recorded and gathered knowledge since time began." His eyes sparkled like a kid on their birthday after they opened the gift of their dreams, "So I spent time in our library here and because of my title, the one in the Vatican which is online and available to upper echelon church leaders."

Moore rolled his eyes and shook his head. He looked at Samyn's face. Samyn whistled under his breath. He stared at the bishop. "I guess titles in the church are like ones in the military, important door openers that give you freedom to bend rules."

O'Malley's face darkened. Where it once was jovial and excited, it now looked like a storm cloud ready to burst open with rain and lightning. "I don't see this as a joke or a chance to fulfill my childhood dream of being an investigator with a police force or crime scene unit, sir. Nor do I see my title as privilege to be used to get what I want."

He swelled up to his full size and looked Samyn directly in the eyes. "I see this as the only way available to find the truth regarding this man's sudden death and perhaps answers to questions the church might prefer to leave unknown."

Father Talmano laid a hand on the bishop's arm. "Sir, they should be told."

Bishop O'Malley stood still and remained at attention. He said nothing, but the clouds covering his face drifted off. After what seemed an enormous span of time, he released his breath, relaxed his stance, and nodded. "Yes, Father, yes. You are right, my dear brother." He patted Talmano on the back.

"Gentlemen, you should know a few things first. I've been keeping something from you because I felt you should approach this problem with outsider eyes. But Talmano had a different opinion, and I'll admit he is right." He gestured for them to gather in. They obliged.

"I am an ordained priest called bishop, but that is only a title given to me recently to open doors. The church has many layers and many people who serve in ways other than ministering in churches and administering in parishes and dioceses. The Vatican sends me to churches to investigate them, most times their staff. I study what they are doing and use that knowledge to help other churches who struggle with a similar issue. Sometimes I am tasked to investigate allegations and sometimes I uncover actions that need to be corrected, all discretely, of course." He paused.

"Twenty-seven years ago in my homeland of Ireland, I helped one orphanage deal with its past. It was there that I met Father Newman, the past bishop here. The children well liked him and he loved them. Newman would have made a fine pediatrician. He was gentle, listened to kids well and had a talent for engaging them in conversation and thought. The nuns worshipped him too, but I think it was more in a nonreligious way. Two of my sisters commented on how gorgeous he was. Movie star looks is the way they described him." He chuckled and weighed his next words.

"One of my sisters had come to the orphanage to place a baby in its care. She's a nurse and social worker. The other who came with her is a nurse and a midwife. They work for the same hospital and often together with single moms." He glowed with the pride siblings get for each other after they've grown and live apart.

"When they arrived, I was monitoring a class-room. The teacher was new, and I wanted to make sure we had chosen well. I had left instructions with the nursery to tell my sisters I would be over there soon and while they were waiting for me, they could make themselves useful if needed. You can never have too many nurses around when kids are your population." He smiled at first, then his brow wrinkled and his puckered.

"I was looking for them when I ran into one, the oldest one, Eileen. She was a little disheveled, and that's not the word I want." He paused. "You know, it's when a person has been put in an awk-ward position, when they have a rumbled compo-sure." He clicked his tongue. "I can't think of it." His lips pursed up more. The next words were spat from his mouth like a bit of rotten food, not chewed, only a bite that hits and disgusts the tastebuds.

"I asked what happened. She wouldn't say, so like a dutiful protective brother, I shook her until she spoke. She told me Father Newman had grabbed her and forced a kiss on her. He then tried to grope her breasts, but she introduced her knee to his manhood." At this he grinned. "Our Eileen was always a fighter. Da called her his lit-tle warrior princess."

"I put my arm around her and walked her back to my office. We passed a nun, and I asked her to find Maureen, my other sister, and bring her to me. When I got to the building where my office was, one of the kitchen help was leaving. She told me she had brought tea and scones as Maureen requested. Right then, I suspected something was wrong. Maureen only eats scones when she is crying or in distress."

"What was wrong?" Samyn spoke up.

"As a midwife, she notices women's figures, and she was convinced we had a pregnant nun on our hands." Bishop O'Malley tapped his fingers together. He looked at each one.

When he hadn't spoken for a while, Samyn nudged him with words. "And was there a nun in the family way running around?"

"I'm not sure. I had Maureen point her out before they left. Her habit didn't look as loose as it should be, but had she gained weight from indulging in food or from pending motherhood, I couldn't say. I promised to check it out. At the time, I was more concerned for what Eileen had endured. Maureen was too, so she didn't push the issue about the nun."

"I took the girls to the train station after we had dinner. When I returned I pondered how to proceed with this. The next afternoon, I asked the mother superior to bring the nun and come to my office for a chat. She told me the order had transferred the sister that morning to another house. That confirmed it in my head. She must be with child. Before I could confront Father Newman about his actions with my sister, I got called back to Rome for a new assignment."

"And you're here because…?" Samyn left the question open.

"The Vatican sent here me to investigate allegations made in private to the archbishop regarding Bishop Newman. Imagine my surprise when I found out our mother superior here had been at the orphanage the same time as both myself and Newman. I checked to see where else she had been assigned and learned they sent her to other parishes where he served. That's very unusual." He rocked back on his heels.

"I was more surprised when I realized this nun was the same one who my sister Maureen guessed to be about five months along with child. The same nun who was hastily sent away."

"Are you inferring something more than confessions were happening between them?" Samyn half grinned. He didn't care if the priest broke vows or not. He was more concerned that this bishop wanted to avenge what happened to his sister even if the revenge he got was one-sided.

Moore's jaw dropped. "Whoa. That's heavy."

Blakes eyes widened so much they made his face resembled a pug dog. He could only repeat one word, "Wow."

Samyn leaned against the wall. He relaxed his tense body. His arms crossed against his chest dropped to his sides and sought his pants pockets. He thought about this situation. His mind switched to what was looming on the horizon for him. *Retirement. That word has a nice ring to it. Let's see, spend my days fishing or playing in crypts with priests? Which do I prefer?* His arms came back up to their normal crossed position. The fingers on his right hand tapped a tune on his upper arm. He snorted.

"So you need help to do what? Find out if the mother superior here was carrying a holy infant over twenty-five years ago? Bring a dead priest up on charges of sexual assault which happened not only in another country, but so many years ago he wouldn't be held legally accountable for? Place another smudge on the Church's reputation and give people one more reason to stay away from a cold house?" He stopped for a minute but began speaking again when he saw the bishop's mouth forming a word.

"Could it be you want to shake up the Vatican and pope in hopes they'll do away with the celibacy vow, which as you are aware has been broken by many. Wasn't it one of the Pope Innocents who had twenty illegitimate children, one of which grew up to be a pope?" Samyn decided he would let O'Malley speak now. He waited for the bishop to justify papal and priestly behavior. His acid tone told on which side of the church aisle he sat.

"When I came here, it was to find out if he, Newman, was a pedophile or had used his authority over nuns or other women to satisfy normal physical desires. I had trouble accepting my sister was the first and the only woman he groped. Now I need your help in learning more. I want to know what he was up to and for that I may need help in tracing where his private bruising came from and if he had any other hidden secrets. Staff say he was a gym rat, but he never used the workout rooms in the high school like the other priests. Where was he working out? But I am most interested in you figuring out was his death natural or did he have a little help crossing the bridge and if whoever stole the ring from his finger was the one who helped him depart?"

Samyn nodded. "Anything else?" He was disappointed O'Malley had not tried to dismiss the faults of priests and popes.

"You can't go about this in your typical way. I don't want anyone getting suspicious about you poking around. Also, no statements to the media. You must keep quiet. Bishop Newman was a respected pillar of this community and a high official in the church. He was to become an archbishop in a few months. In fact, on the day they found him dead, the announcement was to be made by the pope who was already campaigning for him to be welcomed into the College of Cardinals."

Samyn bounced his head from shoulder to shoulder. The fingers of his right curved to hold his imaginary coffee mug and the left hand formed the natural shape of a smoker holding a cigarette.

"I can only investigate from inside the church and now that I must assume some duties here, even that will be limited. But you can go deeper and can explore anything I find in more detail. We'll work together from two different sides." Bishop O'Malley pled his case. When Samyn didn't swallow the bait, only nibbled it, the bishop continued laying out his terms.

"You cannot tell your boss what you are working on for me. Anything you discover must remain secret. Despite how trivial the information may seem, it can rock the church and send lawyers into fits of giddiness."

Samyn laughed. It was a shivery hollow sound.

"Talmano will come up with a plausible cover story for the other priests, the lay ministers and nuns as to why you are around. But don't come here often. Too many visits will make our darling mother superior ask questions and pry for information."

Samyn went back to a nodding motion. "As I have no respect for this institution, or the media, and am not a fan of my boss, I'm in." He held out his hand. The bishop shook it. They had reached a deal.

Talmano smiled his blessing. "I knew you were the right man to call."

"Well boys, are you in or do you want to sit this hand out?"

"Don't I always have your back?" Moore offered his hand to the bishop, but his eyes were on Samyn.

Blake reluctantly agreed. "I'm in, not happy about what you're asking us to do, but I'm in."

The bishop grabbed his hand and pumped it up then down.

"You're doing the right thing. In time you'll understand that. I'm not planning on covering up his past son. I will share it with those who need to know and I guarantee where needed, the church will make restitution."

"Money can't buy forgiveness." Blake said.

"It does in the Catholic church," Samyn said. "Always has and it always will."

Samyn pushed himself off the wall. "Let's get busy. We've got work to do."

Chapter Eighteen

Father Talmano laid the contents of the back-packs onto a wall shelf by the tomb. Samyn nodded his head in approval.

"Looks like your research adventure went well."

Blake picked up the camera and light equipment. "This is nicer than mine."

"Why spare expense when it's the church's money you're spending?" Samyn's sarcasm sounded hollow.

"Does the police force set budgets for investigations? Don't they use as much resource as needed to solve a crime?" The bishop too had a sarcastic side.

Samyn snapped back, but this time he kept his tone conversational. "It depends on the crime." He tilted his head and scrunched up his mouth.

"For a serial killer, a high profile suspect, a politically motivated murder, money is no object. The priority is to get it solved quick with airtight evidence for conviction."

He inclined his head. "For low profile ones, say a murder of an unimportant, ordinary taxpayer, yes they look at how money is spent, and that determines when it gets put in a file and for-gotten. Typically, a few weeks is the max time an investigator has to solve it unless it's getting me-dia coverage then possibly a week or two more is acceptable as long as it doesn't cost overtime pay."

He relaxed his face and continued. "The ordi-nary crimes like domestic disputes, assault, B & E's then yes, money is an issue. No overtime will be paid, no expert witnesses can be contacted. They only pay the detectives assigned their forty hours a week salary, and they better not spend more than a week on it."

The bishop thought for a minute. "Interesting. I never thought about cases having priorities or levels of importance before. Sounds like police work and absolutions could have similar degrees of, how to say this… laxity." He paused a mo-ment and smiled. "Similar, in that the more im-portant or greater the sin, the more a priest must work in the confessional booth. He must unearth the underlying cause, then determine the amount of remorse felt by the confessed." He grinned at Samyn. "Likewise, the more important the sin-ner is to the church finances and profile, the less weight the sin carries, no matter what the sin is."

Samyn chuckled, but Moore laughed hard, hard enough to wipe a tear from his face. Blake looked at Father Talmano, who was struggling not to laugh out loud.

"Have I missed something?" The others didn't understand his confusion.

"Bishop, I like your thinking." Samyn chuckled some more.

"Are you saying it matters who is confessing? I thought no one was supposed to know which priest or congregant was in the confessional box?" Blake's puzzlement caused more laughter and comments about crimes and sins. He snorted.

"I'm sorry, so sorry. I am not laughing at you, son." The bishop faced Blake. His tone was gentle yet sincere. "Yes, in theory, a person is not supposed to know which priest they are confessing to and a priest is supposed to be clueless about the identity of whom they are absolving." He struggled to contain another round of guffaws. "In reality, however, priests become familiar with their congregants. You learn to associate voices with faces, along with sounds that people make. Congregants too learn to distinguish priests from their voices and posture. Only a non-Catholic still believes confession is done without identities."

"Is that why you want the police department to investigate something, maybe a crime, maybe not, with no one knowing what an investigative team is doing on your property but also without this investigation being on the forces radar?"

Talmano and O'Malley stared at each other. Samyn recognized this looks of mental mind reading that passed between them. It was the same looks he and Moore had shared many times. He didn't know if Blake realized what he had just done with his question. Samyn crossed his arms and watched the mental chess match being played by the priests.

O'Malley drew in his breath, exhaled slowly, and stood erect. "Yes." Everyone waited for the rest of his answer. Time moved like sand, trickling through an hourglass. But the bishop said nothing else. He stood with his hands folded.

Blake sputtered sounds not words. Moore studied each priest. No one spoke

Monsignor Talmano shifted his gaze to the floor.

"If we're going to play your game, you'll have to play by our rules." Samyn narrowed his eyes and stared hard at the bishop. "First, we know what to look for when collecting evidence, so stay out of our way."

The bishop nodded.

"Next, you suspect something happened regarding his death."

The bishop said nothing.

"You also suspect he was involved with something unethical for a priest, that is besides what he did to your sister."

The bishop's pupils increased in size a bit. Samyn pursed his lips. He knew he was on the right scent.

"You want this to remain quiet until you have the evidence you need."

The bishop gave a slight nod.

"And if we find out someone who is married to the church stole the ring, we'll not be able to uphold the oath we took because this investigation isn't on our case log."

Samyn stood with his arms crossed and his face blank. The bishop and detective locked gazes. Neither wanted to give the other an advantage. A faint sound of church bells broke the silence.

"We'll collect evidence our way, but later when the time is right, I want you to tell me why we're putting ourselves on the line with our boss for a church that has resources it could use and why you wanted my team?"

The bishop offered his hand. "I accept those terms."

They shook, but still kept sizing each other up.

"You understand what we find may not be useful to you. There's only so much evidence left on a body once it's been embalmed and interred."

"Don't forget, I'm waiting for the results of the autopsy that wasn't officially performed." Talmano spoke.

"If you want us to do as complete of an investigation as possible, then get us a copy. We also need access to his laptop, if he had one. Our boy wonder will trace his actions on it. Blake loves puzzles. He'll be able to piece it all together." Samyn grinned at the rookie. "What do you say, Rookie? Are you up for this challenge?"

Blake's face showed he was not following what was about to happen. "Sure, Boss. I guess?"

"I can agree to everything except handing over his laptop. It should have been wiped clean by now, but I have delayed in doing that. However, if Blake will give Father Talmano or myself instructions on what to look for and where, we will get him the information he needs."

"Sure, but it might be faster if I do it and you watch." Blake's tone said he wasn't sure this was right.

"He gets the laptop." Samyn was not going to compromise on this point.

O'Malley nodded. "It's in my private rooms. I'll hand it over to the young man."

The game was on now. Samyn didn't care if it brought down the church or not. All he wanted from this was another reason to justify not attending services. Organized religion disgusted him by its willingness to cover up the sins of the priests and preachers.

Chapter Nineteen

"Blake, start shooting. Moore put the tweezers to expert use." Samyn barked out his orders. "Here," he tossed a pair of magnifying glasses to Moore. "You might need these, old man."

Moore caught them with one hand. "My eyes are at least a year younger than yours. Maybe you should wear them instead." He flicked them back to Samyn.

Samyn sent them back. "No thanks. I'm playing with the dust." He pointed to a brush, and a container of powder used for lifting fingerprints.

"Is there anything I can do?" O'Malley said. He sounded like a kid eager to take part in some rule breaking adventure.

"Here, take this." Samyn handed him a notebook and pen. "Write everything that has struck you as odd at this church. People, services, interactions…"

Moore interrupted. "You could fill it with stories of that mother superior. She's one feisty mother."

Samyn cocked his head while he replayed what he had witnessed and heard. "Yes, talk about her. Why are you suspicious of her?

Does the incident twenty some years ago have anything to do with that? Or is it because she always popped up at whatever parish they assigned this dead bishop to?"

"Yes, to both." O'Malley kept his teeth clinched.

"Then write everything you remember about the events at the orphanage and give me a confessional piece on why you are here. Absolution does wonders for the soul, I'm told."

O"Malley eyed Samyn. His face froze. Neither spoke nor moved. They stared at each other.

O'Malley broke first. "When's the last time you confessed?"

Samyn sucked in air. "Let me see." He paused, more for dramatic effect than for gathering thoughts. "Blake wasn't born. Moore was a gangly, girl obsessed teenager. Talmano was still a hot-blooded teen and you, well you were still an innocent acolyte who was working hard to keep mommy convinced you were a good Irish boy." He cocked his head. "Or it might have been longer ago than that. Doesn't matter. You're the one with a story to tell, not me, so get busy writing."

Bishop O'Malley kept his face sober but he couldn't stop his eyes from sharing his inner emotion and he struggled to keep the laughter out of his voice. "At some point, you and I need to have a very long talk, with a dram of good Irish whiskey. I suspect we both had some not so innocent times in our past." He walked over to another crypt, far enough away from the others to write his memories in peace.

Samyn watched him. If they had met under different circumstances, would they want to talk to each other, he wondered. Samyn walked away from the church years ago. He tallied in his head the number of years which had passed since he darkened a churches sanctuary. He looked at O'Malley scribbling away on another tomb top. *I was walking out the doors about the same time he was entering the priesthood.* He continued to watch the bishop. Samyn shook off his thoughts and picked up the brush. He dipped it in the powder and stroked it over the dead bishops left hand. *Funny how time moves and connects others to your lives, especially to ones who walk different paths than you.*

Chapter Twenty

Two hours passed as they worked together in a silence that was only interrupted by questions from Father Talmano on evidence collection or by Blake on church history. Samyn and Moore concentrated on their tasks, not the conversation. The only noise from Bishop O'Malley was the sound of his pen on the notebook paper, broken by his turning to a fresh sheet. At last, they were through..

"Ok boys, let's pack it up." Samyn nodded to his cohorts. "I think we've done all the collecting that's possible."

Moore looked over the dead bishops body. "Are you sure?" He raised an eyebrow. "Looks like you missed a few spots on the body."

"What?" Samyn watched Moore's face. He couldn't tell if he was serious or not.

Moore pointed to the body. "Look and see."

Samyn glanced at where he was pointing. He moved his eyes over it, letting them linger briefly at each place he had dusted and lifted for prints. "I give because I see nothing."

Blake took an interest in the exchange and stopped commenting to Talmano on the superior camera and lights he had purchased for this. He leaned over the body, looked and then stepped back and looked again. "Father, may I use the camera again, please?"

"Certainly." Father Talmano stopped packing up the equipment and handed the camera to Blake. "Do you want me to turn the lights back on?"

"Please, but after I've shot a few pictures in low light first."

"Say when." Talmano plugged the lights back into the small portable power source and waited to turn them on.

Blake snapped away, moving every so often to get different views.

"Would someone tell me what they are seeing, please?" Samyn hated it when Moore and Blake saw things he missed. Usually it was a feeling that rose up for an instant, then passed. This time it was making him angry.

Moore was busy making notes, picking up the evidence bags, and writing more down after eyeing where they had been collected from.

"Will someone please tell me what the bloody hell you see that I don't?" Samyn's voice was cold. It bounced around the room. Each stopped what they were doing.

"Hey boss, your language?" Moore shrugged his shoulder towards the bishop, then towards the father.

Again, Samyn was thankful for the dark. "My apologies padres, but I want an answer. Tell me what I missed dusting."

Moore spoke. "It's not what you missed. It's where you didn't lift. Look." He pointed at the body. "Stand next to me and look." His finger moved in a very agitated fashion.

Samyn moved next to his buddy and stared at where the finger pointed. "Holy Hades."

The bishop cleared his throat.

Samyn absentmindedly uttered an apology. "What the hell?"

Again the bishop gave a discreet cough.

This time Samyn didn't acknowledge him. He was too busy staring at the body.

"Have you've ever uncovered something like that before?" He cast a sideways glance towards Moore.

"Nope." Moore shook his head. His eyes never left the body. "Can't say that we've ever had this happen to us, but you know what they say about first times." His voice didn't lighten the atmosphere, and no chuckled followed his words like it always did.

"Did you get this rookie?"

Blake checked the shots on the camera. "Yeah but I want to get some with the lights up. Father, would you?"

Talmano turned on the lights and moved next to Moore.

"Damn. Am I seeing…?"

"Seeing what?" Bishop O'Malley put down his pen and joined them. "Oh my good God! Is that… how can that be?"

Samyn nodded. "Yep, I say it is."

They stood and stared at the dead bishop. His body laid in repose as it had done since being placed in the coffin. However, the dust Samyn had brushed over the body for prints showed he had not lain there alone. The dust revealed a partial image of an arm. A smudged handprint rested on the dead bishop's heart. What appeared to be the point of a chin and tip of a nose displayed itself on his chest.

"How do we lift and catalog that?" Samyn asked his colleagues. Blake just shook his head. He was still in a slight state of disbelief.

"Beats me." Moore looked at Talmano. "Got any prayers or a saint you can pray to for this?"

Talmano's eyes widen. "Not a single one." His head right to left, back and forth, not stopping and not wanting to.

"I thought the church had saints for everything." He gave a half grin to Talmano. "Here, help me measure this, father. We can try to get an estimate of the person's height based on the length of the arm and hand size. We can use it to narrow down the list of nuns who like to sleep with dead men." The measuring tape in his hand showed a two inch measurement ready to be extended.

Talmano grabbed the metal edge. "Why do you say it's a nun, not a priest or a monk?" He laid the tape on the body.

Moore's eyes widen. "Nah, can't be." He recorded the hand measurement and motioned for Talmano to move the tape to get the arm length next.

"A man shouldn't be ruled out. Throughout church history, gay men have become priests to hide their sexuality from the world. Priests and brothers can't marry and neither could gays, so the church became the perfect hiding…"

A voice interrupted Blake's history lesson. "Blake, are you done?" Samyn's voice carried a hard edge.

"I think so. I was only stating…"

"Good. Gentlemen, we must clean up this mess." We've been here long enough. Samyn spoke to no one in particular.

"True dat, boss." Moore pushed up his lips. A high pitched squeaky sound escaped. "Hey Padre, got a vacuum handy?"

Talmano reached into one of his bags. He pulled out two small vacuums used for cleaning keyboards. He extended one to Moore, who stood chuckling. "Gotta ask, father. Were you a boy scout?"

"Nope, just a teenager who understood the value of protection and never leaving a trail to follow. Shall we begin?"

Chapter Twenty-One

They spent the next thirty minutes packing up gear and removing all signs a crime scene investigation had taken place in the crypt. After agreeing everything looked undisturbed, they gathered up their bags and moved towards the chamber's entrance.

"Gentlemen, I must remind you of your promise to keep silent on this," The bishop looked at the police officers. Before they answered him, a deep chime rang out, followed by two higher pitched ones. O'Malley raised his hands.

"I'm sorry. I lost track of time. You gentlemen will have to stay down here until the office is over. I can't have anyone seeing you come out of the crypt with bags."

Samyn nodded. "Wise advice."

"I'll send Talmano to fetch you when the coast is clear." He turned and floated soundlessly up the steps. The monsignor walked a few paces behind.

"Yo boss," Moore said. "Never thought you'd be in a church service again, much less under the church with prayers happening above, did you?" He laughed. "The Lord moves in mysterious ways, at least that's what my grandma always told me."

Samyn ignored him. "Blake lets see those pictures you took. Boys, we need to figure this out. There's something mysterious going on here, but God ain't involved."

"Nope, there's someone sick here. Who wants to lie with a dead man?" Moore shook his head.

"A dead woman." Blake answered. He was busy scrolling through the shots he had taken.

"Here, look at this one." He shoved the camera towards Samyn.

"What do you make of this Moore?" He passed him the camera.

"Not sure, but then I'm not sure what I should see. Want to give me a clue?"

"See this, where the hand laid, is clear not messy." Blake waited for them to study what he was talking about.

"Okay." Both men answered, but their tones showed neither were sure they understood what the rookie was referring to.

Look down the arm. See, it's a swirled, unclear pattern".

"Hey rookie, tell me what you suppose that means. I don't want to play guessing games." Samyn sounded cranky.

"I don't think we'll be able to tell if it was a man or a woman. Nuns are always in habits and priests in robes or suits. Both have long sleeves on this time of year. Long sleeves may have caused the swirled wrinkle looking areas."

He looked at both men's faces. Moore's eyes focused on Samyn, whose eyes were half closed.

"Nuns are no longer wearing traditional habits. Sometimes they wear a short sleeve blouse with a cardigan. And don't ask how I know that." Samyn said.

"Do you see what I'm getting at? If the pattern wasn't so unclear it would be easier to determine the sex of the person. All I think we can determine is the unsub was not wearing a robe but had on a long-sleeved garment. We'll have to rule out a suspect based on hand size. At least we should have a decent fingerprint to use as evidence, though."

"No, we won't. Remember, we're not here investigating a crime. They, not us, will use everything we collected." Moore reminded Blake.

"So we still don't have much." Samyn pondered for a few minutes. "We can bring the priests to us. Interrogation rooms have a way of making people talk and I'm tired of the games. I've never enjoyed being a pawn." The temperature in the room dropped.

"Boss, let me talk with them in private. If the media got wind of you grilling the bishop, you wouldn't be a golden boy for long." Moore looked at Samyn.

Samyn thawed. "You're right, partner. You take Talmano. I'll take O'Malley. We'll talk to them separately, but on neutral territory. Blake, you're the whiz kid. Dig up everything you can on those two men and on everyone who fits the estimated hand size based on Moore's measurements. There's a lot they haven't said. The church hides it sinners and its sickos."

Talmano's prescience filled the doorway of the crypt. "Gentlemen," he whispered. "I can get you out unseen now. Everyone has gone to their dormers. Bring the gear too, please."

Samyn motioned for them to grab a bag and hand him one. They left the crypt with no apparent evidence, but at least now they had a game plan. Samyn felt like they were in charge now.

Chapter Twenty-Two

"Thanks for meeting me here today bishop or do you like to be called something else when you're in civies?"

The meeting was taking place in the coffee shop owned by Moore's niece. It was the one place Samyn trusted the walls to hold on to secrets.

Bishop O'Malley cocked his head. That statement puzzled him. "I don't understand this term, civies?"

Samyn puffed out imaginary smoke. His left hand held a pretend cigarette. His right one wrapped itself around a water glass the way it had always cradled a cup of coffee.

"You're not in clerical garb today." The hand holding the nonexistent smoke flicked itself towards the priest's neck before heading towards Samyn's mouth.

O'Malley grinned. "Sometimes it's good to be inconspicuous. The dog collar draws attention."

Samyn laughed hard. "Dog collar, eh? Never heard it called that. Do you call it that because of the choke hold it has on you?" Sarcastic tones underscored.

"It's a choke hold I embraced willingly but one that's no tighter than the badge you opted to wear." O'Malley deadpanned.

"Touche, padre." Samyn conceded the point. "You are right though. Sometimes uninterrupted conversation is best, and all conversation happens best when it's unnoticed." He took a sip of water. "That's why interrogation rooms are well loved by cops."

"But not you, or that's where we would be."

Samyn nodded. "Touché again."

The waitress came over. "What would you fine gentlemen like today? We have fresh coffee, just brewed it myself. An apple pie came out of the oven recently, a blueberry one that I can heat a slice of for you or are you wanting a late lunch?"

"It's my treat, get what you want." Samyn said.

"I would love a piece of me mum's apple crumble but I know," he held up his hand to silence the waitresses protest, "That's not available."

"The apple pie has a crumble top. Are you from Ireland?"

"Aye, that I be."

"So's the baker who made the pie." She teased him with a smile. "Bet you'll like it."

"Well now lassie, that's a wager I canna re-fuse." The Irish lilt hinted at laughter.   He re-turned her smile. "What say you, Samyn? Care to partake in this offer?"

"I'm a blueberry man myself."

"Anything to drink fellows?"

"Coke." Samyn said.

"I'll have coffee, please. Black."

"That's the only way it comes here." She flounced away from the table.

"I would have pegged you for a coffee drinker, Samyn."

"Why's that?"

"Your right hand is used to holding a cuppa something and I don't see many American men drinking hot tea. Also, unless TV and films are wrong, cops like their coffee."

Samyn sucked in his mouth. "I see, said the blind man."

The waitress returned with their drinks and pie.

"Do you fine gents need anything else?" She looked from one to the other. Both shook their heads.

"Well, if you do, then just wave. I'll be behind the counter sorting silverware into baskets."

"Excellent deduction skills, padre. You didn't learn them in seminary."

"I read too much Sherlock Holmes as a lad." Bishop O'Malley made himself fully erect in the booth before quoting Doyle. "When you have eliminated the impossible, whatever remains, however improbable, must be the truth." He re-laxed. "Ergo, I suspected from your hands natural inclination to cup something and you didn't touch the tea I offered in my room. That lead me to de-duce that you must be a coffee drinker."

Samyn nodded his head in agreement. He clapped and said, "You deduced correctly. I drank coffee, but I gave it up months ago. Trying to break the habit." He grimaced with those last words.

"Will it bother you if I have some? I can get tea instead. I got hooked on Starbucks mocha Frappuccino's when I was at the Vatican. Every once in a while I crave one and take coffee instead of giving into my desire." He hung his head for a moment.

Samyn shook his head. "No, It's fine. Just be warned, I may inhale the aroma a little too deeply and frequently." He gave the bishop a toothy grin.

"Why did you want to quit drinking it?"

"That's a topic for a different day. We're here to discuss other matters."

"So you became addicted to coffee, perhaps to escape another addiction?" The priest pressed him.

Samyn ignored what the priest said. He braced his elbows on the edge of the table and leaned over.

"Tell me about you. Why did a bishop come from the Vatican, the highest church in the Catholic world, to an insignificant town which rests in the shadows of a larger diocese?" He picked his fork and let it hang over the slice of pie before stabbing it.

"What dark secret were you sent to discover?" Samyn devoured the bite while watching the bishop who hadn't answered yet.

"You can call me Seamus." O'Malley picked up his fork and speared a piece of the apple crumble pie. "Close to my mother's but still not quite it."

"Can we stop dancing and start talking?"

Seamus finished his pie and pushed away the plate. "What do you want to discuss?"

Samyn had kept himself busy with his slice. He chewed the bite in his mouth and leaned away from the table. "Tell me why you're here, in Richmond. You told me you were a bishop in title only. They assign you to investigate churches. So what did you come to our cathedral to investigate? Or should I say whom?"

"I should watch my words around investigators, I see."

"Do you need anything else, more coffee, another coke?" The waitress gathered up the plates and forks while she waited for a response.

"That was a mighty fine pie. Not quite as good as me mum's but memories have a way of becoming enhanced with time, don't they?" He grinned. "Might I partake of another piece, if it's not any trouble?"

"I'll bring it right over after I heat it up. And what about you, Lieutenant, do you need anything else?"

"I'm good for now, Cookie."

She noticed him eyeing the coffee she had poured for the bishop.

"If you want some, I'll give it to you. Uncle Melvin will never find out."

"Nay, I'm fine." Samyn wondered if his craving showed on his face. *Is that how dealers tell when a junkie needs a fix?*

"Okay, but if you need one, holler. I'll go get that pie, sir."

"You know the staff? I guess cops do hang out in coffee shops. I thought it was just a Hollywood created stereotype."

"She's one of officer Moore's nieces. Another niece and her husband own this place. I invited you here because the food and drinks are fresh and these walls never talk."

"I see, said the blind man." Samyn chuckled at Seamus' repeating words he had stated earlier. He made a mental note. The bishop was good at listening and remembering.

"So spill your guts. What was going on here in our podunk town that got you sent here from Rome?"

Seamus cut his eyes over Samyn's left shoulder but said nothing.

Cookie sauntered up with two slices of pie. She put the apple one in front of the bishop and laid another slice of blueberry by Samyn.

"He might not like to eat alone." She laid down forks and left.

Samyn reached for his fork. "You confess, I'll enjoy."

The bishop nodded his head. "I'll talk in-between bites." He drove the fork into the warmed up steaming pie. After he had chewed his bite, he began his tale. Every so often he paused for another bite of baked heaven. When done with both pie and story, he laid down his fork and wiped his mouth.

"So that's my tale. What do you think of it?" He asked.

Samyn had stopped eating his pie sometime much earlier. The story being told was too riveting for him to eat and listen. He chose to listen.

When Seamus finished, he picked up his fork, tried to put it in his slice of pie and couldn't. He still felt overwhelmed by what he had heard.

"What's wrong?" Seamus asked.

"I think I need a drink." He waved his hand for Cookie. In it was an empty cup she had left for him.

"A dram or a coffee?" Seamus eyed Samyn's hand.

"I'm not going to drink it, just going to inhale it."

Chapter Twenty-Three

Moore called the private number the monsignor had given him.

"Father, we need to talk away from the parish, please."

"Yes, I believe that is best." Father Talmano said. "When and where should we meet?"

"I'm thinking we could go to a coffeehouse near the precinct, that way we could use your cover story, that the church or the cops are seeking donations?"

"Yes. Good idea to keep the same one." Father Talmano spoke in phrases, not sentences.

"Is this a bad time to talk, padre?"

"No, it's fine. I can meet you to go over things."

Moore guessed either someone was near or someone was trying to eavesdrop. "Is someone nearby?"

"Yes, but if we could do this soon, that would be best."

"Is it the mother superior?" His words danced to a jovial tune.

"Of course. Does the bishop need to tag along or will you trust my decision is one he will approve?"

"No. I want only to talk with you. Do you need an address?"

"Yes, that would be helpful."

Moore heard the faint sound of paper being ripped along with the rustling noises of a phone being held by a jaw. When Talmano said he was ready, the sargent gave him the address and asked when they could meet.

"I'll be there around 1:30 then."

Sargent Moore said ok and hung up. He looked at the clock on the wall. That gives me an hour to kill. He decided to seek out Blake. *Maybe he had dug up something useful.* Moore had to admit he admired Blake's ability to find the most obscure bits of trivial information. More than once, it had helped to convict a guilty party. Sometimes his cyber sleuthing had provided the evidence they needed for an arrest warrant.

He pushed away from his desk and wandered down the hall to Blake's favorite hiding spot. He claimed the internet connection was better here. Moore suspected it was something else.

Once Moore had looked out the window. He saw it gave him a perfect unobstructed view of an administrative assistant's desk and from where Blake like to sit a clear shot of her.

Moore whistled when he opened the door. He glanced at the window. No one was at the desk in the opposing office. Blake was focused on his computer screen.

"See anything good today, rookie?" Moore grinned. His face told Blake he knew why this was his favorite spot to work.

Blake blushed. "How did you find out?"

Moore laughed. "I was young once too. So have you asked her out?"

"Not yet. I don't even know her name."

"Tell you what. I'll get her name for you if you promise to take her out."

Blake didn't answer. His attention was on his screen.

"Hey rookie. Did you hear me?"

"Yes, I heard you. You give me her name, I take her out. Here, look at this." He turned his laptop around for Moore to see.

"Is that who I think it is?"

"Yep," said Blake.

"Whoa. How could, why would?" Moore shook his head. "I guess the church practices forgiveness, big time."

"It says they acquitted him." Blake pointed out.

"Come on, rookie. You know cops can't arrest someone on a charge like that without powerful evidence of guilt. Especially if the suspect wears a collar."

"We can't let it cloud our vision. I mean, a court wouldn't let an attorney use it against him. That's presumption of guilt."

"No, we can't but it changes our card hand."

"Is that why they called us in on the sly?"

"Maybe, not sure, but now we may know why the good Bishop O'Malley was sent here."

They re-read the article detailing the acquittal of the charge of sexual harassment against Father Newman. For almost half and hour, they discussed the implications it could have on their investigation. Moore checked his watch.

"I'm meeting Talmano at the coffee shop in fifteen. Text me if you find out anything I should talk to him about."

"Sure." Blake's answer was automatic.

Moore turned the handle, opened the door, took a step before he paused in the doorway. "Her name's Clarissa Madigan, she's single, and holds a BS in Criminal Justice from Louisville and will start UVA law school this fall. She's with her family in North Carolina today. She'll back at her desk Wednesday." He stopped talking.

Blake's mouth dropped. "How did you know... I mean, I never said?"

Moore tapped his head, then reached in his pocket. He dropped a piece of paper on the table. "They'll be back tomorrow tonight. Call her Wednesday." He took a step out of the door.

"She thinks you're something, whatever that means in girl lingo."

Moore whistled *Strangers In The Night* as he walked down the hall.

Blake caught his meaning when he looked up the lyrics online. He put the slip of paper in his wallet and got back to doing what he did best, computer snooping.

Chapter Twenty-Four

Melvin Moore whistled his way to the diner that sat on the corner of Cherry and Fifth streets. Empty storefronts, graffiti, alleys with trash greeted him. Every few buildings there was an occupied space that operated as a sign the local citizens refused to give up on this part of town.

Sargent Moore had grown up near here, but things were different then. This had been a vibrant area. Shops stayed opened after dark. Stores stayed busy, and they kept the streets and alleys clean.

Old infrastructure fought with cheaper, larger homes outside the city limits. The promise that new offers over old, lured youngsters away. Now older, less mobile, people lived here in homes some had been born and raised in. Businesses left when they had nothing to offer to residents with fixed incomes. Some shops closed that had been around for generations when a younger family member didn't want to keep it going. Time brought changes that ate history and culture, drained away livelihoods, and left rotting shells of buildings.

Moore kept whistling. He stopped in front of one dusty, forlorn building and stared inside the window. When he was a kid, this was where the action was. He remembered hanging out here almost every afternoon. His grin displayed the teeth made straight by the metal he had worn as a young teen. Over to the left had been the soda fountain counter. *Best milkshakes I ever had came from here.* Comic books were on a spinning rack at the front of the store. Kids pulled them off and sat on the floor to read them. The bottle return basket sat by the back door. He spent many a day walking the alleys looking for soda bottles to bring. On a marvelous day, he'd collect enough to buy a drink and the latest issue of his favorite comic. On a grim day, he'd have to make a hard choice. Usually the comic won.

He'd recently found out some of those old comic books were worth a small fortune. Little did he know when his mother insisted he put them in the trash he was throwing away a retirement plan. *That was the only time I shouldn't have listened to her.* He chuckled.

He moved on from the past. Outside the coffee shop, he looked around the intersection. On the opposite corner had been a small grocery, across the street from that had been the butcher. On the other corner had been the laundry and dry cleaners. The one place that hadn't changed was the building he would enter. It had been a coffee shop when he was a kid, and it still was. *Some things can't ever change, and that's good.*

He pushed the door open.

"How's life, Mr. Harry?" Moore spoke to the ancient man half hidden by the counter. Harry had been a fixture in this shop since Melvin's youth.

Harry peered up. "Well now, life is a card game, young man. He, who knows when it's time to fold, walks away with money in his pocket. Me, I plan to sit in on another round."

Melvin grinned. All he could do is laugh at the wisdom in these words. Mr. Harry had lived much, spoke little, saw all. Melvin learned that when he was a kid.

"Want your usual?"

"Yes, sir."

"Go sit down, I'll get it to you in a minute."

Melvin looked around at the open seats. He wanted a booth. Near the back, he spotted a familiar face in unknown attire.

"Father, I see you beat me here."

"I just got here myself."

"Have you ordered yet? Mr. Harry makes a mean sunny side up egg sandwich and his fried chicken is better than my mama's but don't tell her that." He winked.

"I wasn't hungry until you said chicken." Father Talmano licked his lips. "I grew up in an Italian house. We ate pasta all the time. Since moving down here, I've been busy trying to eat my fill of fried bird." He patted his stomach.

Mr. Harry appeared with two glasses of sweet tea and a pitcher. "Thought you might need this."

"Yes sir. Thank you, sir." Moore picked up his glass and swallowed some. He pulled it away from his lips. "Best tea around pops."

"Watch your words, boy."

"Just giving you a compliment."

"Just telling me I'm an old man." Mr. Harry slapped his leg. "You ain't gotta do that, son. My body tells me every day." He turned to Talmano. "Know what you like, young man."

"I heard you got better fried chicken than his mother."

Harry stuck out his skinny chest. "Yes sir, I do. But don't go saying that around women folk."

Talmano laughed. "No sir, I won't."

"You're not from here, are you?" Harry paid closer attention to him now.

"No, sir."

"Let me guess." He tapped the side of his head with a pencil. "I'm going to say New Jersey, northern New Jersey. No, no, Little Italy. That's where I think you come from."

Father Talmano's mouth dropped to his chest. "How did you know that? Have you been there?"

Harry shook his head no. "Nope. Never been to New York, but I served with a man from Little Italy. Talked so much and so loud I can't ever forget his voice. We spent six years side by side together in Nam. Never thought I hear a voice like his again." Harry's eyes watered up. He changed the subject. "Whatcha want with your chicken?"

Moore answered before Talmano could. "It's time to make him a southerner. Serve him some collards, mashed potatoes, and biscuits, lots of biscuits." He winked at Talmano. "Trust me. I've eaten here since I was a kid."

Talmano shrugged. "Whatever you say then." He grinned. "We rarely get those greens at the parish, but one of our older women will bring some occasionally when she's cooked them and I," He kissed his fingers. "love them."

Harry ambled away, wiping his eyes. When he was out of earshot, Moore asked "Eat then talk or talk then eat?"

"We could do both." Talmano laid an envelope on the table. "I went to the post box before coming here. This was in it." He turned it over. Moore looked at the corner. It was from the Medical Examiner's office.

"What did they say?"

"I waited to open it. Shall I do it now?"

Melvin Moore's head gave him a solemn nod of assent.

Talmano picked up the envelope. He held it for several minutes. "This could change things for me and for Bishop O'Malley, you know. I broke church procedure. I overstepped my office."

"But you did, and so now what? Do you not want to know the answers now? Did the enormity of what you were doing just register with you?"

Talmano let his head move left to right. "I knew, but I also felt I was doing a just thing and justice should be something the church seeks." He looked out the window. "What is in here will determine whether I can trust the Church and if it can trust me?" He stared at Moore. "Have you ever pondered if what you were doing was right, not just by not breaking a law, but with your life? Have you ever been in a position where one misstep could end your career?"

Moore's face was solemn. "Father," he said. "More times than you'll ever know."

Talmano weighed Moore's words.

Moore continued. "Sometimes there's a line we must cross for the greater good of justice. But I understand your point. Both the church and legal forces have long arms. The church has a longer reach, I think, and can strangle those on the legal side."

Talmano took a deep breath, held it for a short eternity, then exhaled. He turned over the envelope. "Let's see then what's inside." He opened the envelope. As he withdrew the papers, Harry returned with plates of food and a basket of biscuits stacked high.

"Here you go. Fried chicken for the Italian and the local," He placed Moore's meal in front of him. "Fresh biscuits too."

Melvin's face glowed with anticipation. He picked up a breast from his plate and savored the smell. "Oh yeah. This makes life good." He gave Harry one of his famous smiles that showed most of his teeth. "Mr. Harry, you da the man. You served your country well but you serve me best when you put a plate of your fried chicken under my nose and biscuits within in my reach."

Harry hung his head from embarrassment. "Did what we had to. No big deal." He shuffled back to his counter.

"Let's see if we can discern from those papers whether you and I need to look for another job. But first, let's eat." Moore took a bite of the chicken.

"That's fine eating."

For almost a half hour, the only sounds heard from their table was the click of glasses being sat down, silverware hitting plates. An occasional "um, man that's good" followed a deep release of breath.

Moore pushed his plate away first. He patted his belly. Talmano put the last bite of collards in his mouth before leaning back. He shook his head at Moore.

"That was so heavenly, it should be sinful."

"Father, I agree."

"We never ate collards when I was growing up. We had spinach, kale, cabbage but not those."

Woe showed on his face as he moved his head from side to side. "To think, I missed out on eating something so delicious for more years than I'll ever have to make up for."

Moore laughed. "Padre, I'm sorry but hey, think of it this way; if you hadn't met me, then you wouldn't have been introduced to the best greens in the land." He radiated his contentment. "See wonderful things always come from unpleasant situations. You just have to know where to find them." His fingers pointed at the stacks of plates and napkins cluttering the table.

Talmano burped. "Sorry. That only happens when I eat too much." He adjusted his clothes and moved to get comfortable on the bench. "Does he serve them every day?"

"Pretty much they're a staple."

"Good. I'm coming back soon." Another burp and a sigh interrupted him. "Tell me. Are they hard to cook?"

"Nah, just got to put them in some salt water and flavor them with love. My momma liked to add bacon grease. My granny put in a ham bone."

"Which is better?"

"Both taste good but I'm partial to the bacon way."

"Did you gents need more tea?" Harry asked before he got to the table.

Moore inched his glass towards him. "Well, since you're here." He gestured to Talmano. "My friend hadn't eaten collards before coming south, and now he's hooked on them."

"They were," he kissed his fingers, "Delicisio. How do you cook them, bacon or ham bone?"

"Depends on what's available."

"Today's, how did you do today's?"

"Fatback grease."

"Fatback? What is this, fatback?"

Moore spoke up. "Another southern thing." He nodded towards the papers. "We're here to learn something else."

Talmano held up his hand. "Please, I am learning about southern things." He looked at Harry. "How will you cook them tomorrow?"

"Not sure yet. I'll think about that when I need to." Harry poured more tea in Talmano's glass. Harry shuffled his way back to the counter.

"Padre, we need to talk about those papers."

"Yes, yes. You are right." He picked them up and scanned the first page, flipped to the second and looked up at Moore. "Here, you look."

Moore took the pages, read the first, then the second, then the first again. He glanced up. Talmano was reading another page. Before either could comment on what they read, Harry was back at the table. He sat two pieces of coconut cake down in front of them, placed two cups down and poured coffee into them.

"Thought you might need something sweet." He smiled at Talmano. "Bet you had nothing like this in New York either, Mr. Italian man." He winked.

"This piece is on the house. Second, and you will want seconds, is on Moore." He chuckled at his joke and left them.

"Lord give me room." Moore picked up the fork and dived in. Talmano copied his actions after he pushed the last paper over to Moore."

Moore read it while shoveling in his cake. When he got to the last paragraph, he dropped his fork and looked up. Talmano's face fluctuated between rapture and sorrow.

"How could that have happened?" Talmano shrugged.

"You realize we have to investigate now."

He gave a solemn nod.

"Any ideas on who could have done this?"

Talmano took his last bite of cake, then a sip of coffee. He wiped his mouth and looked out of the window. The weather had turned from sunny with a gentle breeze to dark clouds with rain falling. "No, and no idea how either."

Moore rested his chin on his hand. This would be a sticky situation for everyone involved. Retirement looked better now. "I will have to have those papers."

"I know."

Talmano folded them up and put them back into the envelope they had come from. He pushed it over to Moore but left his fingers on it.

"Just one favor, please."

Moore didn't answer.

"Do what you must, but be discreet."

"That Father, I can do."

"I'll set up a time for you and your team to talk to the bishop. An evening would be best. People are in their rooms."

Moore agreed. He picked up the envelope and stood by the table. Talmano rose as well. "I'm sorry, father."

"So am I." Together they walked out into the rain and headed in different directions to another storm.

Chapter Twenty-Five

"So who's it going to be?" Samyn's boss asked. An unlit cigarette dangled from his mouth.

"It's not Friday yet." Samyn looked at his watch. "According to my watch, it's Wednesday, 3:07 pm." He leaned against the closed door of his boss's office. His face was unreadable, his body tense. Anybody could see by the way he folded his arms across his chest he was not caving to demands put on him by his superior officer.

"You said I had until Friday to give you an answer. That means I still have at least 48 hours to go." Every word he said was distinct, clear, and precise, similar to how a nail gun delivers each piece of metal when operated by a skilled carpenter.

Captain Martin glared at him. "What difference will that make? Someone has to go, pick who, just do it." The unlit cigarette fell from his mouth. Martin, from instinct or habit, twisted his foot on the helpless roll of tobacco until it no longer had an identifiable form. He fished his pack of smokes out of his front left pocket and tapped the pack against his palm before slamming them down on his cluttered desk. "My boss wants an answer and the sooner I get it to him, the sooner he gets off my back."

"Tell him he'll have his answer on Friday." Samyn's voice was calm, his face cold, but inside he was anything but passive. On the one hand, he loved the sense of control he had on his boss at the moment. On the other, the sense of destiny regarding his pals futures ate at him. Samyn had never aspired to be a boss. He had never wanted to be in charge of anyone but himself.

"That's your problem, not mine."

"It is your problem because I say it is." Martin's voice erupted in volume and tone. His hands shook. His face went red and sweat popped out on his bald forehead.

"Hey, don't work yourself up. You'll have a massive heart attack if we're lucky, a recoverable stroke if we're not." Samyn spoke as if he were giving a weather report to a colleague. Anyone listening realized Samyn was unmoved by the happenings in front of him.

"I want an answer." Martin's voice increased in decibels.

"I don't have one." Samyn's stayed level.

"Give me one now." Martin's skin turned redder.

"Can't do that." Samyn looked serene.

Martin fished a coin out of his right front pocket. "Here heads its Blake, tails it's Moore." He tossed the coin in the air.

"Sorry, not deciding that way. You'll get a decision on Friday." Samyn opened the door.

"I want it Friday first thing in the morning."

Samyn shrugged his shoulders. "You'll get it on Friday." He walked out of one fire and into another one.

Moore was seated at his desk. His feet were propped up on it. The envelope from Talmano bearing the autopsy results was lying on his chest. His eyes were veiled.

Everyone in the office tried to look busy. They did what they needed to avoid eye contact with Samyn. It was obvious they had heard the commotion and part of the verbal exchange.

"I don't want to talk about it." Samyn uttered.

"Don't need to boss." Moore put his feet on the floor and leaned toward Samyn. His hand held the envelope out. "We do need to talk about this."

Samyn took the envelope. "Is this the…?"

Moore nodded. "Yep."

"What's it say?"

"Read it."

Samyn removed the report. He skimmed the pages, looked at Moore, and then at the results page again. "Who else knows?"

"Talmano, but no one else. He's setting up a meeting with the bishop. This changes things, huh boss."

"Holy crap. What the hell else can…?"

Moore's phone rang. Samyn slapped the papers down. He walked away.

"Perfect timing, Padre. When can we meet?" Moore watched Samyn head toward the break room where the coffee pot lived.

When he had finished with the call, he picked up the report and put it back in the envelope. He then texted Blake with the meeting details. Samyn hadn't returned, so Moore headed to the break room. His boss, friend, partner, sat at a table, head down, a cup of fresh black coffee cradled in his hand.

"I haven't had a sip. I'm just holding it." Samyn's eyes never left the table.

"Okay, boss."

"I want to."

Moore didn't reply.

"It's not like the worst addiction in the world. It's only coffee for God sakes." He lifted his gaze to Moore's face.

"True dat, Boss."

Samyn picked up the cup. Moore watched him.

"I could drink something else."

Moore's impassive face stared at Samyn's anguished one.

"True."

Samyn's grip got tighter. His knuckles turned white. Moore stood still, watching. The cup inched closer to Samyn's lips. Moore tensed.

"I almost drank a cup when I was with the bishop today. I needed to inhale one until I could digest what he told me."

"You're strong, but if you need a crutch, then this one is better than your other one,"

Samyn kept the cup near his mouth. The smell of fresh-brewed java teased him. The dark liquid dancing in his cup aroused his tastebuds. The anticipated sensation of warmth sliding down his throat and comforting his soul drove him almost to the point of abandonment. Moore's birthed words 'you're strong' echoed in his ears.

"Damn it." Samyn flung the cup across the room. It shattered against the wall.

Moore walked out. Over his shoulder, he murmured. "We have a meeting in twenty minutes with the bishop."

Chapter Twenty-Six

"Where's Blake?" Samyn said.

"He's meeting us there." Moore put the car in reverse.

"Got a reason for that?"

Moore didn't speak until he got on the main road. "Yes." Sargent Moore made a left turn at the first intersection.

"And the reason is what?" Samyn's right hand fingers tap-danced on his leg. His left forefinger beat their rhythm on his lips.

"How do you want to handle this?" Moore changed the subject. "We need a game plan, boss."

Samyn glanced out the passenger window. "Does the bishop know about the autopsy report?"

"Nope."

"Then we've got to tell him."

"Okay. Then what?" Moore's eyebrows shot up. "This is the church boss. They investigate themselves."

"The church." Samyn snorted. "They don't investigate, they cover up."

They rode in silence for several minutes. The cathedral's steeple rose in the distance. "I used to be an altar boy." Samyn looked out his window again. "Grew to hate the secrecy of the church."

"You were an altar boy?" Moore's mouth dropped.

"Mother wanted me to become a priest." Samyn turned to watch Moore's eyes go from jesting to surprise.

"Seriously, you a priest?" Moore looked at Samyn. "Seriously?"

"Yep. It broke her heart when I refused to get confirmed." Samyn's face conveyed the expression his voice didn't. It had twisted itself until it bared the agony he experienced from the long ago imprinted memory. "Couldn't do it, not after what I had seen, after what I witnessed, not after what happened to my family." He spoke more to himself than to his sidekick.

Moore pulled into a space, a quick walk to the door but not beside Blake's car. Before exiting the vehicle, he grabbed Samyn's arm.

"Hey boss, Shirley and I have been talking. We agree it's time to get me out of the force and see the world some. I'll put in my papers Friday."

Samyn protested. Moore left the auto after giving Samyn a salute. He sauntered over to Blake's car and tapped on the window. Samyn could do nothing but follow. He hated not being in charge.

When he got to where his partners stood conversing, Blake spoke a greeting before searching him out on what they were about to do. "I'll follow your lead, but I have to say, we shouldn't give the church free rein on this. Someone in there committed a crime. Who did it and their reason doesn't matter, does it? It's still a broken law, no matter if it's tried in a civil or a canonical court."

Samyn agreed. "First let's see what the bishop says. Then I'll decide. But you're right. They preach about following the commandments, but they think they can break them with no consequences."

The group moved to the entrance of the parish. Samyn lead the way. Without turning around, he uttered to Moore. "It's not up to you to decide for me. I'll give an answer on Friday, not you."

Blake gave Moore a puzzled stare. Moore put his hand up. Blake knew better than to ask what was Samyn talking about. Instead, he told Moore he had called Clarissa. They were going out Saturday. Moore patted his back. "Way to go, Rookie."

Chapter Twenty-Seven

Monsignor Talmano was waiting for them outside by the front parish door. He dropped a cigarette butt under his foot and squished it when the trio walked up.

"Sorry. Awful habit I've had since my delinquent teen years. I tried to conquer it but…" He shrugged his head against his right shoulder.

Moore cut his eyes toward Samyn. "Addictions never go, they just hide in closets waiting for an excuse to escape." Samyn ignored the look and comment.

"You speak as if you have one you battle with." Father Tamano said.

"Not me, but I've watched a friend struggle to kick two destructive habits for years. I always get a dreaded angst when I see him close to giving in to one." Moore was conversing with the priest, but his eyes stayed fixed on Samyn.

"It is hard to watch a loved one deal with an addiction. Some are harder to overcome, some are more deadly if you don't." Talmano pointed to the remains of his cigarette resting on the ground.

"I watched my sister deal with alcoholism. I swore off having over one glass of wine or whiskey a week. However, tobacco has a stronger hold on me. I can't seem to quit them, but I have stopped smoking a pack a day. I'm down to a pack a month and was doing good until today. I've inhaled three cigarettes and the days not over yet." His voice expressed how guilty he felt about his actions.

Samyn changed the subject. "Have you said anything to the bishop?"

"Not exactly. I told him the autopsy report had arrived and that Sargent Moore had seen it and asked to meet with him." Talmano raised his right hand at Blake. "Yes, I didn't speak the entire truth, just enough to get the meeting arranged."

The monsignor dug for his pack of smokes in his cassock pocket. "Bishop O'Malley suspects this will not be news he wants to learn." He pulled out the pack, tapped out a smoke, but shoved it back into hiding.

"Then let's go show him the papers." Samyn lifted his foot to take a step. "Unless you need another one." He's eyebrows raised and his lips pulled down.

Blake had been silent this whole time. He watched the surrounding men. From the conversation he discerned a few things he never knew about his boss. Samyn's comment to Moore regarding Friday confirmed the rumors flying about the office were true. One of them would be unemployed next week. He was the new kid, unproven therefore dispensable. He was sure it would be him.

While he and Moore had a good repartee, he and Samyn not so much. The truth was, Detective Samyn intimidated him with his experience and street smarts. Blake had book knowledge and technical skills, but that seemed insufficient when they were investigating cases.

Ever since he witnessed Annette Williams' suicide, the suspect in the first case he worked with Samyn and Moore, he wondered if he was cut out for detective field work. The police counselor had helped him deal with his feelings and he had put them behind him, he assumed. Now this case involving the Catholic church was causing him to have second thoughts again. He could go back to school, maybe become an engineer, or transfer to cyber-crime. Staying in the background was more his thing.

"Sirs," Blake said. "Perhaps we should go up now. The bishop is waiting and we're just wasting time here." He meant it to be polite nudging, instead he blushed. After he spoke, he realized how much his tone and words sounded like Samyn.

Moore and Samyn glanced at each other then turned their surprised faces to Blake.

"I'm sorry, I just meant we're doing nothing. I mean only standing here." Blake tripped over his sentences.

"Young friend, do you ref for sports games?" Talmano said.

It was Blakes turn to be surprised. "No sir. Why?"

"Perhaps you should, in your spare time, I mean."

Blakes face twisted in puzzlement.

"You are a person who calls things as they see them." Talmano patted Blake on the shoulder. He pointed towards the doorway. "Gentlemen, if you please follow me."

Moore looked at Samyn. "Hey boss man, you're rubbing off on the rookie. He's starting to sound just like you." He chuckled. "Definitely got to do some paperwork now. With two Samyn's at work, I'll never be right."

Samyn and Blake pierced him with hostility before they stomped off. Moore whistled and strolled into the church behind them.

Chapter Twenty-Eight

Monsignor Talmano knocked on the door to the bishop's office. When given the invite to enter, he opened the door, took two steps forward, bowed and then stood aside for the others to come in. When everyone was inside, he walked into the hallway, looked both ways, retreated and shut the door. The click of the lock connecting startled the officers.

"Is that necessary?" Samyn looked at the bishop.

"Is it legal?" Blake whispered to Moore, whose enormous eyes just looked around the room.

The bishop was standing behind his desk. He extended his hands to each man while he spoke. "Gentlemen, I understand you have the autopsy report which Monsignor Talmano requested against the wishes of the church."

Samyn nodded. His eyes remained fixed on Bishop O'Malley's face.

"Each of you must understand what we say here today, what is revealed in that report is shared in confidence. I don't want, need someone to walk in on this conversation."

The bishop appeared to be in control and confident. Samyn knew he wasn't. Telltale signs, ones used by expert poker players, revealed he was spouting bluster. Samyn had spent many nights at a card table. He learned those small giveaways of bluffery. A fine line of glistening on the forehead, pupils dilated, tense shoulders, fingers and feet that couldn't stay still told other players, who was bluffing their way to a winning hand. For now, he would play along with O'Malley.

"Sir, I can promise you what is said here will not be used against you or the church."

He wasn't exactly agreeing with the bishops terms but showing a willingness to cooperate.

Bishop O'Malley sized up Samyn. He too was a card player, and this was the best ante he could get from the detective. O'Malley decided he was in.

O'Malley gestured they should have a seat. Arranged before his desk were four chairs. The officers looked at each other before selecting their seats. Samyn chose the one in front of the bishop. Moore went to his left, and Blake sat on the right of him. They left Father Talmano with the chair closet to the door, but next to Moore. He waited for the bishop to lower himself as that was church custom. The bishop gave his permission for the priest to sit first, as that was Irish politeness. The other men were not practicing Catholics. They made themselves comfortable and waited for this dance to end.

Samyn held the report envelope out to the bishop.

"Have you read this yet?" O'Malley took it from him.

"Yes sir. I have and so has Moore."

"I guess it's my turn then." The bishop put on a pair of reading glasses and removed the papers. He read the first sheet, cast his eyes towards Talmano and proceeded on to the next one. "Have you seen these?"

Father Talmano's head dropped. "Yes, your Grace. I have. I am sorry."

The bishop dismissed his apology with a wave of his hand. He leaned back after reading the last page of the report. His glasses slipped down his nose. Bishop O'Malley's elbows rested upon the chair arms and his hands raised up with his fingers lightly touching each other. His head bowed. To the casual observer he looked to be in deep mediation. Those who had seen his face before reading the papers supposed otherwise.

Each man suspected him to be in turmoil over the results of the autopsy. After what felt to be hours of waiting, the bishop let his hands drop and he looked at the men around his desk. "Gentlemen, we have a severe issue here, one that must be handled delicately."

Samyn broke in. "You get what happened was a crime, right? Even a holy person can't break the sixth commandment and get away with it, not in this age."

The two men sat, eyes focused upon the other. O'Malley broke first.

"I'm aware the church has a grim history and people are suspicious of it, but you are right. Even the holiest cannot break the commandments." He leaned forward. "Can I propose something?"

Samyn nodded. He still stared at the bishop's face.

"I think, and I could be wrong that what we found in the crypt relates to the crime."

"Go on." Samyn gave a quick glance to each of his partners.

"I'm not sure how but it seems logical, it's not a coincidence that a bishop dies and someone has opened his tomb."

"Are you suggesting the owner of the arm outlined in our dust is the killer?" Moore asked.

"The missing ring then could have been taken by the killer as a memento." Blake said.

"Possibly." The bishop focused on Samyn. "I can't help but wonder if the start of this all began at the orphanage in Ireland. Too many little instances aligning in one spot doesn't work for me. I believe in divine destinies and manifestations, but I don't believe in coincidences."

"I don't either." Samyn agreed. "But as an officer sworn to uphold the law, I can't let you cover up a murder just because it happened on church grounds."

"I'm not asking you too. I'm only asking for mercy and your help. I want to know what happened and why. Bishop Newman's death may have been an accident."

Samyn opened his mouth. A snort escaped.

"Silence." The bishop ordered. "I will not allow the church to take control of this, but I do not want a media circus. This investigation must take place quietly, discretely, and with reverence to the church. If Newman's death was an intentional action committed by a person in holy orders, then I will support them being prosecuted by the legal system. If they are brought to trial and convicted only upon evidence of their crime and not the other ones committed by the church, gentlemen.

I also want assurance they can be housed in a facility which will be suitable for their mental state."

"If I don't agree?"

Bishop O'Malley scooped up the autopsy papers. He walked over to a shredder.

"Then these never existed." He held one page over the entrance and turned the machine on.

Samyn grinned, only it had no warmth and was not jolly. It was cold, hard, but respectful. It was a look he gave when bested at cards.

"I like your moxie." He nodded at the bishop. "Where would you like us to start?"

Chapter Twenty-Nine

Moore headed back to the precinct to go over the bishop's notes and Blake tagged along to find anything out about the websites he had discovered on the late bishop's laptop and search the web for information on people whose names popped up. Samyn stayed behind. It was time for him and the bishop to have a conversation in private.

"Would you like some coffee, no excuse me, I remember you said you don't drink coffee. Tea then, can I offer you some tea?" Bishop O'Malley didn't wait for his answer. He reached for his phone. "I need a cuppa Irish Tea." He sent a text and laid his phone down on the desk.

"Why don't we sit over here?" He gestured to the area the officers had sat the first time they were here.

Samyn stopped in front of an antique mahogany case. He peered at the contents peeking at him through the glass doors. "Yours, I presume."

"They are." O'Malley tried not to let his pride be too obvious.

"What position?"

The Bishop chuckled. "Would you believe I was a hooker?"

"Good-looking guy like you should have made a bundle or at least more than the church pays." Samyn deadpanned.

O'Malley laughed hard. "You think it's easy working the streets? Women are never satisfied. They always want more." His eyes watered.

Samyn struggled to keep a straight face. "So bloody true, at least that's been my experience. Nothing I did made my ex happy. Please tell me you didn't make the mistake of promising them forever?"

"Only after I donned my cassock." Samyn lost it. He worked to keep the laughter from his voice. "Was that before or after you took their money?"

O'Malley drew back his shoulders. "After, of course."

"So what did you do when hooking didn't work for you?"

"I flanked when I had too."

"And after that?"

"Got ordained when I finished seminary and left rugby on the field when I took a position with the Vatican. Still like to watch it as often as I can and when I'm home play in a pickup game if possible. Like to fantasize I still can move like a youthful man."

Samyn considered making a retort but passed. It was time to move the conversation towards the goal. He sat on the settee in front of the window and sighed. "I have fantasies about still being young then my back or knee will remind me I'm not."

A knock on the door startled them. Before the bishop could give his customary response to enter, the door opened to reveal Monsignor Talmano and the mother superior tugging on a tray.

"I have it, mother superior. You may go back to your duties now." He turned to the bishop. "I apologize your Grace. I tried to bring by myself."

The mother superior pushed past him. "I told him if he were holding a tray with both hands, he could not knock or open your door. I am here as his helpmeet." She eyed Samyn. "Haven't I seen you here before? With some other men?" She looked around the room.

Talmano entered and sat the try on the table. "Yes, I told you they were here trying to get a donation." He looked at Samyn and cocked his head towards the nun.

"Yes, yes, we are seeking money for a charity."

"What charity?" Her voice pronounced she did not buy that story.

Without missing a step, Samyn spoke before Talmano. "Two actually. One is the Play Cops and Kids or PLACK as it's called on the streets and the other is Widows of Officers Wishes, or WOW for short." He gave her an angelic grin, sincerest pleading look, and even batted his eyes at her.

She glared back. "They sound phony. Have you checked him and these groups out?" She glared now at the priests. "I suspect they're scammers." She turned back to face Samyn. Her eyes dared him to argue with her. Instead, he smiled sweeter.

"Oh no, Ma'am." His head shook emphatically. "No PLACK is an inner city organization aimed at getting street kids to trust us. We teach them how to play sports, take them to a movie sometimes, mentor the ones who have no fathers around. If we can show them cops are not bad guys then perhaps we may keep them out of trouble later." He spoke in an earnest, grave tone.

"WOW is an offshoot of our Police Fraternal Society. As brothers in arms, we promise to look out for one another. When one brother dies in the line of duty, or even when he passes away from an accident or disease, we take care of his widow and their home for as long as she remains single and in that house. We become the men she calls for her honey-do list." He struggled to stay solemn.

"Didn't Christ say to take care of the widows and orphans?" He shrugged his shoulders. "And didn't he also say to do unto others and love one another.?" He pushed one side of his lips up. "I sure he did, ma'am. At least, that's what my nuns in school taught." He gave her a beguiling gaze. She wanted to speak, but he let his words go first. "Sister, please, we are serving Christ the only way we can in this life and aren't we all called to do that?"

He opened his palms up and talked before she could say anything. "Now you're aware of why I'm here." He wrapped his hand around her elbow as he shepherded her towards the door. "You'll understand why I need to plead my case for a substantial donation from the church to these fine priests in private." When they arrived at their destination, Samyn gave her a gentle push and then put his body in the doorway. "Perhaps the nuns would like to contribute something to the widows or put together a box of snacks for the kids? Go talk to them about it. You can tell the bishop later what you will give."

He shut the door, leaned on it for a moment as she rattled the doorknob from the other side. When he heard her walk away, he moved back to the settee. Talmano and O'Malley clapped their approval.

"Well done." O'Malley nodded. "How many sisters did you have?"

"Can you teach me how to dominate her like that?" Talmano realized what he said. "Sorry your Grace. I meant guide her away and not let her talk." O'Malley frowned.

"O come on your Eminence. Admit it, he has a gift for dealing with the mother superior. She's a beast."

"True, she is."

"She's more than a beast. She's Satan personified, my purgatory on earth. Why can't I learn to handle her the way he did?" He dropped his head before the bishop. His clasp hands reached skyward. "Oh please, please, please let him teach me his ways."

"Italians, such lovers of drama in the operas of life." O'Malley chided, then chuckled and motion Talmano to stand.

"I didn't lie. Those are real charities that the police force supports and we can always use money and sometimes help, if the church is interested. Let's first discuss what to do about the problem someone in this institution created for you?"

Talmano moved to the door.

"No, stay, if Detective Samyn doesn't mind." O'Malley looked at Samyn for his answer.

"Not at all. I think an Irishman, an Italian, and a streetwise Polish cop will come up with an ingenious way to solve this conundrum. Are you in?" He looked at Talmano, who nodded.

"Good, then gentlemen lets play this game."

Chapter Thirty

Moore and Blake set to work in an empty conference room. Piles of papers laid on the table. Blake got busy googling names highlighted by Moore that were mentioned in Bishop O'Malley's notes regarding the orphanage in Ireland. Occasionally he'd scratched through something on his list or make a note on the iPad next to him. Moore kicked back in a chair with his legs stretched out and crossed in front of him. Every so often he adjusted himself or underlined something on the page he was reading. Their work was progressing with the same speed of molasses flowing in winter. Moore stood and stretched. His arms reached above his head, and he yawned.

"I need some caffeine. Want something?" Moore said.

Blake shook his head no, then changed his mind. "Yeah, a coke would be great and some chips or crackers." He twisted his neck from side to side and rolled his shoulders. "Find anything interesting yet?"

"A few things. Let me grab some drinks for us first." Moore headed out.

Blake looked at his phone. They had been busy for ninety minutes. He stood and walked around the table. His research had created all the piles of printed sheets. Seeing it in stacks made him suspect he had once again been too zealous. One stack was information on the families whose attended St. Stephens or sent their children to school there. Another pile was the biographies of the church and school staff. Next to it were lists of names of everyone who in the last ten years had been affiliated with the convent or abbey. The largest pile was church history and religious traditions. Blake picked up a paper-clipped bunch and thumbed through it.

"Ok, one coke for the research king." Moore offered him a can. He then dropped the load of chips and snacks he had in his arms. "Pick your poison." He grabbed a bag of peanut M&M's and sank into a chair. "Learn anything yet?"

"That I overdid the research."

Moore laughed.

"But I've traced some names from the orphanage and a few crossed paths over the years. What about you?"

"The bishop tells an excellent story. Although he doesn't say it, he implies things at the orphanage under Bishop Newman appeared kosher but weren't. Three times they sent adolescent teenage girls from that home to one of the church-run laundry facilities. Twice nuns asked to be placed elsewhere, and once a nun was sent away. That was the one his sister thought pregnant."

"Were the circumstances the same for the others?"

"Good question, rookie. He's not saying they were, but my gut says he suspected something suspicious was happening."

"You don't suppose what O'Malley was investigating at the orphanage has anything to do with the murder of the bishop here?"

Moore leaned back and put his feet up on the table. He threw a few pieces of candy in his mouth. "Yep, I do. Just seems odd to me that strange things happened wherever this Bishop Newman ventured. His karma caught up with him."

"True dat." Blake spoke with a forced straight face.

Moore looked at him through squinted eyes. "Say what?"

Blake's face turned red, but he held his ground. "True dat." He enunciated each word.

"Homey." Moore said before chuckling.

Blake grinned, then grew solemn. "Why would someone open a coffin though? Would you do that?"

"No man. I don't believe in disturbing the dead. I don't even walk on graves in a cemetery if I can help it. I say let the dead rest."

"That image we found bothers me. It has to be someone who had more than normal friendly affection for him. Right?"

"I love my wife but I don't want to crawl into her coffin for a hug. Hear what I'm saying? Somebody who had or has that desire, they have some serious issues."

Blake nodded. "Myself? I can't picture what kind of person would feel like that. Do you know someone who would want to lay their head on a dead man? Or touch a body after it's been buried."

"The whole idea of necromancy fascinated as a kid. I think it was in some story I read. Anyway, the word sounded cool, and I was a big enough geek to like cool words. Shirley and I have been to New Orleans dozens of times. Lots of voodoo and dark stuff in that city," Moore shook his head. "Bad mojo, my granny would say. She was a creole who believed in Christ and superstitions." Moore grinned.

"I always thought the Catholic church was good at using superstitions to keep their faithful in line. Maybe Newman practiced it on some of his followers and one just couldn't let go of him when he died."

Moore couldn't tell if Blake was joking or trying to make a valid point.

"What do you mean?"

"All right, suppose this: Newman sees that someone beams when he speaks or follows him around and hangs onto his every word. He realizes he has power over this person and uses it."

"How would he do that? I know little about Catholicism, but I understand what you mean. How would an adored catholic priest use, let's say idol worship, to his advantage?"

"Idol worship?" Blake laughed. "Did you mean to make a joke?"

"You know what I meant. I'm not talking about the idol worship they do during prayers and such, but I've seen people swoon when the pope is nearby. There are some who truly treat these guys the same way girls do who go crazy over musicians."

Blake's face went slack. He stared at the wall over Moore's shoulder.

"Hey rookie, are you ok?"

Blake kept staring. His lips moved, but no sound came out.

"Rookie? Talk to me, man. What's wrong?"

Blake raised his hand. He grab a bunch of papers, flipped through them and threw them over his shoulder before picking up another bunch. He dropped those and frantically searched his piles. At last, he found what he was looking for.

"What are priest expected to give up?" Blake looked at Moore. His thoughts excited his eyes.

"Well, it's not whiskey or any alcohol I guess. We saw Bishop O'Malley had some in his lair."

"Keep going."

"I've seen the way some of these guys live when they hit the upper ranks, so I don't think it's the desire to have wealth. I mean, I saw the Prada loafers Pope Benedict wore. I couldn't afford them without maxing out a credit card."

"Keep on."

"They don't give up licenses or cell phones or apparently satellite TV. I saw a dish at the parsonage or parish hall, whatever they call their residence." Moore pondered, then shrugged his shoulders and held his palms up.

"Mull on this." Blake looked intensely at Moore's face. "What do you have that no priest has, at least, not outside the church walls or private inner sanctum of his rooms?"

Moore's eyes grew larger, so large they appeared to be the only feature on his face.

Blake nodded.

"You mean a wife, a woman, a home life?"

Blake kept nodding. "Bingo."

Moore's head moved in the opposite direction. "Nah, he can't have. I mean, they take vows on that. Do you really suspect he may have had a woman, a wife on the side?"

"Yes, they do, and yes he must have. I've checked some websites with Talmano that the bishop had visited regularly. They're pretty bizarre, but the one thing they have in common is women. He even had a site where he's posted pictures of women in either workout attire or in habits and all were in strange poses, not just ordinary snapshots."

"Like what?"

"One was grafting a tree. Several were of women in various yoga poses. The weirdest one was the backside of a nun removing her habit."

Moore arched his shoulders back and stared at Blake as if he had grown another nose or his head had shrunk to the size of a dime.

"Whoa." Moore's usual grin disappeared. Instead, his face looked like he had tasted food he didn't enjoy eating.

"It's possible."

"My Shirl loves me but I don't think when I go she'll stay at the funeral home and lay on my cold dead body. I ain't loved that much. More likely, she'll stand there and remind me of all the things I promised and didn't do."

"Here." Blake handed him the papers he held. "All the kids sent from the orphanage were girls and of course, there're the nuns who asked to leave. He was in his prime then. All the orphans he counseled were girls between the ages of thirteen and seventeen . Boys were in the orphanage too, but there's no record he was involved with them."

"Incredible." Moore skimmed the papers.

"What if Newman saw some youthful woman gaze at him with awe and he took advantage of her? Suppose he seduced a woman so completely, she had trouble letting him go after his death? "I'll buy it for now. But who would it be? Church member, mother of a student, you can't be supposing a nun?"

Blake shook his head yes.

"A nun? A woman who runs around in a penguin suit?"

Blake kept up his affirmative motion.

"Seriously?" Moore looked at Blake in amazement. "Okay lets say I agree with you but why do you assume a nun and not some other female associated with St. Stephens?"

"It makes sense that a nun would be the most likely suspect. They live on the grounds so they have access to the crypt at all hours, I'm sure. They would be more familiar with the routines of the priests and possibly where the bishop might be at certain times should they wish to accidentally met up with him. I guess a teacher would be able so do that too though, but not a regular parishioner or a mother of a student." Blake scrunched up his lips, looked at his papers again and decided. "Yes, definitely a nun makes most sense."

"So which nun do you want to investigate first? Perhaps the charming mother superior?" Moore's tone tried to hide his normal jovial self.

Blake hadn't caught on that Moore wasn't fully in agreement with him. "I think we should investigate them all until we narrow down the list. To me, they're all suspects, even the mother superior, though she's seems most unlikely."

"Why? She's female, we assume, and she lives on the grounds, and if anybody knows what is always going on at St Stephen's, it's her." Moore was biting the inside of his mouth as he spoke.

Blake pondered these facts. "Yes, she fits the perimeters of a suspect but well, I, I mean… what I'm trying to say is wouldn't you have to be capable of loving someone immensely to want to hold them when they are dead?"

"You would guess so."

"Right and I don't see the mother superior as a person who gives and gets love. But if you want to put her in the suspected murderer column, I'll go along with that. I can see her killing the bishop. Heck, I'm sure she's tried to kill us with her stares."

Moore lost it. He laughed until he choked. "Sorry rookie. I'm just surprised by your thinking. I agree whoever was in that crypt would have to some knowledge of the church activities, but I can't fathom the mother superior as not knowing one of her nuns was gaga over the bishop, and not putting a stop to it. Somehow I just can't picture her as letting anyone feel anything like love while she's on duty. She's a scary mother, man."

Blake considered this. His face showed his defeat. "Your right. She would have put an end to anything, and she certainly knows what is always happening on those grounds. It must be a parishioner or a lay person, not a nun. Maybe someone he met off grounds."

Moore picked up Bishop O'Malley's notes again. "Who says it has to be a female, rookie? I've always heard being a priest is the perfect cover for a man not wanting to be known openly as gay. Wouldn't it be a fit place to live in peace if someone was transgender?"

Hiding Behind Robes

It was Blakes turn to be surprised and speech-
less.

Chapter Thirty-One

Samyn hoped he would avoid being seen by his boss at the precinct house. He wanted to go in, catch up with Moore and Blake, then hide somewhere while he sorted through this church mess. The last thing he wanted was to deal with the demand to fire one of his partners.

He and Moore had been together for nearly thirty years. How could he break the partnership up now? Samyn reasoned. Moore had been there when his marriage fell apart. He was the one who got Samyn help when he most needed it. He was the only one who knew what coffee meant to Samyn and why. Samyn had been there for Moore when his only son was killed in Yemen. He was with him when the call came about his father's heart attack. They were more than work partners or brothers in arms; they were friends closer than family sometimes.

Blake was like a son that Samyn never had. He was young, green, and uncynical. Samyn had been like that at one time. Life changed him though in ways he hoped Blake never experienced. *Kids got game and I want to teach him how to break the rules.* Blake came along when both Moore and he, needed a freshening. The rookie kept them on their toes, and he liked that. That kid wasn't like most of the youngsters who graduated from training, Samyn thought. *He has an old school dedication and the desire to serve, not use his badge as an authority shield.* The lieutenant was not in favor of letting him go.

Samyn kept his head down when he walked into the precinct. He guessed which room Blake and Moore were in and headed that way. He slinked down the hall, not speaking or making eye contact. It was the only way he could try to be invisible.

"Samyn, get in here." The one voice he did not want to hear pounded his ears. For a moment he considered keeping to his plan. He knew though that voice would follow him, then his team would have to explain what they were working on. *Make the church angry or the boss man?* Both were tempting. He chose boss man.

He entered the office with a sullen face and a lifted arm. He pointed to the old analog watch he wore, which showed not only the time but date and day too.

"It's not Friday."

"Who's going to leave us?"

"It's not Friday."

"What's a few more hours? Just give me a name."

"It's not Friday."

Captain Martin slammed a file drawer. "Damn it. Why are you drawing this out? Pick one and tell me."

"We agreed I had till Friday. It's not…"

"I know it's not Friday." Martin mimicked.

Samyn walked out. He had thirty-five hours before he had to give an answer officially. The pressure, though, would start first thing in the morning to speak a name. The only name he wanted to say was his. He really was ready to retire. This garbage with the church, the pressure from his boss, all the tech jargon spewed out by the rookie kid. He was getting too old to be a cop. He'd file his papers in the morning. Boss couldn't stop him. Samyn smiled. His day was looking up. He whistled the rest of the way to the conference room.

"So guys, what can you tell me?" He said when he walked in.

"That you're whistling off key." Moore said without hesitation.

Samyn looked at Blake. "Tell me something, kid."

"You sound fine. Moore's ear is out of tune."

Samyn cackled. "Touche, Moore."

He loved these guys. These were his friends. There was no way he would sacrifice either of them to appease the muck mucks who ruled the force. They were the only family he had. He would retire, but for now, there was this whatever you call a case that's not an official investigation to deal with first. "Anything new, any clue who's responsible for a murder that's a non criminal case?"

Blake looked at Moore. Moore held up his right palm with his index finger pointing to Blake. "Go ahead, rookie. Spill your thoughts."

Blake took a deep breath. "I don't know where to start. We have made some headway on this."

"Start by explaining all this." Samyn gestured to the papers piled on the table.

"This is everything I could think of to consider. I ran backgrounds on all the parishioners, all the parents of students enrolled in the school, names of all the nuns and priests who live on the grounds, names of the people mentioned in O'Malley's notes, events that happened in the church…"

"Got it. You researched everything."

"He's the research king, bossman."

Samyn sifted through some papers. "Good thing we aren't charged per page. Our department's budget is sitting right here."

Moore grinned at the jest. Blake looked at the ground. "Sorry. I got carried away. I was trying to be through. Guess I should have analyzed what I found before I printed it out."

Moore tried to ease his embarrassment. "it's no big deal, rookie. Samyn's upset you know how to print things from your laptop. He still doesn't understand the relationship between printer and computer and that the printed pages don't come out of the desktop machine." He winked at Samyn.

"No, I overdid it but it helped us narrow down things today or at least I thought I had narrowed down who may have been the person in the crypt with the dead bishop until Moore put another obstacle up."

"I was only weighing things out."

"But you brought up a valid point."

"it's just a matter of experience."

"But it was so obvious once you said it."

Samyn's head swiveled like a spectator at a tennis match. He did not understand what they were talking about.

"Stop and one of you speak."

"Go rookie." Moore said.

Blake coughed and explained his idea that the person who had been in the crypt was a nun. Samyn listened without interrupting. Blake spoke until he felt he had talked too much, then he shut up.

"Do you think the same person was responsible for his death or not?" Samyn asked.

"I don't know, maybe."

"Okay so if it's a nun who was with the dead Bishop and she didn't kill him did another nun off him or was it a priest and could they have taken his ring?" Samyn again quizzed Blake.

Blake mulled over this. Samyn had nothing else to do, so he picked up some papers to read while he waited.

Blake cleared his throat. "I suppose it's possible it may have been a priest if we assume he was interested in the nun who was with the dead Bishop."

"A motive for this would be what?"

"Jealousy. People do stupid things when blinded by envy." Blake said.

Moore looked at Samyn. His eyebrows raised. The telepathy that takes place between people who have been close for years was happening now. At last, they reached a conclusion and nodded at each other.

"He's got a valid point." Moore said.

"A love triangle, in a church?" Samyn scratched his face by his right ear. "So you're supposing the nun wants the bishop, but another priest wants the nun. The priest removes the bishop from the equation."

"Yes. That would be a plausible theory, but what if there's a nun who was in love with the dead bishop? He never noticed her, but was chasing someone else?" Blake said.

"That fits what we know as well." Moore said.

"How are you going to prove either? Do you have a nun for a suspect yet? What about at a priest?"

"No, not yet." Blake was pensive. "We should first find the person who got into that coffin and I think that person is a nun. A person wouldn't have to be very strong to slide the top of the coffin enough to get to the deadman's hands."

"How are we going to do that?" Samyn wrinkled his brow and locked eyes on the innocent face before him. He enjoyed testing the kid.

"By spending the night there. If the nun comes back, and I believe she will, then we can snag her."

"Sounds very simple, rookie." Moore said.

"It will work. I think she's visited that sight often, probably every night. Those candles have burnt for several hours and I don't deduce it was in one night."

"Well, if you want to stake out a coffin in a church crypt, then I say do it. I'll call the Bishop

O'Malley and tell him the plan. He may insist Monsignor Talmano be with you. You know, he'll want his own witness."

Blake nodded, "Where will you be?"

"Boss, I don't know about you but I see this as a one-person job. There's two ways in but the activity is focused on one area only and it's a place full of dead people. No one goes willingly into a crypt at night unless they got problems. Know what I'm saying?"

"I do and I don't do dark cold places myself." Samyn extended his hand to Blake. "Great idea, kid. Go catch our creepy nun. Moore and I will back you up from our homes. Excuse me, gents. I have a call to make."

Chapter Thirty-Two

Blake arrived at the church and parked in the back of the parish. Monsignor Talmano was outside smoking. Blake heartily greeted him, and Talmano shushed him in response.

"It's a period of silence now." He whispered. "Sorry, Father." Blake was grateful the priest couldn't see his red face.

Talmano dropped his butt and twisted it under his foot. He pointed to the door and in they went. He gestured to the fridge, and a counter where a basket of fruit was sitting. His gestures asked if Blake would like anything.

Blake shook his head no and lifted his shoulder, indicating he had what he needed in the bag he carried on it. Father Talmano grabbed an apple for himself and a bottle of water. He walked out the kitchen with Blake close behind. No matter how lightly he tried to step, the floor squeaked under his feet making him cringe before he touched it. He felt foolish creating noise in a place of solitude.

Blake expected to be taken to the bishop, but instead Talmano headed down a side passage. When they got to a door, he stopped and indicated for Blake to wait there. Father Talmano opened the door, and a cool breeze entered. He glanced left and right before taking a step outside. Hidden in his robes was a small flashlight which he turned on and aimed towards the ground. He signaled Blake to follow, but to pay attention to what was below him. Three steps appeared in the dim light. He nodded and moved down each one when Talmano placed the light on it. They were now outside under a stone archway that led to the Cathedral.

Blake had never seen the church up close at night before. He stared in awe. It looked cold and imposing. If a building could look intimidating this one did. Blake now understood why horror writers enjoyed using Gothic buildings in their stories. It was easy to get a sense of evil from this place.

They tiptoed down the walk leading to a church entrance. Again at the doorway, Talmano paused to turn on his flashlight and signaled for Blake to wait. When he gave the okay sign , they stepped into the church. Talmano pointed which way they were heading. The sleeves of his robe obscured the beam from his light, but it gave off enough for Blake to see the ground and step cautiously around candleholders and lecterns. Once they had gotten passed the sacristy, and into the hall leading to the crypt entrance, Talmano let the flashlight escape from his robe. The full beam now showed them the way.

Again Blake was taken in by the cold stones of the church. He felt himself being swallowed up by the history this place represented. It hit him what he was about to do. He may leave here feeling inept and stupid for assuming the nun would be back tonight. If she did make an appearance, then he would have to deal with the biggest church in the region, a branch of the largest, oldest church in existence, whose arms reached everywhere. Recent media stories made people believe the church desired to cover up crimes that happened under their roofs, not admit to them. He wondered if he, the rookie, was being used as a scapegoat tonight, if he was the expendable one on the team. Rumors flew that someone from his unit would be let go soon. *Why not axe the kid who thinks somebody in robes committed a crime?*

Down the steps and into the future, or rather into the past he headed.

"Can we talk in here? If we whisper I mean?"

"Yes, if you want to."

"I'd like to ask you a few questions, about some things."

Monsignor Talmano pointed to one of the wall shelves. "I put a sleeping bag down here earlier. I say we spread it on the floor. Those stones get damp at night and I personally didn't want to stand all evening, nor do I want to curl up on one of the empty wall shelves."

"I brought one for the same reasons." He took the bag off his shoulder and pulled out his sleeping bag.

Father Talmano nodded. "Great minds, they say. I picked out a place today where I thought we could wait. We can see the coffin and not be seen by a visitor. We can also see if any lights appear on the stairs. No one would try to come down here without some kind of light, even if they are familiar with this place."

The place he suggested was ideal. It was tucked away from the main walk. Anyone would have to be intentionally looking to see them. They spread out their bags and settled down for what might be an interminable night.

Talmano took a bite of his apple. "What made you decide to do this?"

"Be a cop?"

"No, spend a night in a crypt."

"I thought about it. Why would anyone open a coffin and touch a dead person?"

"They're disturbed." Talmano took another bite.

"Yes, obviously, but are they overcome with a powerful sense of guilt, grief, or both? I decided they could be, must be. So now I need to learn who that person is."

"I have seen people who do grieve deeply and go to burial sights daily. So I'll agree that can happen, but I've not seen it take place in a church crypt at night before." Talmano pulled his legs up to his chin. His hand holding the apple, laid on his knee.

"What if this same person killed the bishop? What if it's that pain that makes them want forgiveness? Grief can make people do crazy things." Blake reasoned out his thinking.

"So you're saying the outlined arm on the bishop could be the same person who poisoned him, accidentally, perhaps?"

"It's just a working theory for the moment. No one came up with a better possible way of finding out who committed this crime and as police officers sworn to uphold the law, we have to try to solve it." Blake pulled his water bottle from his bag. "Even if no one in the department knows we're working on it like a regular case."

"Will you arrest this person?" Talmano looked at Blake.

"I should, I guess, but I don't know what to do. Technically, it's not a matter of police record, but it is a crime." Blake took a sip of water.

"We put you in quite a conundrum, didn't we?"

"What would the church want me to do?" Blake saw a way out of this mess and took it.

"Bishop O'Malley and I agree. The church has covered up too many sins in its past. If this was an accidental act, then the church should handle it. The offender would be given a lifetime of penitence and solitude. If it was intentional, well that's different. Neither O'Malley nor I believe wearing a robe, habit, or collar, should protect you from your crimes. It's why he investigates clergy so diligently and gets angry when the church wants to protect them."

A shaft of light by the steps suspended their conversation. They looked at each other. The wait had ended. The expected guest was here.

Chapter Thirty-Three

Father Talmano suggested he move to a place near the entrance but still out of sight. Blake agreed. Talmano worked his way to the back wall on the left side of the stairwell. Blake worked out where the monsignor's line of sight would be. He moved to get a different view of the tomb.

The rustling sound on the steps told them someone was now descending. An unsteady light beam bounced ahead of the intruder. A figure draped in dark, non-revealing attire entered the room. It glided effortlessly to the coffin of Bishop Newman and knelt beside it. The figure extinguished the light they used to get down the stairs and to the tomb. The room escaped back to deathly darkness.

Blake thought Talmano had moved, but he wasn't sure. His eyes had adjusted to the lack of light, but still all he made out were shapes of ebony. He blinked, trying to get his eyes better focused. The kneeling person disappeared in the dark. Blake looked around. He couldn't see anything resembling a human, nor did he hear a noise that would give away the person's location. He made a decision and took a risk. Up he ventured. *Found you.*

Blake watched as the unknown person stood at the foot of the bishop's resting place. He saw how they stroked the top and laid their head down upon it. A movement out of the corner of his eye caught his attention. Monsignor Talmano was inching himself along the wall with more stealth than expected in an untrained person. Blake admired him for that. He wished he could be so silent in motion. *Do they learn this in seminary?*

His attention turned back to the guest. They had climbed onto the coffin and were tracing the Chi Roi carved on it with a finger, moving as if it were drawing it. *Strange, so very strange. Why do that?* Blake himself had traced headstones, but paper and pencils were involved and it was on the graves of his ancestors. This action creeped him out.

The person pushed back a little on their hood. The face was still obscured. With catlike mimicry they jumped off the tomb. Next they pushed the top open to reveal the upper part of the body. They leaned in and kissed the dead man's hands before crossing themselves. This macabre scene fascinated Blake. It was like watching a horror film, but not on a screen. *This is sick, so very sick.* Who, those thoughts addressed, him or the robed person, he wasn't sure.

A glint appeared. He looked to see where Talmano was. He guessed the Monsignor was standing by the wall between two other coffins, but he wasn't sure. All he knew was he was closest and he would have to apprehend this person.

The metal object was poised in the air. Blake tried, but could not make out what it was or where it was aimed. *Please Lord, I need Talmano to turn on his flashlight.*

Blake moved gingerly from his spot. He hoped that whoever this was; they were intent on their actions and were ignoring any noises.

On clicked Talmano's flashlight. A thin slice of silver in the act of striking down paused. The figure stared ahead, mesmerized like a deer by the sudden brightness. Blake lunged toward the robed person. The unknown person stayed in the act of suspended motion until Blake's hand touched their arm. Fear caused the robed one to turn. The object in their hand moved again. Blake ducked, intending to scoop this person up in a classic fireman carry. It struck down again and again. Blake screamed from the pain. He let go, and the robed one ran.

"Go. I'll be behind you." Blake urged Talmano, who took off after the unknown assailant.

The monsignor grabbed the robed one as it put a foot on the bottom step. Talmano wrapped his arms around their waist. They twisted and kicked to get away. The hand with the object thrashed about. Talmano's grip remained tight while he bobbed and weaved his head out of danger's way. The robed figure dropped the weapon. The hand that held it now reached up and clawed at Talmano's eyes. His eyes were untouched, but his face took the blunt of the scratches.

The hand retreated, and the body went limp. Talmano spoke to the person in gentle whispers between gasping for air.

"You're safe. Be calm and breathe. You're safe."

He was turning the body towards him when the person tensed up, dropped their head and bit Talmano's hand. Pain, then blood. His instincts made him let go. As the body turned to run up the steps, Talmano made another effort to grab them. He got his bleeding hand on their arm. The robed figure tried to pry Talmano's fingers off, but the blood made them slick.

Monsignor Talmano put his divinity aside, fished his flashlight from his pocket and used it to whack the wrist of his assailant. The unknown person yelled whether from pain or from the shock of being struck the priest did not ask. His concern was keeping his hold on them until Blake could get there or the robed one gave up.

The battle of wills continued until the assailant wiggled free. Whoever they were pushed Talmano back. His flashlight struck the wall hard enough to break the lens and dent the metal casing. The unknown one squealed, then spit in Talmano's eyes and on his face. His face, where he had been scratched, stung from the hot germy liquid. By the time he had cleared his eyes and wiped away the pain, the robed one had gone.

"Blake, Blake, where are you?"

A moan was the response. Talmano's familiarity with the surroundings guided him to the sound. He stopped long enough to light one candle sitting on a shelf. When he lifted it, he saw feet pointing towards a wall. He moved that way. Blake was lying on the floor. One hand pressed against his neck. Blood trickled through his fingers. A pool of it was gathering by his hips.

"Call for backup. Officer down." The automatic words were slurred.

Chapter Thirty-Four

The mother superior was having difficulty sleeping. She decided instead of tossing about in bed, she would get up and read. Beside her bed was a nightstand with a hidden drawer. She reached down and pulled it open to retrieve her book.

Although people considered her hard and unfeeling, she loved nothing more than a good romance. She preferred one in which the hero was a buff, youngish lad. The book she was enjoying now centered on a very narcissistic man sporting a lusty desire for power.

Mother Mary Angelina settled into her armchair by the portable heater and propped her feet up on the well-worn plaid ottoman which she had purchased at the church's yard sale several years ago. She threw a blanket she knitted last winter over her legs. Settled, she readied herself for giddy delight.

Headlights from a vehicle pulling into the church's parking lot distracted her briefly. She was too involved with the female yearnings of the love-lorn Lady MacTavish who desired the gorgeous well-proportioned ne'er do well Lord of Argyll, Somerled McNeill the IV. Otherwise she would have made her way downstairs to find out why someone was outside after hours.

When the mutterings of voices and flashing lights invaded her privacy again, she tore herself away from the fictional world and peered out onto the real one. She grabbed the binoculars hanging from her bedpost and focused in on the action.

An ambulance was parked on the lawn near a back entrance to the sanctuary. Its rear doors were open. Two men dressed in paramedic clothing pushed a gurney out the church doors. It was hard to make out who was on the mobile bed. Another person following the paramedics came into view. She zeroed in on their face. It was Monsignor Talmano. What had happened at church? She wondered. It was long past the last office and nowhere near time for the next one to start. No one should have been in that building. She lowered the binoculars. *If I go down there to demand what's going on, I'll be accused of spying. But if I wait until morning, I can discreetly question Talmano. If something has happened to the bishop, that news will spread at breakfast.* She decided accusations leveled against her was not what she wanted. *I'll listen to the whispers at breakfast.*

With her decision made, she picked up her book again and flipped to the marked page. Before she read the first word, she panicked. *What if something has happened to the bishop?* "Oh Deus meus." Mother Mary Angelina crossed herself three times with her left hand. Her right one was clutching the small gold crucifix she wore around her neck.

She couldn't go ask Talmano if anything had happened to O'Malley without admitting she was spying with binoculars, but she was too anxious to wait until morning gossip. Another thought hit her. *Where is the child?* The mother superior was aware she became easily agitated when she was afraid. *Be in your room. Be in your room asleep like a good girl.* She took off. Down the hall she ran. If anyone heard her and opened their door, she would tell them she was going to the bathroom.

She rounded the corner and stopped by the third door on the left. It was closed. Mother Mary Angelina crossed herself three times, placed her hand on the knob, took a breath and turned the handle. Her heart pounded. All she needed to do now was push against the door. She steeled herself and finished the act.

A body was lying on the bed, curled up with a blanket clutched against its cheek. The chest moved up and down in slow rhythmic motions. *Thank God.* Again she crossed herself, but only once this time. The mother superior's eyes adjusted to the dark. She looked around to make sure this person had not returned recently from a nighttime excursion. The clothing on a hanger was properly placed on the rack anchored to the wall opposite the bed. A glass of water half full was on the table. Slippers were partway under the bed. Mother Mary Angelina crept into the room. She picked up one shoe. It was dry. She thanked God again. If something had happened to O'Malley, it was not by this person's hand. She left calm and contented.

Back in her room, she looked out her window. The ambulance was gone. She would find out in a few hours who had been on the gurney and what had happened. Right now, there was a seductive adventure awaiting with the dangerous boy of her dreams in the starring role.

She settled down with her book and pictured herself as Lady MacTavish.

Chapter Thirty-Five

The buzzing noise woke Samyn. His hand snaked its way out from under the bedcovers and up to where a clock sat. He hit the top button, but the sound continued.

He fumbled his fingers around, searching for that small black disc that made the morning sound. The noise irritated him. He opened his eyes. The clock showed it was only 3:37. His alarm always went off at 6:30 so why was it bothering him now?

Samyn rubbed his eyes, squinted them and looked again at the digital numbers shining from the noise box on his bedside table. He noticed his phone moving like Mexican jumping beans. *Who calls in the middle of the night?* He grabbed the phone. "Samyn."

A melodic voice spoke. "I am sorry. This is Bishop O'Malley. You must come to St Luke's hospital now. The young man, Officer Blake, has been seriously injured."

Samyn, still not fully awake, repeated what they had said. "How?"

"Just get here quick. I don't have all the answers, but Father Talmano was with him and is on his way here."

"On my way." He hung up and threw on the clothes he had worn yesterday. Out of habit, he grabbed his badge, wallet and phone. He busied himself by trying to figure out what Blake did to end up in the hospital. *Did he trip and hit his head against one of those stone coffins? Did he fall down those slick steps?* He so worried about what may have happened, he never reflected on how he would explain this to his boss? He also did not think about the fact it was Friday.

Samyn arrived at the hospital in record time thanks to the flashing blue lights which had been recently installed on his unmarked car. He parked between two spaces but didn't care. He ran in the front doors with no clue where the bishop or Blake were. A security officer was by the unmanned information desk. Samyn headed that way.

Before he got out his questions, the elevator doors in the lobby area opened. Bishop O'Malley called to him.

"Phillip, Thank God you're here. Come with me now." He held the doors.

Lieutenant Samyn ran into the waiting elevator. "How bad is he?" He spoke before the doors fully shut.

"It's bad, but how bad? Well, that's not known yet. He's in surgery now."

"What happened? He was at the cathedral on a whim of his."

"I'll let Father Talmano tell you what he knows. He stayed behind to seal off the crypt. He called to say he's on the way. Apparently, the whim, as you called it, paid off."

"Tell me everything, O'Malley?"

"Someone came into the crypt and took the top off Bishop Newmans tomb. They stabbed Blake and got away."

"Blake's been stabbed?" Samyn digested this. "It must be bad if he's in surgery."

"I don't know. I do know he lost a lot of blood."

The doors opened, and the gentlemen headed toward the waiting room. "I told the ER doctor and surgeon that I expected to be told what his status was when the surgery was over, and that I would be in this waiting room." He motioned to the room's door. "Go on. I'll be there in a second." He stopped at the nurse's desk to see if anyone had been looking for him. A few minutes later he came in with two cups of tea.

"Sometimes being a part of the church hierarchy has benefits." He held out a cup to Samyn. "Here."

"Thanks. Can I use your privilege to make a call from here? I need to tell Melvin."

"It's not my privilege to give." He held up his palm. "But we are the only ones in here, and you own the badge."

Samyn pulled out his phone and hit Melvin Moore's speed dial button. Samyn thought he would never answer.

"I'm at the hospital. Blakes been stabbed."

"Be there shortly." No questions were asked, no details given. Officers know there's time to talk later.

"You're aware sir, we will have to bring in the force now. If he had fallen down the stairs or tripped and hit his head, I could have kept this under wraps, but not now."

"Yes, I understand. Perhaps though you can listen to Father Talmano's story first. We didn't call the police just a rescue squad, and we didn't tell them Blake was a cop."

"What did you tell the paramedics?"

"That we would talk to the police later. Our first concern was the wellbeing of our guest."

Samyn looked at O'Malley who showed signs of distress in his face and his voice. Samyn, however, glared at him. All the contempt he had for the church came out from where he had hidden it long ago. His anger robbed his voice. He opened his mouth and nothing would come out, not even a sputtering sound. His head moved left to right.

His gaze focused on the floor while he tried to get words together. His disgust erupted at last. The cup of tea flew from his hand. It hit the opposite wall. The foam cup bounced off. The liquid made a large watery stain with little rivers of wetness flowing down towards the floor. Samyn now spoke.

"You, you, you," came out first. "There's a man in surgery because of your precious church and all you could think of was covering the church's ass." He pummeled his legs with his fists. Samyn's face switched from red to colorless. His icy eyes glared at O'Malley.

"Do they teach you how to protect the church in seminary? Is it a required class?" He thumped O'Malley's chest with the middle finger of his right hand.

"Are you so brainwashed that you believe everything that happens in the church is ok? Is that why your pedophiles and rapists and now assailants never get convicted because you're all taught that robes make you immune from the law, that because you wear a dog collar you can do no wrong?" He pushed O'Malley away, then himself off the chair. Every inch of his 6'4 frame stood towering above the slumped priest. He fought his inner demons, willing them not to let him lose control and give into the locked up hatred he carried. He flexed his fists in rhythm with his breaths.

"If that boy is permanently harmed or worse dies, I'm bringing down your house if it's the last thing I do as an officer of the law."

Bishop O'Malley sat with his elbows resting on his knees and his hands clasped together. His forehead rested against his fingers. Samyn's words had hit him like a whip. When the tongue lashing stop, he raised his face, wet from tears.

"I sought to make changes within the church, to make priests and nuns become accountable for what the church calls sins and the legal profession calls crimes." He held up a hand.   "Please hear me out. You are right. The church has for centuries hidden the shortcomings of its ordained clergy, while its lay people and parishioners suffered for theirs. Do what you must. I will support you even if it means my defrocking." In his hand hung his rosary. He had wrapped it around his palms and entwined his fingers. The sterling silver crucifix swung, reflecting the ceiling lights.

Samyn crossed his arms and his body went rigid. Hate beamed from the narrowed slits where his eyes usually were. It zeroed in on one spot; the hypnotizing motion of what many call the symbol of ultimate love.

Father Talmano stood silently at the doorway. He put his fingers to his lips and turned only his head when Sargent Moore's booming voicing and pounding footsteps interrupted the tension-filled solitude.

Chapter Thirty-Six

Sargent Moore entered the waiting room, more subdued than he had been when he came through the hall's doors. His usual smile was replaced with a grim line of worry. "How is he? What happened?" He glanced at the priests and nodded his head in acknowledgement before he honed in on his partner. "Talk to me, bro."

"We don't know how he is yet. Still in surgery, but the doctor knows we're waiting." Samyn said. "As for what happened, that's a good question, one I'd liked answered now."

Bishop O'Malley gestured for Father Talmano to speak. "You were with him, tell these gentlemen all you saw."

Talmano took a lengthy breath to steady his nerves. He closed his eyes, breathed out and opened them. "First let me say, I am sorry this happened. Neither of us expected anything so violent."

"Yes, violent accidents seem to happen in that church." The acidic tone in Samyn's voice was unmistakable. It was obvious he laid the blame on them for Blake's injuries. Samyn was angry. Fresh anger from tonight, pent up anger from his past, but he blamed it all on the church. He was ready for battle against his enemy, even if he could only fight with words.

Talmano and the bishop did not respond. Talmano instead began his story with how they each reacted when they saw a light and heard the footsteps.

"I moved to the back wall by the steps. I stayed in the shadows like Blake had told me to. I moved closer myself when the person knelt down in front and Blake stood up. Unfortunately, too many tombs were in my way. I couldn't get to him quick enough to help grab the person so I made my way back to the steps and thought I had secured them, but they fought back. I tried to help him. Please understand, I tried."

"What happened to Blake? What else did you see?" Moore was insistent.

"Why did you run?" Hard and cold, Samyn could be nothing else now.

"This person, I couldn't tell if they were male or female, wore a hooded robe. They kissed Newman's body. The hands, probably as that's traditional, then lifted a knife or scissors up. That was when Blake lunged for them. He tried to grab them by the knees but, the whatever it was, came down on him. He dropped the person, and they took off for the steps. I almost had them, but they bit me. I hit them with the only weapon I had, my flashlight."

"Blake's been stabbed? By a church person?" Moore looked puzzled. Samyn got angrier.

"What kind of holy orders do your people take? First someone poisons a bishop, now they've attacked and stabbed a police officer. Any more crimes you want to tell us about?" He said.

Bishop O'Malley let his Irish come out. "May I remind you, sir, you said there was no proof that the poisoning was intentional."

"May I explain to you sir, my rookie got stabbed on your church grounds by someone most likely in Holy Orders, someone who came down to your indoor cemetery to slash the dead bishop?"

Samyn sent rays of contempt to O'Malley. "May I also point out that this incident changes things? I will investigate your precious church and I don't care if the Vatican likes it or not. If Blake dies, I will bring down St. Stephens if it is my last act as an officer of the law."

Any other time Moore would have tried to diffuse the situation with a joke or a grin, but this time he stood solemn faced by Samyn. "I think he means WE will bring down your church."

Before more harsh words could be spoken between the parties, a weary doctor wearing sweat stained scrubs entered the room. "Are you here for the stabbing victim?"

"Yes," said everyone.

The doctor looked at each of them. "Are any of you related to him?"

"He's our partner." Samyn pointed to Moore and showed his badge.

"He's a police officer? I wasn't told that."

"Does that matter?" Samyn said.

"No, no. I thought he was brought here from a church."

"He was." Bishop O'Malley was somber.

"Look Doc, tell us how he is? Is he alive?" Moore was getting inpatient.

"Oh, yes. Sorry. He's out of surgery. Lucky for him, the object either had a small blade, about four inches, I think, or else the person using it didn't push it in too deep. He's lost a lot of blood because of where he was hit. One strike in the neck nicked his carotid artery, but that was easy to fix. One landed above his kidneys but did no permanent damage to any organ. The last blow is the one we will have to watch." He stopped talking.

Samyn let his anger loose. "What do you mean watch?"

"Sorry, I'm mentally drained right now." The doctor said. "The blade entered his lower back at an angle which caused it to hit his spinal column. I was more concerned with repairing the ripped vessels and stopping the blood loss than fixing nerve damage."

"What are you saying, doctor?" Moore said.

"I'm sorry but there is a very good chance your friend may be paralyzed. We will know more when he gets out of recovery and we can access the injury better."

Shock overtook everyone but the doctor. "Do you have questions?" He didn't give them time to answer. "I'll drop back in when he gets out of recovery and I have more news. Right now I need a cup of coffee." He left the room quicker than he had entered.

"Paralyzed? Oh, man!" Moore looked at Samyn who sank down in a chair.

Bishop O'Malley rose. "I'll be in the chapel."

Monsignor Talmano sat next to Samyn. He laid a hand on his leg. "This should not have happened. I am so very sorry. I'll go now and join the bishop in prayers. We'll have the church saying masses for him." He got up to leave. Before he made it to the door, Samyn spoke.

"Prayers. Yeh, go do that. Better pray for whoever did this to my rookie though. I will find them. Accidents happen, especially on your church's property."

Talmano left the room and Samyn's words followed him.

"Listen, I get it, you're upset, so am I, but you can't threaten anyone boss." Moore said.

"Maybe it's time for someone to threaten them. The church has been covering up crimes for centuries." He spat out the words. A snort escaped his nose.

"You believe in divine destinies, Moore." Moore shook his head yes. "Then perhaps this is how God plans to make the church own up to its sins. Suppose I'm the cop who will bring them to their knees, those holy hypocrites."

"Before you get busy dismantling a two thousand year old institution, why don't we wait to find out how Blake is?"

Samyn looked at Moore, the man he had worked with for years with eyes that emitted nothing. "You do not understand what the Catholic church is about and hides my friend. Don't tell me what I can do where they are concerned."

Moore grasped this went further than what had happened to Blake. He also knew when to stop pushing an issue. "I need some coffee. I know you were trying to quit, but do you want a cup? I'm buying and I'll not hold this slip off the wagon against you."

"I want whiskey." Samyn looked at the ground. He raised his eyes to meet Moore's. "But I'll take coffee. Better to fall off that wagon than the other one."

"You're right, boss."

Chapter Thirty-Seven

Moore came back bearing two cups of coffee. He handed one to Samyn who looked at it, hesitated, then took it. "I'll quit again when this is over."

"I know, boss."

They sat in silence next to each other. Moore began conquering the barrier Samyn had built between them.

"Bossman, does he have any family we should contact?"

"I'm not sure… I think his mother is still alive but lives in another town."

Moore took that information in stride. He couldn't remember Blake every talking much about his family.

"I guess I should tell Clarissa about this. He had a date with her tomorrow night, or maybe it was for tonight."

"Clarissa?"

"Yes, she works as an admin in the records department. He finally asked her out."

Neither spoke for several minutes.

"I guess I need to inform the captain about this." Samyn looked at his coffee.

"You can wait until we learn more."

"True dat." Samyn was trying to build a bridge. Moore helped him.

"True dat." He raised the cup before he drank some.

Again they were quiet while the hands on the clock moved. Moore decided it was time to have the discussion Samyn had been avoiding this week.

"Boss, don't you have to talk to Cap about my retiring today? I was thinking if you didn't mind, I'll still retire, but I want to finish this case first."

Samyn sipped the coffee he had been studying. He forced himself to swallow the heated liquid that was burning his mouth. The clock made five ticks before he spoke. "I wasn't going to tell him you want to retire."

"But you're supposed to give him an answer today?"

"Yes, I guess I am." He took another sip, and this time savored it.

"Philip, listen. No conversation held in that precinct is ever private. Everyone knows he's been told to keep you and that either me or Blake must go. I've put in my time. I'm ready to fly."

"And I've got one, two years on you."

They each drank from their cups. Ten ticks were made by the clock.

"I plan on staying until this case is through and you better be by my side. Blake's out of commission for a while until he recuperates. We can deal with what the muck mucks want then." Samyn shifted his gaze from the floor to Moore's head. "Deal?"

Moore lowered the paper coffee cup he held in his left hand. He formed a fist with his right and bumped his against Samyn's raised one. "Deal Boss!" Each sipped from their cups. Moore guessed it would be better to keep his mouth closed than speak now, but the quiet bothered him.

"How's the coffee?"

"I've missed this, but I won't let it control me again." Samyn felt guilty for breaking his vow to give up coffee, and it was showing on his face.

"Shirley tells me I need to watch my caffeine intake. We can quit this together later."

Twenty ticks sounded, and the hands moved from number to number.

The doctor poked his head into the room. "He's awake and still in recovery. He'll be moved to ICU as a precaution first, then maybe to a regular room tomorrow. You can see him." He pulled away from the door.

"Wait." Samyn said.

The doctor stuck his head in again.

"Is he paralyzed?"

The doctor entered. "You're not next of kin, so I shouldn't tell you his status or prognosis."

" I'm his boss and my boss will need to be told and as he is an officer of the law with a sworn duty to protect and defend..." Samyn politely conveyed his authority.

"Yes, I guess you need to and I could let him tell you." The doctor paused, then continued after giving it some thought. "At the moment, he can't feel his legs. Will that change? We're not sure. It is possible, as he heals, that sensation will return and he'll be able to use them again. But..." The doctor shrugged.

"Thank you." Moore said.

The doctor moved out the room before Samyn could ask anything else.

Moore looked at Samyn. "Well, now we know." He chuckled. "Hey boss, God must really like you."

Samyn raised his right eyebrow and cocked his head.

"Look at it this way. You got handed the gift of time. This accident just bought you a postpone-ment. Can't have you make a choice about whom to let go when ones out of commission, can they?"

Samyn shook his head.

"And while God only likes you he obviously loves me because in three weeks, I'll have another year in on the force and my retirement package gets sweeter. Even if the captain insists on you cutting me now, I can take my vacation and sick time and still hit the three weeks." Moore attempted to laugh but failed.

"Let's go see the kid before we have to head to the station."

In the hall, Moore again tried to use his humor to lift the feelings they were both experiencing. He pointed to Samyn's sneakers. "Like those shoes Samyn but glad I'm not wearing them today. You're going to walk on some mighty big toes." He shook his head. "Lucky for those people, you didn't put your boots on."

Chapter Thirty-Eight

Blake was awake, but he didn't want to be. *Why can't I just go back to sleep? This can't be real.*

He stared at the ceiling through half-opened eyes. *What happened tonight?* He must have done something wrong to have caused this.

"They shouldn't have sent a rookie." He spoke to the monitor next to his bed.

"Why not?" A voice boomed and disrupted the quiet. Blake tried to lift his head. He raised it only a few inches, not enough to see who was filling the doorway with their body.

"Why not send the person who suggested it was probable the culprit would return to the crime?" Again, it sounded like a voice bouncing off the walls. It echoed loudly.

The person who had spoken moved from the door and next to the bed.

"Sir?" Blake said.

"Yes, kid. What can I do for you?"

"Sir, I'm sorry. I did something wrong. I must have."

"Nah. I don't think you did because I trained you in the field."

"And I corrected all the knowledge he got wrong." A different voice, melodic, peaceful, now made itself heard. "How you doing rookie?" Moore's face came into view for Blake.

"Why are you… I mean how did you… Who told you?"

"Bishop O'Malley awoke me with a phone call so I thought it was fair to disrupt Moore's rest with one. Though I probable shouldn't. He really needs his beauty sleep."

Samyn gestured to Moore's face. Blake tried to laugh but choked instead.

"Hey boss man, the kid knows you wish you looked as good as I do."

"In your dreams, my friend."

The bantering continued for a few minutes before the soberness returned.

"So rookie, how are you doing?"

Blake looked at Samyn and shook his head. His eyes swelled with tears until they overflowed and fell onto his cheek. "I can't feel my legs. I can't feel anything past my hips."

"Hey kid, it's okay. This is probably temporary. You've been through a lot tonight."

"But what if I never walk again?"

"We'll worry about that then." Samyn said. "Focus on getting out of here."

Blake nodded. He pushed the water off his face. His hand moved in awkward motions.   His partners looked at each other, the walls and machines, anyplace but at him. Each made comments, nothing but idle chatter. It was all they could do for the moment.

"Look rookie, what happened tonight… well, what happened is something you'll be able to brag about later when you're back at work. Not everyone can say they got attacked in a church crypt by a person wearing robes." Moore started to pat Blake's leg. He realized what he was about to do and moved his hand towards the arm.

Blake gave him a half smile. He lifted his upturned hand. It met Moore's. "I guess I've got a story now. Scars too to prove it." His hand felt the bandage on his neck.

"We will find who did this kid. They'll pay." Samyn's voice was tight, controlled.

"Monsignor Talmano was there. He saved my life, sir. He called for help and tried to stop the bleeding."

"I'll be talking to him and getting his version of events. Later, when you're rested some, I'll get yours."

"I want to do it now, while it's fresh." Blake insisted as much as possible for a man on pain medications.

Moore looked across the bed to Samyn. "He's got a point, boss. Anyone else we would want a statement from."

"Only if you feel like talking kid."

Blake nodded, stronger this time. "I do."

"Okay, then talk. Tell me what happened."

Blake started his tale. He detailed the evening in the crypt. Most of what he said was irrelevant, but Samyn and Moore understood the kid needed to get everything out of his system. Moore recorded it all on his phone.

"Then we saw this light and heard someone tiptoeing down the steps. Talmano pointed to the back wall, and I said stay in the shadows. Father Talmano complied. This robed figured wearing a hood came down and moved towards Bishop Newman's resting spot. You could tell they knew their way around by how easy they navigated in the dark." He stopped talking to cough.

"Want some water kid?" Samyn said. Blake nodded. Samyn picked up the glass with a straw in it and held it out. Blake took it with shaky hands. Water sloshed on the bed. "Here let me. You just drink." Samyn grabbed the glass back. Blake raised up enough to sip some and fell away.

"Ok where did I stop?"

"The robed person had come down the stairs and headed to Newman's tomb." Moore said.

"Ok. They moved the top off and acted reverent, like."

"Explain that kid."

"Well, they stroked his face and kissed him, on the hand maybe and then from out of nowhere they had this blade raised over his head. It was like they loved him, then hated him the next minute."

"Weird, rookie."

"Anyway, I tried to grab them and halfway through lunging I decided to pick them up. That's where I made my mistake." He stopped again.

"I may have done the same thing, rookie. Don't second guess your instincts."

Blake shrugged. "I guess. So that's when they stabbed at me. I didn't think they had got me, and I reached out to grab them again. That time when they struck me, I felt it. I let go, and they ran off. Father Talmano had moved along the wall nearer the tomb. He ran to the steps and tried to get them, but I think they fought. I couldn't see, only heard struggling sounds. Then he came back, and I told him to report it, then I blacked out."

"Ok kid, that's enough for now. Get some rest. We'll find this person. I mean it." Samyn said.

"Hey, do you have any family we should contact?" Moore said.

"Clarissa, I have a date with her."

"I'll talk to her rookie. But is there anyone else?"

"No, just my mom and a sister but they live in another state."

"They should be told." Samyn said.

"My mom's in a home. She has dementia. She doesn't remember me anymore."

"What about your sister then? I can call her."

"We don't speak. She's angry that taking care of Mom fell upon her shoulders, not mine. She cut me out of her life and changed her number. I don't know how to reach her." Tears again fell down his cheeks.

"I'll see what I can do to find her, son. Rest now." Samyn said. He spoke like a father when he's not sure what words to say to comfort a child.

"See you later, rookie. If you want something, ask me, ok."

"Okay." Blake closed his eyes. This time his partners exhausted him with no effort. He drifted off to sleep before they had left the room.

At the nurse's station, Samyn left his card with instructions to call if there was a change. The concern on his face, his badge, and his implied reference to being Blake's only family made them agree.

"Time to go get your whipping boss man."

"Yeah Yeah. Don't remind me."

235

Chapter Thirty-Nine

At the precinct doors, Moore and Samyn parted ways. Moore headed to records to tell Clarissa about Blake and Samyn inched his way to where the detective unit was housed. He shrunk his 6'4 frame as much as he could, hoping no one would notice he was there. He failed.

Captain Richard Martin was waiting for him. He stood in his office doorway. When Samyn entered the room, he yelled for him to get in his office. *So much for subtlety.*

Samyn erected himself and walked in. He ignored the others who were watching the drama.

"It's Friday. Who did you pick?"

"Yes, it's glorious weather today."

"Come on, Samyn. Tell me your choice."

"I like the Hornets tonight. Think they can take the Lakers. I mean, they are playing on their court and LeBron's out with a strained muscle."

"Samyn." Martin's voice rose two notches. "Don't play stupid with me."

"I'm not boss. I thought you were talking about the big game tonight." It was all he could do not to smirk. He loved verbal battles. *Feigning ignorance can be so relaxing.*

Martin dropped into his chair. He picked up a pack of cigarettes laying on the desk.

"Hey Captain, weren't you going to give them up?"

"Samyn. It's Friday."

Samyn looked at his watch. "Your right. It is."

"We had a deal."

" If you say so."

"You tell me which member of your team will leave today." Martin spoke through clinched teeth. Each word struggled out of his mouth with reasonable calm but over enunciated syllables.

Samyn decided it was best not to play with his prey any longer. "Boss, we need to talk."

"You better have a decision for me."

"I do, but not one you're going to like."

Martin leaned back in his chair. The cigarette pack tapped against his leg. "Go on."

"This morning something happened to Blake."

"What happened?"

"He got stabbed, underwent surgery and is in the hospital now."

Martin's chair dropped. He leaned over his desk. "What happened? Where? When?" He tried to keep his voice low.

"Let me start from the beginning." Samyn filled him in on what they had been doing with the church. He emphasized why he kept from this knowledge from Martin by blaming it on the bishop.

"You broke police procedure."

"I know."

"Now Blake may not walk again."

"That's right. I've told the bishop this changes things. We would be actively investigating his parish now."

That statement appeased Martin. He leaned back in the chair again. Two of its legs left the floor. His feet plopped onto his desk. He folded his arms behind his head and stared at the ceiling.

"Looks like Blake who's leaving us then."

"Wait, a minute. You can't fire him. He's injured."

"Yes, but if he's disabled now, he can't do his job here. You guys are investigative detectives."

"Before you make any decisive moves, wait until you know his long-term prognosis." Samyn fought to keep his bitterness in check.

Martin whistled.

"Let me put it this way. If you file separation papers now, it will seem like you're firing a disabled member of our squad. That gives him grounds for a very winnable lawsuit and you get to suffer through an internal investigation. Are you prepared for that?"

Martin looked at Samyn. His eyes sent out sparks of contempt. "When will you know something about him?"

"Doctor didn't say yet, but I would think a few weeks at least before they can see anything definitive."

"Okay, I'll wait, but he's who's going."

Samyn turned to leave.

"You're a lucky man, you know that. You didn't have to decide who to axe. Somebody else did it for you."

He shut the door hard enough to rattle the glass in the office walls and shake the windows. Storm clouds gathered around Samyn. The buzz in the office shut down. Everyone froze at their places. Moore was at his desk, which sat behind Samyn's. Lt. Samyn's vision had narrowed into a tunnel aimed at the exit. He headed that way. Moore grabbed his phone and jacket, then fell in behind him.

Chapter Forty

Moore kept his mouth shut. He followed Samyn to the car. Lucky for him, Samyn waited until he had buckled up before screeching out the parking lot. They had worked together long enough to appreciate when to talk, when to listen, and when each other was struggling with an issue, either case related or personal. Moore dug into his memory vault and could not find one where Samyn had acted like this. He assumed it was because of Blake's injury.

"Do you want to talk about what happened in there?"

"Nope."

"Do you want to talk about how we're going to handle this mess with the church?"

No answer came.

"Would you like to stop for the red light?"

Samyn slammed on the brakes. "Are you happy now?" Samyn's icy voice cooled down an already chilled car.

"Look Phil, I know you're upset over Blake. I know you're angry with the captain. However, I am in the car and I have no wish to die today. So either pull over and let me get behind the wheel or pay attention to getting us safely to wherever we're going." Moore kept his hand on the handle above his door. He turned his body to face Samyn. Instead of yelling, he spoke in a conjuring tone that brought Samyn's focus back,

"Sorry. I'm not thinking about driving."

"I can see that."

"He wants to fire Blake because of what the doctor said."

"He can't do that legally, I mean."

"I reminded him of that."

"Hey, I still want to retire. What happened to Blake has made me ponder about this job. Shirley agrees with me. The world is too crazy now, and it's time for me to get out. When we get this case wrapped up, I'm putting in my papers."

Samyn nodded. "It is a crazy world."

"How are we going to handle this? You realize I'll follow your lead, but a heads up as the direction we're going would be nice."

"Talmano said he may have injured the guilty party. I say we visit the bishop, then if necessary, get a warrant to search for a person with an injured wrist or arm. But I'm thinking since the church doesn't like to air its laundry, he'll be okay with us doing a visual search. Hell, I'm even willing to be generous and question the suspect in front of him."

"And if we don't find a suspect, then what?"

"A warrant to go through the records and see who's missing from yesterday."

Moore's eyebrows raised. "You don't suspect O'Malley would have sent that person to another church?"

"I know the church has a habit of quietly sending the guilty ones to another parish."

"But O'Malley? He came over here to investigate Newman, who died before he arrived."

"So he says. I asked Blake to do a little background check on O'Malley and find out if his story tallies up, but he hasn't said if found anything or not."

"He had stacks of info the other day spread out in the conference room. I remember there was some papers on O'Malley. I'm sure he had some on that orphanage."

"Where are they now?"

"Beats me. Looks like we've got to go to the hospital boss to find out."

"I had planned to go by anyway to check on him."

They pulled into the church parking lot. Samyn skidded the car into a parking space.

"Boss remember you have a precious cargo in this car."

"What?"

"Me." Moore got out before Samyn decided he might want to park behind the parish.

"I don't understand what you're worried about. Shirl and the department carry enough insurance on you, you'll be easy to replace." Samyn gave him a quick smirk. When his eyes glimpsed the looming towers which awaited them his smirk disappeared. His anger came back.

"Boss, control your temper. This is still an investigation and we need nothing happening that can give someone legal technical grounds to have it dismissed."

Samyn glowered at the church. He leaned back to take in the full height of tower bearing the church bell. "Why would people want to build churches that give the impression they peer upon those who enter as unworthy?"

"I've got no clue, boss."

They headed towards the parish's back door. Like a guardian angel, the mother superior appeared before them.

"May I question why you are here and who you are seeking?" Her demanding voice boomed across the lawn.

"May I ask you to address me as sir and not yell when you're in front of me?" Samyn said.

"Would you answer the question?"

"Which one?" Samyn gave her an innocent stare.

"The one I asked." The mother superior showed her impatience by removing a ruler from her habit pocket and tapping it against her palm.

Samyn turned to Moore. He wore a devilish grin radiating pure evil. He showed it now to the nun. "Excuse me, but you asked two. I'll answer whichever one you want."

"Why are you lurking around this building?"

"Now you've asked three. "Which one do you want me to answer?" She tapped the ruler harder.

"If I recall correctly ma'am you're supposed to rap the ruler against your legs not your palm. Are you still allowed to rap a student on their knuckles, or has that changed?"

Samyn was enjoying the exchange.

She thumped the ruler on his chest. "Answer my questions."

"Ma'am, I have a witness here who will swear you assaulted an officer of the law with your ruler. I advise you to return it to your pocket, NOW." Samyn was polite until the last word. He retrieved his badge and flashed it. "That's right I'm a cop and tapping me in the chest, like you would a student, is against the law. Now what I am here for and who I'm going to see is none of your business." He pushed past her. Moore tipped his head as he followed Samyn to the parish.

"I'm guessing, boss, you had an unpleasant experience with a nun once."

"More than once. Used to hold the record for hand slaps at St Mary's."

"What are hand slaps?"

"It's when a nun tells you to hold out your hand, and she smacks it with her trusty ruler."

"What was your record?"

"Sixty-three administered by the darling Sister Nasty, who only stopped because the mother superior told her too."

"Why did she hit you so many times?"

"Because I kept asking for more."

Moore gave him a puzzled glance, "Why would you do something stupid like that?"

"When Sister Nasty slapped you she made you say 'please may have I another'. She wanted to make you cry. I refused to cry or quit repeating her phrase."

"I get what you have against nuns now. What do you have against priests?"

Samyn stopped walking. He turned around. Standing in front of Melvin Moore was a man whose face bore long suppressed pain. "You want to know why I dislike this so-called holy institution? Do you?"

"Hey bro, it's okay. We've known each other more than half our lives, and I've never seen you act this way. Something happened that hurt you, but you don't have to tell me." Moore put his hands on Samyn's shoulders. "Just keep a cool head for now. You don't want to give an attorney grounds for dismissal of a case. Think, pull your-self together."

Samyn nodded. "You're right." He patted one of Moore's hands before pushing them away. "A priest abused my only brother. He told my parents. My dad called him a liar and told him to go to his room and get ready for a whipping. My mother cried and begged my father not to punish him but to ask the priest what happened. While my father was busy yelling that priests don't do things like that and how his lying perverted son took after her side of the family, my brother ran from the house. They found his body the next morning in the river."

"I'm sorry, but I get your anger now." Moore laid a hand on Samyn's right upper arm. "We can't get justice for your brother, but maybe we can right a wrong for someone else. What do you say, boss? Are you ready to find our suspect?"

"Let's do it."

They entered the rectory by the front door. A younger man wearing a collar greeted them.

"I need to see the bishop."

"Is he expecting you?"

"Does it matter?"

"He sees no one without an appointment, sir. He is a very busy man."

"Is he upstairs?" Samyn started up the steps.

"Sir, I must ask you to stay down here. I'll be happy to find out if he's available."

Samyn continued up the stairs. The younger man pulled out his phone.

"I wouldn't do that." Moore showed his badge. "I would suggest you cancel any appointments he has. He'll be busy the rest of the afternoon." Moore moved up two steps.

"Hey, why don't you find Monsignor Talmano and have him join us?"

He whistled a blues tune as he climbed the stairs.

Chapter Forty-One

The door to the bishop's office stood open. A recording of Chopin's Nocturnes drifted out into the hall.

"Hello gentlemen." O'Malley spoke before Samyn and Moore crossed his threshold. He was sitting at his desk, his legs stretched to their full-length, with his head tilted back and eyes closed.

Samyn and Moore walked in. Monsignor Talmano sat across from the bishop. He too leaned back in a chair, seemingly lost in the music.

"I hope you don't mind if Father Talmano joins us today." Bishop O'Malley straightened his body, aligning it with his desk chair. Samyn shook his head. "Good, and any word on Officer Blake?"

"He may be paralyzed. We won't know for a few weeks."

"I'm sorry to hear that. The church will continue to pray for him."

Samyn neither responded nor showed an interest in what the bishop had said.

Seamus O'Malley lowered his head for a moment. He tried again to thaw the ice wall Samyn had built. "Shall we move over to there?" He pointed to the sitting area. On the table, coffee and tea pots along with cups and sweets were waiting for them.

"Sir, I'm here for two reasons. First to debrief Talmano and then find this person who stabbed Blake. I'm not here for a social visit."

Bishop O'Malley moved to the other area. "I'm not expecting this to be a social call but while we talk, there is no reason we can't be courteous."

"I can't speak for him," Moore pointed his thumb at Samyn. "But I can use a cup of coffee. It's been a long morning."

"Please sit then." The bishop poured a cup and offered it to Moore. "And would you like a cup?" He addressed this to Samyn, who shook his head no. The bishop handed the pot to Monsignor Talmano, who took it and poured two cups, one of which he gave to O'Malley.

"Help yourself." The bishop gestured to the plate of cookies and scones. Moore thanked him and took a scone. He sat back, took a bite, then another. He was waiting for Samyn to begin the questioning.

Samyn looked at Father Talmano. He was still standing. "I need you to tell me what happened in the crypt. This time I'm taping you. When I need to clarify something, I will interrupt and ask you a question. Do you understand?"

Before Talmano agreed, O'Malley laid a hand on the monsignor's arm. "Is this necessary? Should he have counsel?"

"No, it's unnecessary but considering what has happened, it is best to record this talk." Samyn pulled out his phone. He punched the app and pulled on his reading glasses. As he was typing, he answered the second question. "Only the guilty need counsel. Are you guilty?" He waited for Talmano to respond.

"No, of course I'm not."

Samyn finished his typing. "Then he doesn't need an attorney. Are you ready to begin?"

"If you are."

Samyn pointed to a chair for Talmano to sit in. He took the opposing one, laid the phone on the table between them and hit the record button. "Okay what happened last night in the crypt?"

Talmano repeated the events he had told them about earlier. Moore made a few pen strokes in the small notebook he had pulled from his inner coat pocket. He handed it to Samyn, who read what Moore had written.

"How many tombs were between you and the suspect when they stabbed Blake?"

Talmano scrunched his face in recollection. His right elbow rested on his knee. The raised arm allowed his forehead to rest on his fingers.

"I want to say there were four." He lowered his arm. "Everything happened so quick. I remember I moved down the wall to get a better view. That's when I caught a flash of what must have been the knife. After Blake yelled, the robed figure ran to the back, and I followed them. I almost had them, but…" he stopped talking.

"But what?" Samyn prompted.

"I'm sorry. Something dawned on me."

"Would you mind sharing this revelation you've had?" Samyn showed his anxiousness. He tapped his feet impatiently and stared hard at Talmano.

"I grabbed the person by the upper arm."

Samyn threw up his palms. "And?"

"I think it may have been a female who attacked Blake or a very young unphysical man."

"An upper arm tells you that how?"

"It was slender but not thin, toned but not muscular like an athletic man's would be. I had tried to get them around the waist but they moved quickly, which is why I only grabbed the arm."

"Did you get a look at the hands?" Moore asked.

Monsignor shook his head no.

"Not even when you hit them with the flashlight? You said earlier this morning you had struck the attacker. Did that not happen?"

"It happened. Yes, I hit them on the arm, but it was dark. I must have seen the hand, but I can't recall it. I'm sorry."

Samyn stared at the monsignor's face. He was angry but didn't show it. The monsignor had to know more than he was telling. All witnesses did. It took patience to get them to recall an event, and patience was not Samyn's forte. Samyn clinched his fists, relaxed them, then repeated his motion. He wanted to grab the man and shake the needed information out of him.

Moore noticed Samyn's actions. He knew from their years together that was not a good sign. He took over the questioning.

"Monsignor, we know it's hard to recall an incident, especially when it was violent and it involves you. You are trying to, and we appreciate that. Studies have proven when you close your eyes while trying to remember a scene, it allows you to see it again, recall more details that can provide investigators with clearer pictures. Would you close your eyes and picture the stairs and the person you wanted to catch?"

Talmano closed his eyes A minute or two elapsed before he spoke. "The hood fell off. The hair was short, not close cropped to the head. Light colored, a blonde. Their skin was reddish, which sounds odd. Maybe it was from the exertion they had with Blake?" He opened his eyes and looked for approval from Moore.

"That could very well be."

"So they were fair skinned?" Talmano raised an eyebrow at Moore.

"I would concur with that, sir. You're doing well. Close your eyes again." Moore kept his tone level.

"They were on the first step when I reached them but if I subtract out the height of the step, then I would say they are about this tall." He raised his hand to his shoulder. "when I'm standing, I mean."

"Are there any men who are that height in your seminary here?" Samyn leaned forward.

The bishop and monsignor looked at each other. Both shook their heads no.

"Any nuns?" Tension mounted in the room.

"Yes." Bishop O'Malley conceded. "Several."

"Okay, the nuns have it then." Samyn threw down a gauntlet with his words. No one picked it up.

He rose with Moore. "We'll need to see them, and Talmano, since you bashed one on the wrist perhaps someone is wearing a telltale bandage today. I want you to come with me. You may be able to identify them. A movement, a step, some-thing may trigger a recollection."

"Wait." O'Malley said. The men stopped.

"I'm going to put a kink in your plans."

"What will that be? And if you would like, I can get a warrant."

Bishop O'Malley ignored his comment for a minute. "Look, get what you want or need to. The church will not impede your investigation. I said wait for a different reason." He eyed Talmano now. "We have a priest, a third-year seminarian whose cancer is in remission. He lost his hair, but it has started to grow back, and he is very slight. Also, he's not tall. If you're looking for suspects, based on the monsignor's arm description, then you might include him too."

"That's right. I forgot about Brother Mark. He could pass for a female if he was in a hooded robe and in a dark room."

Samyn tried to hide his embarrassment with a gruff thank you.

They had almost made out to the door. "Oh yeah, the mother superior caught us coming on to the churches grounds. I guess we need not be dis-creet now."

Bishop O'Malley slapped his forehead. "Jesus, Joseph and Mary, why her today?" He made the sign of the cross. "May you go in peace. I'll find something to keep her busy."

He pulled a flask from his robe and took a long swallow.

Chapter Forty-Two

Breakfast was a disappointment to the mother superior. No one was talking about the ambulance which had arrived and left quietly last night. Both the bishop and monsignor were present and did their customary thanks and readings. Something fishy was going on, and she didn't like not knowing what it was. Her good angel suggested she may have imagined the ambulance. *Dreams can seem real sometimes.* She let the possibilities of this thought roll over in her mind before deciding she had not imagined what took place outside her window last night. Somebody in the room knew something and she would find out who that someone was.

Sister Julian seemed more subdued than usual. She wasn't a big breakfast eater, so her small meal of toast and coffee wasn't surprising, but lately she was eating less than usual. The mother superior watched her for clues. Her gut said pay attention. *She knows something.* Listening to her instincts had served her well in the past. It was the times she ignored them that trouble found her.

When Sister Julian excused herself and hurried from the dining room, the mother superior found a reason to leave as well. She would feign stomach cramps if anyone inquired why she was abandoning her charges, as she called them.

The mother superior, known to some as Sister Mary Angelina, slipped away from the dining room without breaking the commandment about lying. No one was in the hallway, but a door at the end of it was in the last act of shutting. She headed that way. The morning sunlight caught her. Temporary blindness was her punishment. When her eyes adjusted, a flurry of black fabric was moving towards the cathedral. She followed behind. Her curiosity was moving towards apprehension.

Of all the nuns in the convent, this is the one whom she was most fond of. Sister Julian was gentle, with an innocent air about her. She struggled in her studies because of a learning disability, but that made her more humble, more willing to try harder to achieve, thought the Mother Superior. But she also was aware of her limitations and never tried to gloss over them. Once Sister Mary Angelina heard her say to another nun that even a legless person may compete in a marathon, they just wouldn't be running on legs. When that nun asked what she meant, Sister Julian said you can do anything if you change how to define a result or your expectations. She might learn to be conversant in another language, but not write stories or letters in it flawlessly. She then laughed, saying she had enough trouble mastering her native English grammar. Grammar in another language was not a challenge she wanted to take on. It would be enough for her to speak it.

That overheard conversation had stayed with the mother superior. It helped her when dealing with Sister Julian.

Sister Julian entered the building by the east side Facade. Sister Mary Angelina ran to catch up. Once inside the cathedral there were many places where the sister could disappear.

The mother superior entered the building. She stood still to listen for the telltale steps which would indicate where Sister Julian was heading. There were none. She moved her head, raising it up and scrunching down, leaning her body left and right, searching for this elusive nun. That the church was dark and Sister Julien in black didn't make this a simple task.

There she is. Sister Julian was rising from the center aisle. She crossed herself and moved with no sound towards a confessional box. The mother superior headed down the side aisle to the hidden stairs that led to the one of walkways above the transepts and nave. Once on the walkway she hurried to position herself in the prime spot for eavesdropping on confessions.

The church has set confession hours. It's not time for that, so why is she here? Did she arrange to meet a priest? Sister Mary Angelica now worried. She had seen young nuns fall in love with young priests before and nothing good ever came from it. She hoped that was not the case this time. The soft echo of words fueled her thoughts.

"Forgive me Father, for I have sinned, well almost sinned. I hope you can hear me Jesus and Mary without a priest listening too." She said nothing for several minutes. "Is it a sin if you hurt someone you love, even if you didn't mean to? Is it a sin if they die before you can honor a promise to them?"

The Mother Superior listened to the anguish pouring out of this inexperienced girl. She was right; the child had fallen in love, one that would not be returned. She once had done the same thing. Her heart too had been broken by a priest. She prepared a few words to comfort her, like a mother would their hurt child, when her blood froze. Her face lost all color and her heart seized up. *No, no, she didn't. Please tell me she didn't do that.*

Sister Mary Angelina clutched the buttress closet to her. She willed herself to be steady, to stay on her feet. It took all her energy to hold herself upright. She wanted to let go of the buttress and cover her ears, but she needed to clutch the support beam to keep from falling over the walkway. It didn't take long for her to give up and slump down on the stones under feet. She buried her head between her legs and used her hands to keep it there.

Nausea churned her stomach. She thrust a hand in her mouth. She prayed not to throw up. She was too in shock over the nun's sordid story to pray for her now.

A happy, light, singsong voice, like a little girls bounced off the cathedral's walls. She pulled herself to the columns along the walkway and peered between them. A black shadow skipped around the crossing below before skipping itself out the front doors.

The church bells signaling the start of the school day sounded. The mother superior forced herself to stand. Her stomach rolled about. She grabbed the buttress on her right before leaning over and heaving her breakfast onto the pew below.

Thank God no one was down there. She must make her way to school first. She would come back and clean up her mess after she saw things were running smoothly and gave Sister Katherine Grace instructions for the day.

A bigger issue than vomit on the pew was rearing its ugly head. She couldn't tell Sister Julian she knew of the young nun's dilemma without admitting she had eavesdropped on her confession, yet she also realized this was a situation that must be handled. *I'll deal with it later.* This dilemma was something she would need to think long about. *School first, then my mess. Sister Julian must wait for now.*

Chapter Forty-Three

Sargent Melvin Moore and Lieutenant Detective Philip Samyn, after informing the bishop they were on the church grounds as cops who would use all legal means to get an answer to who attacked Officer Blake, investigated the place where the crime happened. They scoped out the crypt without Father Talmano, then returned with him in tow.

"First, what we want you to do is walk us through what happened with no lights. You move just like you did last night. Then we'll go through it again with you in the position Blake was. You'll tell us what you saw happening to him and you'll reenact his motions for us. After we experience it as you did, we'll fire up the candles and flashlights and collect any evidence we can. Ok?" Lt. Samyn said.

"Thank you for sealing off this room last night. That was wise. Well done, like a cop would have." Moore directed his nod of approval towards the monsignor.

"I guess I've watched too many crimes shows." Father Talmano said.

"I hand it to you, sir. Not everyone would have thought to move a barrier in front of the door and over the hidden entrance at the altar, much less put up a sign that says stay out because of sewage leaks." Moore chuckled. "Brilliant my friend." He patted the priest on the shoulder.

"No one hardly comes in here, especially after dark, but I didn't want this to be the night a priest wasn't sleeping and came in here for the quiet."

"Can we start, please?" Samyn said.

Talmano showed them where he and Blake began the evening, then how he moved down to the wall by the stairs and last where he crept when the unidentified suspect was by the burial space.

"Did you notice anything that might identify the person who stabbed Blake, besides what you told us already?"

Talmano concentrated for several minutes before he shook his head. "No, I'm sorry. It was dark, which is why the shiny object caught my attention. I didn't know it was a knife."

"That's ok." Moore said.

"No, I should have paid closer attention. Things like Blake's attack don't happen in churches, or at least shouldn't happen here." Talmano's voice shifted from sadness to heart-rendering unease. "But that's no excuse. I…"

"Pretend you're Blake now. Get to where he was and reenact what you saw him do."

Samyn could careless for the apology the priest was making. It was a waste of his time. All he wanted to do was catch the villain who hurt his rookie.

Father Talmano stood where Blake had been when the assailant came into the room. He then moved to where Blake had been before the attack.

"He stood up and creeped closer to the crypt. When the unknown one raised their hand, Blake must have ducked. I didn't see him by the suspect. I heard him. Then I saw him holding the suspect below the waist like this." Monsignor Talmano got down in a tackle position.

"The person Officer Blake was trying to grab bent like this." He collapsed his body. "And that's when they brought their hand down. At first I thought they were hitting him with a fist, but then he screamed and let go. I realized it had to be with something else." He looked at both policemen. "My fear paralyzed me and I wish I could go back and change things. I should have helped him not stood by the wall."

"What did you do when Blake let go?" Samyn said.

"The person who struck Blake ran for the steps and I followed. I reached out and got them by the robe and tried to turn them around, but they were clawing at me. They bit my hand and I grabbed the flashlight from my robe and hit them." Father Talmano acted this out in a rush of movements. He stopped. "I remembered something." He glowed with excitement. That beam of light from him faded. "No, I think you know that already."

"Know what?" Samyn was in his face.

"About the hair."

Samyn backed away. "That's not new."

"Moore get your gear. Let's see if we can find something on the body or by its eternal bed." Samyn was disappointed. He didn't bother to conceal that fact.

Father Talmano weaved around to the shelf to light the candles. He pulled out his damaged flashlight. Dangling from the dented casing were several threads..

"I forgot I retrieved my flashlight from where I dropped it last night. Look, there are a few threads on it. Could this be from the person who attacked Officer Blake?"

"Possibly. Let me see that." Samyn held out his hand. Maybe a much-desired break would happen now. He looked at the flashlight from all angles before handing it to Moore. "Tag and bag, please."

"Gladly." He said.

Chapter Forty-Four

Mother Superior spent her morning in a fog. She responded to questions without hearing the words. It was obvious from her absent-minded, polite answers that she had something heavy on her mind. No one had the courage to ask if they could help. Instead, by unspoken agreement, they enjoyed her unusual kindnesses.

After she had seen the school day start well, she told her staff she would be in silent retreat for the rest of the school day. She handed control over to her assistant Sister Katherine Grace and departed while they were still in shock.

Well, I'll be the talk of the teachers' lounge today, I guess. With what she had overheard this morning, she didn't much care. She made her way to the cleaning supply closet, took what she would need and headed to the sanctuary.

The building was now lit by candles around the altar, along with the ones by in the ladies chapel which parishioners and clergy lighted for their prayers. A priest was busy preparing the building for the next office. Since it was a time of silence, he couldn't ask why she was there, so he continued working his way around the building, trimming wicks and lighting the wax columns.

Mother Superior walked to the crossing, knelt and crossed herself, then looked up at the walkway on her right. She gaged where she had been standing on the walkway from the ground. When she felt she had determined which buttress had supported her, she shifted her focus to the pews and counted them from the one closet to her now to where the assumed stomach contents awaited her. She walked briskly. Even though she wanted to run, she opted to practice restraint. When she had arrived at her designated spot; she looked back up to the walkway and guessed how far she may have expelled herself.

She walked a few steps down the length of the pew. Nothing was there. She continued to the end, came out and pondered. *Move forward one or go backward.* She tapped her left cheek with her forefinger. *Forward.* There waiting for her on the pew were the remnants of her breakfast. *Thank God I wasn't hungry this morning.* Undigested bits of toast and orange pulp had dried on the wooden seat and on the back of the church bench. Some of her morning coffee was still puddled on the tile floor. Sister Mary Angelina made her way to the mess. She knelt and mopped up the liquid with the paper towels she had brought.

When they absorbed all they could hold, she tossed them in her bucket and repeated the process. Oddly, she found this repetitive action to be conductive to thought. *Why haven't I realized before that simple actions, repeated mindlessly, can be so freeing for reflective thinking?* She had discovered another way of enforcing discipline for her novices and students. Any other time, a revelation like this would have delighted her. Now she diligently scrubbed using motion memory and engaged her thought processes on the Sister Julian dilemma.

When she had finished tidying up her mess, she stood, gathered her items, and let out the breath she had unknowingly held. Her left hand rested against her forehead while she checked areas around the now cleaned pew. Satisfied she had gotten it all, she stepped quietly into the center aisle and moved to the apse. She crossed herself, knelt, and cried while she fingered her rosary beads.

She was in too much anguish to say rote prayers now. Her time of thinking made her pensive regarding Sister Julian. Some of what the sister had done must be laid at the mother superior's feet. *Why did I not see what was happening sooner? Why did I insist on keeping her with me?*

She rose, bowed, crossed herself and moved towards the doors. She still wasn't sure of all that she should do, but she had a plan forming in her head. *At least Ireland had done away with the Magdalene laundries. Thanks be to Saint Mary the American church had never embraced that style of torture and shame. Sister Julian is safe from being put in one.* The mother superior had never thought she would be thankful for her personal knowledge of such places. Right now it was the only comfort she could claim, but it didn't lessen the grief she carried regarding the eavesdropped confession.

Chapter Forty-Five

Back in her room, Sister Mary Angelina pulled out a box full of memories from her past. Besides photos and letters, there were her degrees and certificates, journals she kept when young, and a pair of crocheted baby booties with a matching bonnet. She took these and a packet of letters tied with a ribbon and laid them on her bed.

She unclasped a necklace she kept hidden beneath her habit and placed it on top of the bonnet. The delicate gold chain, thin from age and wear, seemed small to her now. At one time, a small High Cross hung solo from that chain. Now the cross shared its space with a plain gold disc bearing the initials JEN.

On the floor beside the bed, she stretched out with the packet of letters. They were in the order she had received them. She untied the ribbon and thumbed through the bundle. Each one brought back a memory. *People should still write letters. Nothing stirs the heart than to reread the words crafted for you when you feel alone.*

She began her reading and reliving with the first one. Seventy-two envelopes later, she read the last one. The need to stand and work out a cramp in her leg made her get up and limp around the small bare room. Instead of going to the window where she might gaze at the peaceful outdoors, she hobbled to the little table holding a basin over which a mirror hung. It was this mirror she used to put on her coif and veil. She had not worn a full long habit in years, but the old headdress was a part of her identity she would not give up.

With critical eyes, she stared at her reflection. She was not the same person who had married the church. Back then she was a young lively red haired lass who laughed easily, smiled often and found joy in every situation. *Look at me. I'm withered, wrinkled, and worn.* She frowned more than she smiled. Wrinkles had replaced the tight skin on her cheeks and fine lines had etched themselves around her eyes. *Who would have thought service to the church would take away vitality and youth?* She massaged her upper thigh. I am old, she thought.

She splashed water on her face, checked her headdress and made her way back to the bed. She gave one last look at the items laying there, before she gathered them all and threw them in the box. The packet of letters landed on top. She massaged them and made a vow to burn the bunch when this was over. A firm rap secured the lid. After a quick snatch up, the box was dropped to the floor. A shove with her foot sent it back under the bed. She brushed her hands against her skirt. It was time to visit Bishop O'Malley and hand this issue over to him.

Chapter Forty-Six

Blake raised his bed to a sitting position. He wished he had his laptop. His phone was in reach, so he sent a text to Moore with a request to bring his laptop. *I can work from here, please bring it.*

Moore responded with a thumb up emoji. But when would he be here? Blake wondered. He clicked on the TV, scrolled through the channels, paused briefly on Discovery Channel, and clicked again. When he had gone through the selections twice, he turned it off. Blake had never been an overactive person, but he was feeling cooped up and bored now. Involuntary immobility was not something he was used to, and he hated it.

He grabbed his phone again, this time he checked emails. *How did I get on so many mailing lists? If I could just delete last night.* Blake wasn't much into social media, but he looked up Clarissa on Facebook.

"Wow, she's geekier than me."

While on Facebook, he caught up with some college friends, checked out some pages he followed, posted a message to Clarissa, and grew bored again.

For no reason, an image of *Bob the Builder* popped for no reason into his mind. The words,

"Can I build it? Yes, I can" became an earwig he couldn't escape from. Pictures from his favorite childhood book, "The Little Engine That Could" replaced Bob. *Why am I thinking about childhood now?* His earwig changed too. Now all he could hear was "I think I can. I think I can."

He stared at the ceiling. Repeating the iconic words of the little engine out loud psyched him up. He told his brain to lift his legs. He couldn't feel them, but they were still on him. He saw them every time he looked down.

Nothing happened. *Try harder.* "I can do this," he said to the room. Again he tried and failed. His spirits stated sinking. *Do it again.* He obeyed. His legs didn't.

Instead of getting frustrated, he reasoned there must be some exercise he could do to strengthen his muscles to make them respond. He grabbed his phone. *Surely the answer would be on the internet.* He began with a Google search.

Blake was so involved with his new mission he took no notice of the person who stood in his doorway. "Excuse me," the voice said. When no answer came it spoke again louder. Blake looked up then.

"I'm Kimberly, your nurse for the next few hours. I see on your board you're scheduled for some testing, which begins in about twenty minutes. Would you like to shave before your day begins?"

Blake stroked his face. "Do I look scruffy?"

Kimberly eyed him. "No, I wouldn't say scruffy."

"Good, then I'm not shaving."

Blake's attention shifted back to his phone.

"Is there anything you would like?" Kimberly erased the previous nurse's name and put hers on the board.

Blake dismissed her. All he needed was an answer to his question, how to make his legs work again.

He was making no headway into his search. *Why can't I think of the right keywords?* A frustrated groan came out. His phone slammed against his leg. Yesterday he would have felt that sensation. He hit himself again, and again. Anger grew to rage. Rage morphed to despair. Twenty-four hours ago, he could use his legs. He had plans for his future. Now he had no idea what his future would be. Blake was a planner. It was how he dealt with life. He hated this moment, this uncertainty about what he would now do with his life. *What if I never walk again?*

When the attendant came to get him for the first test, an MRI, he asked them for keyword suggestions, but they gave the same ones he had tried already. As he was being wheeled past the nurses' station, he saw Kimberly sitting by a computer.

"Hey, I know what you can do for me. Find me some information related to my injury." He couldn't hear her answer. He had been pushed into the elevator, and the doors were closing.

When he got back to his room, several printed out pages were waiting for him. They were laying on his pillow like pieces of chocolate. Blake smiled. "Yes." His hands did the thump motion.

"Yes, what?" The attendant asked.

"My nurse came through."

"That's good, I guess." It was an automatic reply. The male attendant's shift was almost up, and chances were they would never cross paths again.

Blake hadn't noticed the indifference in the attendant's tone. He had research to read ,which would give him a clue on where to search for more, if not give him the answers he desperately needed. Three sentences into the first paragraph and, he realized, he had no pen to underline with.

"Can I help you?" A voice crackled out the speaker.

"Yes, please. I need a pen. Can you let me borrow one?"

Kimberly walked into his room. Her fingers held the pen like a prized possession. "You understand, this is most unusual. Patients usually ask for drinks or for help. You are the first to ask me for a pen." Her eyes twinkled with mischief. "I may need to ask for some collateral for this precious pen."

"It's a pen." Blake said. This exchange puzzled him, but not enough to stop scanning the papers.

"I was jesting with you." She laid the pen on the tray he had across his lap. "Will be there anything else or am I dismissed sire?"

Blake looked up. "I'm sorry. I was absorbed." He pointed to the papers in his hand. "Thanks. Thanks for getting me this."

"No problem. I'm guessing you're into medical studies."

"No, not really. I mean, they are fascinating, but I'm more into research. You can say I am a geek. I like to learn." He blushed.

"Cool. What do you do when you're not in the hospital?" Kimberly leaned against the wall. She pulled her hair away from her face, held it up, then let it drop when Blake answered.

"I'm a member of the RPD, Investigative Unit."

"Awesome. My dad was a civil servant too. A fireman."

Blake nodded. "That's nice. When I was in third grade, my class took a trip to a firehouse. I slid down the pole."

"Did you like it? I used to love when my dad would take me to his station and let me tire myself out sliding down it."

"It wasn't as much fun as I thought it would be. I enjoyed answering the calls better."

Kimberly laughed. "Scared of heights?"

"Nope. Scared that someone would come down faster and land on me." Blake grinned.

Kimberly's pager went off. "Ok back to work for me. If you needed something, just page me."

Blake waved in acknowledgement. He picked up his papers and began underlining.

Chapter Forty-Seven

Moore and Samyn finished bagging, tagging and photographing the place where Blake had been attacked. Fortunately for them, Father Talmano had plenty of gloves, swabs, plastic bags, and paper for envelopes, left over from their last forensic soiree in the crypt. He happily supplied and helped them with their tasks.

"I'm not expecting much of this will work as evidence. We might get a DNA hit from the threads, but I wouldn't count on it." Samyn said.

"Perhaps this will give us what we need." Sargent Moore held up a plastic bag holding an object covered in dried blood.

"Is that…?" Father Talmano couldn't say the word. His voice reflected his agony over last night's drama.

"I suspect it is." Sargent Moore wasn't smiling now, nor did his tone hint at a joke.

Samyn showed his bafflement. His eyes squeezed into oval spheres, and lines of exhaustion filled the space around his mouth and cheeks. He looked from one man to the other. "Could it be anything but the attack instrument?" Neither spoke. He directed his next comment to the monsignor. "Don't tell me all priests carry a concealed pocket knife, on them now?"

The monsignor looked at Moore. His face questioned him with a 'Do I laugh or is this a serious question' look? Moore helped him dissect Samyn's comment by clearing his throat.

"Good question, boss."

Samyn ignored Moore. He didn't understand why his partner had made that comment, but he wasn't thinking clearly or quickly this morning. His mind was operating on slow speed. "All right, we've cleared the crime scene. Is there an infirmary here?"

"Yes, one for minor emergencies mainly." Father Talmano said.

"Good. We need to find out if anyone has been in for a sore arm. Take us there next."

"I think you should talk with the bishop, first." There was a resoluteness in Talmano's voice that Samyn was too tired to fight.

"Fine, take us to the bishop." Samyn surrendered. He threw up his hands and shrugged at Moore.

"Why is it when I'm with you I always get in trouble?" Moore said. "Usually it's the captain's office I'm sent to. Now you've up the game with the bishop. Thanks, my brother."

They left the underground burial site for what Samyn hoped would be the last time.

"I'll drop you with the bishop then if you'll pardon me, I need a smoke." Talmano's hands twitched. He reached for his hidden pack of cigarettes.

Samyn looked at Moore. "Don't start."

"I didn't say anything."

Moore leaned his head towards Talmano. "Hey padre, do you have people who assume just because you are privy to their weakness, you hold it against them?"

Talmano laughed. "Are you kidding? I hear confessions. I have more knowledge about our parishioners than they realize sometimes." His voice took on a different, more subdued tone when he spoke. "Lieutenant, I think, I mean, the voice last night," he paused. "I know it was only squealing not words, but it had a vague familiarity to it."

"Why don't you think about that while you're puffing on that cigarette your hand is holding?"

"I'm not..." Talmano looked at his hand. He chuckled while shaking his finger at Samyn. "Very good observation, sir."

"Keep an eye on him, Padre. You'll soon see what his addiction is." Moore slapped Samyn's back. "I trained you well, old man."

They had arrived at the bishop's office. Talmano knocked. He opened the door after they were invited in. Bishop O'Malley stood behind his desk. He gestured to the chairs in front of it. Talmano was pulling the door closed behind him when O'Malley spoke.

"Aren't you going to join us, monsignor?"

"No, not this time your Grace. I'm being summoned elsewhere." He pulled the door shut before O'Malley could ask him questions.

"I wish he could give up that habit."

"You're aware he smokes? On church grounds?" Moore said.

"There's no commandant against it per se and yes I know. The smell gives it away, and I am blessed with a mother superior who knows and sees all. She makes sure I am informed of the things she presumes I need to know."

Moore laughed hard. "True dat." Samyn punched his arm. "Sorry Your Grace. Street slang. It slipped out."

Bishop O'Malley repeated the words to himself. His Irish lilt gave them more textured tones. "I like that phase." He said it again. "Did you find anything helpful?" He looked at each man as he spoke.

"Not sure. But Father Talmano believes he may recognize the voice he heard last night."

Samyn watched the bishop. He wasn't sure O'Malley could be fully trusted yet,

Bishop O'Malley interlocked his fingers and laid his hands on his desk. "I guess that's likely. He is one of the priests who hears confessions of our brothers and sisters."

"We understand there is an infirmary on the grounds. We want to talk to whoever runs it."

"May I inquire why?"

"Talmano states he struck the assailant with his flashlight, hard enough to dent the casing and crack the lens. If he did, then perhaps the assailant sought help in your clinic for deep bruising or a sprain."

O'Malley cupped his face. "Then that person would become a suspect, I suppose."

"Look, someone injured my rookie on your grounds last night. He's lucky to be alive. I intend to find the person who did this. Collars and wimples won't protect them from the law, not while I'm on the case."

O'Malley raised his hands. He struggled to control his anger. "Listen. This is my parish and no guilty party will be protected from prosecution, but neither will I allow you to interrogate people needlessly just so you can find someone to blame." He stared at Samyn. The clock's minute hand moved from one to three before he spoke again. "You can question the infirmarer, but you will do so in my office with me present."

Moore tapped Samyn's leg. When the lieutenant gave him the attention he wanted, Moore nodded his head. Samyn turned back to face the Bishop. "Agreed. I want to see him now."

The bishop picked up his phone, punch in numbers, and waited. He sucked air in and out. After an interminably quick time, the bishop stated his request. An audible click ended the conversation. "He will be here presently. There is no one in need of his care, and his assistant can run things until he gets back."

Samyn leaned back to wait. He kept his eyes veiled while he studied the bishop. He liked him personally, and he wanted to trust him completely, but he was a ranking part of an organization the Samyn learned to dislike and distrust long ago.

Tick, tick, tick. The clock's minute hand moved from the four to the six. It was the only sound in the room until Bishop O'Malley broke the silence.

"May I offer you something to drink?"

The door opened. Father Talmano came in with a tray bearing coffee and scones. "I thought I would bring this on my way up?"

Samyn and Moore shot glances at each other. They were witnessing an act people had accused them of doing, knowing what the other wanted, needed before either had said anything.

"Father Brien is on his way here."

"He's in the hall waiting to enter." Talmano set down the tray. "Didn't you wonder how I opened a door with full hands?" He looked at the officers. "Shall I…?"

Bishop O'Malley cut off his words. "Yes, invite him in, please."

Father Brien came in, bowed, and waited to hear why he was summoned. The bishop introduced the men sitting by his desk. When greetings had been exchanged the bishop looked at Samyn and spoke before the lieutenant did. "Father, has anyone been to see you today regarding a pain in their shoulder or on their arm?"

Father Brien looked at the ground. His hands clutched in front of him. He finally looked at the bishop. "No your grace, no one has been in for anything like that."

"What about for a scrapped arm, or a sprained wrist?"

Again Brien reflected before answering. "No, nothing like that."

"What have people been in for today?" Samyn's tone revealed his desperation.

"We've had one brother come in for an allergic reaction to something he had contact with on his skin."

"Where on his skin?"

"His leg. Around his ankle and calf."

Samyn shook his head. "No one else?" He prompted.

"One brother for some aspirin. He had a headache." Father Brien stopped for a minute. "Oh, and Sister Julian came in for a pain reliever. Cramps, she said. No one else, though."

"Thank you, Father. That is all."

Brother Brien bowed. He shut the door behind him.

"I guess if the person was hit that hard, they would have sought help by now. I can task Monsignor Talmano to keep asking Father Brien about this."

"Yes, do that." Samyn had lost his energy. He looked at Moore. "Let's go. I want to see Blake." They said their goodbyes.

In the car, neither man spoke. Moore knew when to make a joke to lighten up a situation, but that wouldn't help now. Samyn was at a very low point, and there was nothing that would bring him up.

Chapter Forty-Eight

Father O'Brien passed the mother superior on his way down the stairs in the parish building. He greeted her, but she didn't notice him. He tried again after she had moved up five steps. This time he coughed in her direction, making a louder than needed sound. She uttered an automatic reply.

"Pardon me Mother, but may I inquire how Sister Julian is feeling?"

The mother stopped. She pivoted halfway around. Her eyes zeroed in on him. "Why do you ask that?" Suspicion loomed around her. It hadn't always been in her nature to assume guilt, prying, treachery, lustful thoughts, and deceit were the basis of anyone asking her a question. She once assumed people were seeking only general knowledge. Now, she lived her life afraid someone wanted to destroy her.

"She came into the clinic this morning and I was curious if she felt better." Father Brien leaned back against the wall. His fingers tried to clasp the flat surface. His feet moved in inches until he had descended one step. They began their measured retreat again. Like everyone else, he feared her.

"What did she say was wrong?"

"Did you not know of her visit?" He grew nervous.

"What did she tell you was wrong?" She spoke each word distinctly.

The mother superior hovered above him now like a vulture readying to attack. His instinct made him crouch. One hand rose to cover his head, but he quickly directed it back down by his side.

"Cramps. She complained of cramps," was his whispered response.

"I am sure she is better now." Her words sounded shaky to her ears. "I must go."

She hurried up the rest of the stairs. *Why am I so on edge?* She knew the answer. Admitting it was not something she could do. What she had heard Sister Julian say confirmed her previous suspicions. When Bishop Newman had died, things changed with Sister Julian's demeanor, but she had hoped it was only the natural grieving process we have when a friend leaves. This morning's eavesdropping had undone her. "Get yourself together old woman." She shook herself. *I don't know how to.*

She bit the inside of her mouth to keep the tears which were crowding her eyes from escaping. I *mustn't cry. I can't, not now.* She bit down hard enough to release a drip of blood. Her mouth hurt, but she kept pressure on her cheek while she counted to five hundred by twos. When she had reached her goal, she opened her mouth, pushed it around and rubbed the cheek which had endured her punishment.

That's the way to pull up yer big girl knickers.

***

When she felt more composed, though not totally in control of herself, she entered the bishop's office. Heavy footsteps, not the sneaky soft ones she was known for, announced her.

He was dealing with emails when she blustered in. Without looking up he asked, what was so urgent that an invitation to enter could not be given.

"Damn the formalities to hell." Anybody else's face would have turned red when they realized what they had just said to a bishop but not Sister Mary Angelina. Bishop O'Malley raised his head. That statement garnered all his attention.

"Mother Superior, what a surprise. I'm not used to you announcing yourself with footsteps." He wasn't either. He also wasn't use to oxygen remaining in an area when she was in it.

She sank into a chair sitting in front of his desk. He gestured for her to use it after she had taken possession. "Please." He had been at St.

Stephens long enough to comprehend this was not her normal behavior.

"We must talk now."

He held up his hand. "I see something perturbed you, but I suggest you hold your thoughts until I shut the door."

"Yes,.. right.., sorry." The responses came out abstract, automatic. Nothing more than random words chosen from a distracted mind.

Instead of heading back to his desk, he walked to the short filing cabinet. On top of it sat what had become his favorite toy, an electric teakettle. He picked it up to check its water supply. Satisfied there was enough for several cups of tea, he placed it on its warmer, hit its switch and prepared two cups with a measured amount of strong black teas leaves in strainers. For this occasion, he chose Irish Afternoon tea.

When the water had been heated and poured, he carried the china cups back to his desk. He held one out. "Here, you may need this."

"Yes, yes. Bless you, I do." She lifted the cup to her nose and inhaled the scent. It reminded her of home, a farmhouse she had grown up in, where tea was taken around a table in the kitchen under the thatch roof. This smell was from her Ireland. She lowered the cup.

"Bishop, you must send Sister Julian away. I think it's time she was at another convent."

"You have a reason for this, I presume."

"It's only that the child has been with me since she was orphaned. She's not known another." She chose her next words with care. "Mentor you could say or teacher perhaps would be better. Anyway, she has not experienced church service as she should."

"Can you explain, please? What do you mean by experienced church service? Surely you have given her chores and jobs. I am sure she will be adequately instructed before taking her final vows."

"Of course, I've trained her well." Some of the true mother superior haughtiness came out from hiding. It retreated with her next sentence. "She's rather immature because of her learning disabilities, and I feel it would be in her best interests to go somewhere else, a place without a church or monastery attached to it."

Bishop O'Malley had been sipping his tea. He sat the cup on the desk. His finger interlocked. Slowly, his arms moved upward until they connected with the skin under his chin. His chin pressed down on his fingers, forming a flat ridge where it could rest. His gaze never left the mother superiors face.

"You don't mean someplace like one of the old Magdalene Laundries or Mother and Baby homes in Ireland, perhaps". The words were soft, uncondemning, seeking confirmation.

She turned her body towards him. "No," she said empathically. "Possibly." She said sadly. Her eyes showed no emotion, neither did her face. She looked like an empty spiral notebook, one that someone had torn most of the pages from.

"You… you remembered me, didn't you?"

"I was always curious what happened. You left too suddenly after my sisters visited for me not to suspect something."

"One of them had guessed, I suppose. The mother superior sent me away the next morning."

"Both of them commented on their suspicions. I had made a note to talk to you the next day. When I had time, I sent for you, but was told you had left for another school who needed a sister with your skills."

She laughed. There was no mirth in that sound, only pain brought to life from the memory.

"That is one way to sell my story, I suppose."

"I think it's time you shared the truth."

Sister Mary Angelina breathed in a full expanse of air. It expanded her chest, caused her to sit erect, and at last tilt her head back. She held on to that breath until her lungs forced her to give up and release it. She let go in little controlled gasps. When fully expelled she looked at the bishop and nodded he was right.

She slipped out of the chair and knelt on the floor in front of his desk. Her fingers interlaced themselves in her rosary. When her hands aligned themselves in the proper prayer position, she began.

"Forgive me, Father, for I sinned so many years ago." Her story continued. Words fell from her mouth. They mixed with the tears from her eyes. A little quiver of her lips happened sometimes, but never once did she stop speaking. For over an hour a stream of memories were given life again. When there was nothing else to share, her words ended with an abrupt finality.

Bishop O'Malley sat silenced by all he had heard. He felt sorrow for what she had endured. The church had let down one of its own. He came to the front of his desk and offered his hand to her. She allowed him to help her to her feet. When she was standing he embraced her. His tears took up residence on her shoulder. All he could say was I am sorry in endless litany.

She pushed away when she tired of his chant. "You have no reason to be sorry. The person who should have spoken those words did not and now cannot." Bishop O'Malley reached for the Kleenex box on the desk. He held it out to her.

"Thank you." The mother superior blew her nose. She took another tissue to wipe her face, and then blew her nose again. "I made peace with what happened. I accept all the blame can't be laid at his feet. I must own my fault." She wiped under her nose.

"Why did you stay?" He cocked his head and looked puzzled. "How did you… what did you do to make them keep you? Anyone else would have been turned out of the church, but you managed to stay in your order and rise to the top. How?"

Sister Mary Angelina smiled. It wasn't warm, inviting, or joyful. Pity was what it emitted. "At the girl's home where I was sent, I was told I would have to name the father and admit to how many times we had sinned. They took my habit from my body and gave me a scratchy, thread bare sack they called a dress. They were yanking my headdress off when I gave the name of the father. They slapped my face, called me a liar… a whore. These actions continued until another sister came in and told them to stop."

She walked over to his windows and fingered the silk drapes. "I always loved this color." She leaned against the wall. Her hand still laid on the fabric. "Apparently I wasn't the first to be knocked up by him, but I played my trump card. I let them know I would talk to the media if they expelled me. In exchange for my remaining quiet, however, I wanted to not only stay, but I wanted to go to every church, every orphanage, every home he was assigned too. I made a promise to them, mainly to myself, this would not happen to another girl, at least not by him."

"The mother superior at that laundry weighed out my words. She took a few days to decide my fate. But at last she agreed. I then made my last demand. It didn't take her long to see how it could be a punishment for both him and I." Sister Mary Angelina returned to the chair she had occupied in the beginning.

"What was your other demand?"

"I think I have told enough of my story today." She picked up her tea. It was room temperature, but she sipped it. "Now what about our Sister Julian? Can't I find her another place?"

"Your reasons were not clear."

"They are the only reasons you will get."

"Then I will consider your request."

"I suggest you consider them expediently. I've done as much as I can to keep the church safe from evil. I am old, tired, and weary from battles. This church will fall if I can't protect it. Newman may be dead, but his sins still live here,"

Before Bishop O'Malley could ask what she meant, she had left his office. He leaned back in his desk chair. Her confession cleared up the mystery of the orphanage. It gave him the needed piece to his puzzle and confirmed he was right in being at St. Stephens. Not all of his questions had been answered regarding events that happened in Ireland twenty-nine years ago, but he may not need for them to be. He weighed out the mother's request. He had researched part of the records regarding transfers that happened here during Newman's time. What he found made him suspect some of Newman's unsubstantiated habits had been exercised here. Now, after hearing the mother superior's confession, he knew the truth and could report that to his superiors at the Vatican. Bishop Newman's death resolved nothing for anyone, but the church who wouldn't have to worry about buying indulgences and quashing leaks. *It's good that he died. His charisma and charm may have blinded people on earth to his true nature but the judge who decides where we spend our eternal life isn't easily swayed.* He took a sip of the cold tea. "Forgive me father for being thankful some evil has departed our earth." He lifted his cup in salute. "May the Devil enjoy his company."

He decided fresh air would be most beneficial to him now. He took a few steps towards the door. A squeak was spat from a loose board. "Mental note, put that on the maintenance list."

He lifted his foot. An epiphany kept it in the air. "Holy Mother of Jesus, her feet never made a sound when she went from here." The sneaky steps meant the mother superior was back to her proper form. "God have mercy on us all."

He returned to the desk, took out his flask, and swallowed one wee bit, then another longer dram. This day was not going as he had planned. First, the attack on an officer. Then the visit by the police. Now the mother superior confessed sins from her youth.

"Good Lord, what will happen next?" He rushed from the building before another calamity could find him.

Chapter Forty-Nine

Blake, his eyes closed, laid on his back. His chest rose and sank in perfect slow movements. Samyn elbowed Moore. He held a finger over his lips. Samyn tiptoed up to the bed. Moore crossed his arms over his chest. He angled his body to lean against the door frame and watch. Samyn dipped his fingers into a cup of water. When content with their wetness, he pulled them from the glass and positioned them over Blake's face. The water worked its way down the crooks of his fingers until there was nowhere else to go. The trickles formed a pool. When the pool grew crowded, drops of water leapt from the fingertip and landed on Blake's cheek.

"I wasn't asleep." Blake's eyes opened.

"You weren't awake," Samyn said.

"I was in deep thought."

"Is there another kind of thought for you?" Moore stepped into the room. Blake turned his face toward him. He grinned.

"I guess not." He struggled to push himself into a sitting position. It was hard to do with the bed flat.

"Here." Samyn punched a button on the side on the bed. It lifted Blake's feet.

"Wrong end," Moore said.

"Sorry." Samyn gave Blake a half-cocked grin. He pushed another one. This time the feet and the head moved.

"Stop. You're squashing me."

Samyn hit the button again. When the bed quit moving, he hit the last one. "this has got to be the right one."

The mattress section which held Blake's head eased itself up. "Glad it wasn't vital to flip the right switch the first time." Moore shook his head at Blake. "You knew he failed bomb disarming, right?"

Blake tried to laugh, but it hurt to do it. He had spent the day discovering what parts of him were injured. He was lucky, not much damage to anything but his legs.

"Did you bring my laptop?"

"It's right here, rookie." Moore pulled Blake's backpack off his shoulder.

"Great, thanks." Blake's fingers were twitching. His actions said he was still a kid at Christmas, not a grown officer of the force. "Hand it over, please."

Moore laid the burden on the bed. "Getting a little antsy, young man." He nudged Samyn. "I think our rookie is addicted to technology.

Wouldn't you say he looks like a junkie who needs a fix?"

"What do I know about addictions?" Samyn said.

"More than I might." Moore cut his eyes towards Samyn. He then shot a look at Blake, who was cradling his laptop.

"Man, I would love it if my wife hugged me like that."

"I'm overreacting, but guys, I'm not one who… I don't like just lying around. I had a nurse bring me some things to read about paralysis and exercises."

"Why not a magazine?" Samyn said.

Blake gathered himself. "Look, my legs… well, I still can't sense them. If I can't feel them then they must not be movable, right?"

"Son, someone stabbed you last night. Your body doesn't instantly heal itself. You need to give this some time." Samyn said.

"Yes, but I've read once about how people who had been injured forced their body to move. They regained their ability to walk again faster than if they had just laid around and waited. I can't lie around. I'll go nuts."

"Calm down, kid. We want you to walk again too, but it won't happen overnight."

Moore tapped the bed rail to get Blake's attention. "Old man is right rookie. You need to be patient."

"Difficult to do." Blake snapped the words like a rubber band.

"Yes, I agree with that. But while you're going to be busy lying around, then why not get your butt back in the game?" said Samyn.

"I'm not lying around on purpose." Blake's face turned red.

"I was trying to jest like Moore does. Guess I failed."

"Guess you need more lessons." Moore quipped. "Or maybe you should buy a sense of humor like mine." He winked at Blake.

"Anyway, what I was saying..." Samyn paused "We need you to do some of your magic computer snooping,"

"What do you need me to find?"

"See if you can find out anything about a Sister Julian at St. Stephens."

"Okay. Is she a suspect?"

"I'm not sure, but also look for info on a Father Brien and on Sister Mary Angelina and Bishop O'Malley." Samyn rattled off the names without pausing to think between them.

"I printed out some things about them before."
He looked at Moore. "It's in one of the stacks of
info we were going through."

"I need you to go deeper. Find out everything
this time. From where they were born, who their
parents were to what they ate last night. It's important, kid."

"I'll do my best. I'm not sure why you care
about their stomach contents, but since I have
time on my hands, I'll search it out."

"Good, good. I know I can count on you. Not
this chump standing beside me." He pointed his
thumb at Moore.

"Hey. I've saved your behind many times,
boss."

The room phone rang. Blake answered it. His
only responses were I see, I understand and Yes,
sir.

He put the receiver back in its cradle.

Samyn sputtered. "Was that the Captain?"

Blake affirmed with his head.

"I'm on suspended duty for now. I'll be released from the unit in thirty days if I'm unable
to walk." He looked at Samyn. "Guess this means
you won't have to choose someone to fire now."

Moore whistled low. He watched Samyn for
his reaction.

Samyn's temper rose inside him. It showed it-self on his face, in his clenched hands, and in his tone. He spoke too calmly, too clear, too precise. His actions scared the other men. "That bastard, that sorry bastard."

Moore put his hand on Samyn's back. He used his body to shield Blake from witnessing Samyn's anger. "I think we should go now. Rookie looks tired and we need him to rest now."

He steered Samyn towards the door.

"We'll be back tomorrow. Get us some info."

"But I'm suspended."

Samyn pushed Moore's hands away and turned back to see Blake. "No kid, you're not. He can't do that. We won't let him. We're a team. So get busy. Do what you do best. We're counting on you. We'll deal with the Captain." He gave Blake a toothy grin. It wasn't warm or restful. It made Blake think of a hyena getting ready to kill its prey.

"Ok" Blake had nothing else to say. He pushed the call button. He needed an aspirin.

"By the way, how did you know I was sup-posed to sacrifice someone?" Samyn replaced his grin with his usual stone face.

Blake leaned back on his pillow. "I'm a keen investigator and you taught me to pay attention to my hunches."

Samyn's face cracked.

Chapter Fifty

Moore took the keys from Samyn. "I'll drive."

Both slammed the car's doors. Moore turned the key to start the engine. Samyn stomped his foot on an imaginary accelerator. "That bastard."

"Boss, we'll deal with him. Yes, he's wrong to call the rookie and tell him he has thirty days to get his mobility back. Yes, he's wrong to do it only hours after the kid had surgery, but you know timing was never his best skill."

"Don't you try to defend his actions."

"I'm not. I'm telling you we'll deal with him, but first we need to find out who did this to Blake. Agree?"

"Head to the church. I don't care if we have to interrogate every person on that property. I want to find who attacked him before today is over."

"I have another suggestion."

Surprise kept him from speaking. Samyn looked at Moore expecting to see his partner had grown two heads, and his skin had turned lime green.

Moore stopped at the red light. "I'm hungry. I say we grab lunch and make a game plan. No battle is won without a fight strategy."

Samyn threw up his hand. "Sure. Whatever it takes to keep you moving."

Moore knew Samyn well enough that he had been planning to get lunch before mentioning it. Samyn hadn't noticed which direction they had travelled.

"I should have known." Samyn's head shook.

"Hey, you like Tessie's food."

The cafe was owned by one of Moore's cousins. Ever since it had opened, the tables stayed full. It was crowded enough to keep conversations from being easily overheard. Moore had sent Tessie a text asking her to keep a corner table for them.

People were jammed at the front waiting to be seated when they walked in. Samyn's height always got him noticed, even in packed places. Moore's electric grin and size drew its share of looks anywhere he went.

Tessie, holding a pot of coffee, noticed them coming through the door. She waved.

"I got you a place in that back corner." She pointed towards it. "You've got a pot of coffee, two glasses of tea, and a pitcher of water waiting, and I ordered your usual. It should be up soon."

Moore gave her one of his famous smiles. "You the best, cuz." He made his way to their spot. Samyn followed. People in front chatted.

They wanted to learn why they hadn't known you could reserve a seat.

"Guess you must need to tower over others to get seated quickly." A short blonde said.

"He's my cousin, and he's a cop. I take care of him, and he makes sure beat officers patrol often by my shop. You look smart enough to get how the system works, sugar."

Tessie gave her a wink. She turned around and rolled her eyes. The staff who saw her expression laughed. The regulars waiting for a table chuckled. Tessie's had a reputation for serving first responders before others, which is why so many of them frequented her place when on duty.

Moore and Samyn's orders were up. Tessie waved off the waitress who was reaching for the plates. "I got it. It's my cousin's food." On her way to their table, she greeted several regulars, noticed who need refills on their drinks, and smiled at everyone.

"Gentleman and cousin, here you go." She sat the plates down in front of them.

"A Reuben with fries for the gentleman and for the family man, a chicken salad sandwich on sourdough toasted with a side of chips."

"Looks good Tess." Samyn said. "I didn't think I was hungry, but my stomach says different."

Moore took a bite. "Hmm, yes." He pointed to his plate. "Now that's what I'm talking about." He wiped his mouth. "Best chicken salad I've ever eaten, but don't let Aunt Maude knew I said that."

Tessie's eyes rolled again. "Lord no. No one would ever hear the end of it, and she'd quizzed me on my recipe every time we saw each other. Your secret's safe cousin." They laughed.

"Now do you need anything?"

Samyn and Moore said no. "Good. If you do, yell for me. I've told my staff not to bother you. Figured you must have business to discuss if you wanted to be in a corner." She winked and walked away.

Samyn didn't speak until he had finished half his sandwich. "Good decision to stop."

"I thought so." Moore picked up a French fry from Samyn's plate.

"Eat your own food."

"Yours taste better. Besides, those fries were taunting me. Had to eat one." He refrained from taking another. Instead, he grabbed a chip. "So what's the plan of action?"

"We're going back to the church. I want to talk to Father Talmano again. Perhaps he's remembered more about the hooded person. I also want to wonder about the grounds. Somebody's got to be walking around with an injured arm."

"Do we have to talk to the mother superior? That woman scares the heebie jeebies out of me."

"I hope we don't. Besides, she's middle age and the way Talmano and Blake described the attacker's movements, I would think it's someone younger."

"I'll agree to that if it means no dealing with the rabid penguin." Moore ate a bite of his sandwich. "But if it was a nun who attacked Blake, then won't we have to talk to her. I mean she is over them?"

Samyn thought about this. "Maybe." He took a chip from Moore's plate. "It was taunting me." He spoke before Moore could protest. "I got the impression she sees everything that happens and it wouldn't surprise me to learn she eavesdrops." He rubbed his chin. "We may want to talk to her. She may have seen who is walking around with a damaged wrist or arm."

Moore's palms went up. "Oh no. Not me. I'm not talking to her. I promised Shirley some marvelous retirement years. Besides you outrank me, golden boy."

Samyn had been reaching for his wallet. He stopped. "Tell you what. You buy lunch. I'll talk with the mother."

Moore signaled Tessie to bring the bill. "You're planning something, but if paying for your meal keeps me from that woman, I'm happy to treat you."

"Who said you wouldn't be there?" Samyn's face was frosty. "I may need a witness, partner."

"I don't think she did it."

"Neither do I. But I suspect she knows who did."

"I'm not comfortable playing bad cop, good cop with a church person who I swear would terrify Satan."

"Not going to do that. I will remind her of what the church teaches and of her vows. You're just there to look intimidating and take notes."

His body slumped, and his face expressed his sorrow with drooping eyes and lips. His head moved in slow motion from side to side. "I've got a feeling this isn't going to go well boss. Nope, not well at all."

"Maybe not. We shall see, though."

"That's what the blind man said."

Samyn left the table. Moore dropped some bills on the paper Tessie had discretely placed by his arm. He caught up to Samyn outside by the car. "I hope you got a back-up plan. Please tell me there's a backup." He clicked the remote.

"I do."

"And that is…?"

"Wing it."

Chapter Fifty-One

It was quiet when Samyn and Moore entered the Parish building. No one was at the front, so they preceded up the stairs. "Must be their silent time." Moore spoke low. Samyn agreed with a nod. Without being conscious of it, each man was stepping lightly, trying not to make any noise that would interrupt the solitude.

O'Malley's office door was shut. Muffled sounds within the room escaped into the hall. Moore raised his fist to knock. He gave Samyn an unsure glance. He lowered his hand.

"Something's not right."

"I feel it too." Samyn raised his hand. He placed it by the door, dropped it back to his side and gave a look to Moore. Once again he rose his fist. This time he followed through with a rap.

Chairs scrapping against the floor. Footsteps, then a squeak, suggested someone was coming. A tumbling click resonated from the lock being unsecured. The sound of the old crystal door handle turning followed. The door swung open. Father Talmano's arm extended itself from behind it.

"Come in, gentlemen. We've been expecting you."

Moore looked at Samyn. "Did you call? Cause I didn't."

"Can't take the blame partner. I didn't do it."

"It's simple boys. You had an officer wounded on our property. Where else would you investigate but here?" Bishop O'Malley's answer set the tone and the parameters for the visit.

"Please sit." He pointed to the chairs in front of his desk.

Samyn and Moore shot looks at one another, then chose a seat.

"Father Talmano and I discussed who we suspect may be involved. With over 100 suspects, and that's based solely on the nuns who live in the convent, the priests who are part of the abbey order, and the staff, we thought it wise to narrow your interested parties down."

"I suppose I should thank you." Samyn said.

"No, you should listen. I know I wear a dog collar, but you need to accept its one for show. As I told you before, I investigate churches, not serve in them as a priest. I came here to check out reports of missing funds, inappropriate behaviors, and to resolve that nagging sensation I had about the Ireland orphanage. They gave me the title Bishop because it gives me freedom to discover things without raising anyone's caution flags. So while I do not carry a cop badge, I have investigative skills."

Samyn made a fist, then hit his chest. "Mea culpa."

"You'll be happy to know we have a list for you." He slid a paper across his desk towards Samyn. He handed a copy to Moore.

"This is your suspect list?"

O'Malley nodded.

"No other names?"

O'Malley replied with a resolute no.

"How may I ask do you narrow it down to just this?"

"Elementary, Watson." O'Malley said the words with a straight face but couldn't keep from smiling after they came out. "Sorry, I couldn't help it. I devoured Arthur Conan Doyle as a kid."

Father Talmano's grin made a quick retreat.

"All kidding aside, it wasn't that hard for us because we're familiar with these people. If you had to weed out the possibles and non-possibles from the probables, it could take valuable hours. Time, we assumed, was vital. At least, cop shows imply that." He leaned forward. His voice dropped in volume. "And Seamus had a request to send a nun away."

Samyn's attention had been drifting. The last sentence pulled it back. His body half raised for the chair. "Who?"

"Do you mean who requested she leaves or the name of the nun to be sent away?" The bishop spoke as he cracked his knuckles.

"Both answers."

Bishop O'Malley rolled his neck. The tension from the day was bothering him. "Hold on for a minute, please. This day, well," he arched his back, then pushed his shoulders forward and back alternately.

"Please take your time. I'm going nowhere." Samyn's words drew a line he wanted them to cross.

A faint popping sound followed by an "oh yes" was the response from O'Malley.

"The mother superior has requested that Sister Julian go somewhere else."

"Did she say where?"

"Her answer doesn't matter, does it?"

"It might, but that's for me to decide."

"Lieutenant, I ask you to please trust me on this. The place in her mind no longer exists."

"Why would she do that, unless she didn't know it had been disbanded or shut down or whatever you do to no longer needed facilities?"

"It was a type of home, many had existed, now all are closed, at least the ones known by the name Magdalene Laundries."

"Okay. I don't care why all the laundries closed. I'm guessing everyone has their own washing machine. It seems absurd to want to send a nun to a laundry mat, but you Catholics do strange things." Samyn turned sideways in his chair. O'Malley stretching his muscles made Samyn notice the cramping in his legs. He now extended them to their full length. "I'll concede you're right. Where she wanted Sister Julian to go is not important."

"I think we should talk to both of them," Moore said.

"I must insist you do it here." O'Malley looked first at Moore, then at Samyn. "I will not allow you to speak with them alone. It's me and Father Talmano as witnesses or the church will bring in its legal counsel for the interview. Which do you gentlemen prefer?" His eyes ping-ponged between their faces as he waited for their answer.

Samyn and Moore faced each other. Samyn's left hand rubbed his chin. Moore's head cocked towards his right shoulder, then his left. Samyn's hand left his chin and repositioned itself in front of his mouth. His fingers tapped in rapid repeating motions against themselves. Moore's right leg crossed over his left and dangled. Fast, fast, slow was the rhythm it kept.

The clock ticking had been the only sound in the room for the last seven minutes. Samyn broke the silence.

"Let's see your mother superior first."

Chapter Fifty-Two

Sister Mary Angelina decided not to return to the lower school. She couldn't focus on trivial issues right now. She was still unnerved by Sister Julian's pseudo-confession. *The school's in excellent hands.* Sister Katherine would find her if a catastrophe occurred that needed her attention.

Instead of turning left on the path that would take her to the lower school, she chose right. *I must clear my head. I must resolve this problem.* When she had been a novitiate, the nun in charge encouraged them to walk when they needed to think and when they had an issue they were struggling with. She suggested walking a labyrinth. The path the mother superior chose would take her to the one on the abbey grounds.

First she must pass the church buildings and the parking lots. She deliberately strode like a nun on a mission. *Please Lord, Let me others choose not to bother me. Let my reputation put fear into them, as I am too unsettled in mind to deal with others now.* The shadow from St Stephen's Cathedral crossed her walk. The coolness from sudden loss of sunshine caused goosebumps to pop up on her arms. Automatically her hands pulled an imaginary cardigan tighter around her. Her pondering, interrupted from her dilemma, took another route. She stopped walking, but kept thinking. Her thoughts now hurried through her memories on how she, a young nun from Ireland, came to be here on these grounds here, now, a much older and wiser woman in a habit. The shivering grew more intense. Sister Mary Angelina rubbed her arms, determined to warm them up.

With her head back, she could take in the entire tower that dominated the front of the building. She had never noticed how imposing it looked, nor how long of a shadow it cast. From where she stood, the view consisted of one side of the church, the side which abutted the parish hall. She moved to get a better look at this former mansion. There was a time in her past when she had considered becoming an architect. Her mother discouraged her from that profession.

"That's work men do and you're a female, my dear. No one will ever hire a young lady, no matter how well-qualified she is to do a man's job," her mother said. So she had put that dream away.

Now she let herself get distracted from the worry that had laid heavily on her mind all morning and her recent reflections about herself and purpose, by studying the former house's architectural lines. Her view offered the front of what had been a most impressive home.

She changed mental tracks again and imagined what it would have been like to live in such a magnificent dwelling. Now it housed rooms only used by the men for debate and study, the library used by the nuns and priests, dining facilities for the men and the bishop's private retreat. She wondered what those rooms had been before. She knew the room used by the church for large gatherings had been the ballroom. A sigh escaped the body of a person who had dreamed of drafting designs for places like this. In so many ways, it was only a shell of its former self. *I guess it still is a home though, in the sense it houses needed items, provides comfort with food, and protects discussions and debates that take place within its walls.*

She studied the front door. *Now that's a work of art. The shape, the lines, the arch.... Oh My Blessed Jesus, Mary and Joseph, that can't be.* She rubbed her eyes, squinted, and looked at the entrance again. She hunched, twisted, repositioned herself before accepting her eyes were showing her the truth.

At the front door were two of the men she did not want to see, did not want on this property today. The labyrinth walk would have to wait. She now had another worry to handle.

She pulled up her habit sleeve. The watch she wore showed it was 2 o'clock. That told her to head to the music room in the middle school.

A person with her authority should walk and expect things and people to wait for her arrival. She ran.

"I'm getting too old for this nonsense." She panted at the front door of the middle school building. After catching a quick breath, and reestablishing her air of superiority, she hurried through the doors, waved off any greetings and made her way to the room where music was taught. Tidying it was the person she was antsy to see.

"Sister Julian, I want you to go to your room and stay there until I send word to you."

"But I have not finished yet, Mother. Shouldn't I do that first?" Sister Julian's large blue eyes looked at the mother superior. They were innocent, like her tone. The blue of the iris was an inviting color. It made one think of joy, laughter, childlike innocence. So blue and inviting were her eyes, they warmed you with their sparkles, and made one want to protect her.

"What haven't you done?"

"I promised I would tidy the music folders, remove the old music, file it away, and put in the sheets for the new songs the students will perform at the next concert."

"I'll find someone else to take care of that. Go to your room now. Go nowhere else and tell no one where you are going or why. Do you understand me?"

"Yes, Mother."

The obedient nun left. The mother superior sank down on one chair in the arranged semicircle. She rubbed her forehead. One catastrophe averted, she thought. *Now to the labyrinth.* She left by the back door and hurried to where she knew refuge awaited and if all went right, a solution to this mess that bothered her.

Chapter Fifty-Three

Father Talmano had been sent to find the mother superior and bring her to the bishop's office. He decided not to tell her why. He headed to the lower school as that's where she typically was at this time.

He cringed when he placed his hand on the front door's knob. Every person has at least one thing they dislike about their profession. For him it was not celibacy, it was children; They were sticky, snotty, smelly, germ sharing miniatures of regular size humans. He avoided the lower school when possible. He also found ways to not deal with little kids in church. Middle schoolers, high schoolers, he had no qualms about, but the smaller the size of the human, the less he wanted to be around it. Some priests delighted in baptisms; he made excuses to get out of doing that sacrament.

He sucked up his displeasure concerning this confined space of noisy, active, germ missiles. *Just get this done, man. Go in, grab the nun, and pull her out fast.* Right, he thought. As if anyone could make her move quick or pull her from where she's planted.

He stopped putting off entering this lair of his doom. *Thank you, God, for front offices.* He breezed in like a ship ready to handle any storm before it returns to port. The nun seated behind the desk gave him a surprised but pleasurable smile.

"Why Father, how lovely of you to come see us." Gaiety danced in words and mischief sparkled in her eyes. "What saint should we thank for letting us witness the miracle of you willingly coming to a place known to hoard small children?"

Father Talmano turned red. His hands twisted automatically in response. Apparently his aversion to kids, which he thought he had hidden, was known by others in the church. He stuttered sounds and trip over the words his mouth tried to form.

Instead of laughing at him, the nun took pity upon the poor figure who stood in front of her in blatant distress and discomfort. She leaned over the desk, cast glances around the room, then raised her hands to her mouth. They shielded her lips from others viewing them. "Don't worry, you're not the only person at this abbey who doesn't like the wee bairns." She winked.

One finger on her right hand tapped her chest. A slight shake of her head confirmed she too was not a lover of little kids.

Father Talmano's jaws unhinged. "You." The disbelief was clear. "Why then are you here?" His conspiring whisper combined with an astonished face encouraged her to share a long-harbored secret. "The mother superior put me here for punishment. She overheard me say I hoped to never be assigned to an elementary school. She said I needed to overcome my dislikes if I am to live up to the image of Christ who taught we must love everyone."

From Father Talmano a hearty, booming laugh emitted. "I'm sorry." He wiped his eye. "I just pictured her standing over you and saying those words." He kept laughing.

The nun joined in. "Scares me to death she does."

When they had gotten control of themselves, she spoke again. "I've been in this purgatory for three years now. Maybe I'll be released when I die."

Her last word reminded him why he was there. "Where is the mother superior? I am to bring her to the bishop."

"OOH is she in trouble?"

"No, he just needs to find out something."

"Oh dear, she's not here. She came in to talk with Sister Katherine this morning regarding what needed doing today, and then she left. She's not been back. Could Sister Katherine help him?"

"No, no, he needs the mother. Any idea where she may be? Was she going to another school building?"

"She left no instructions on where she would be. That's odd, isn't it? She always tells us where we can find her." The nun stopped talking. She tapped her pencil on the desk. "Try the gardens, sometimes she goes there to weed them while she meditates."

"Thanks." Father Talmano turned to make his exit.

"Stop."

He did as commanded.

"The only other time I remember her not saying where she could be found was once when she was disturbed by something happening with a young nun. She went to walk the labyrinth. Try there first."

"I will." He got away before some little child to touch him.

Chapter Fifty-Four

The spaces between the concentric lines that formed the circular patterns in their labyrinth had been planted with small perennial flowers blooming in vibrant colors. While they made a beautiful filler, they took away from the purpose, she thought. *They should have used all white flowers. This is a place where we focus.*

She blamed the flowers for her mind refusing to stay focused on the burden her heart bore, but she reasoned that was only an excuse. She didn't want to deal with what troubled her because the solution would affect her. Her life would change soon, and perhaps not for the better.

A whisper of wind roused the sleeping flowers. They released their scents to the only one around. The mother superior, who had just expressed her dislike in her thoughts, now experienced remorse. A smell she knew well rafted up. She knelt to confirm her nose was still in working order. "Lavender, how very appropriate for a place where peace is sought." Another little breeze lofted up a scent also known to her. *Chamomile.* She adjusted her earlier thoughts to now thinking perhaps whoever had chosen these plants picked wisely.

She crossed herself, clutched the crucifix she wore around her neck, and took the first step. "I must concentrate." She took another. "I must concentrate." Another, more purposeful step, followed. She repeated her mantra and step ritual halfway through the first section.

Her nerves grew steady, her mind cleared, all distractions had been put to rest. She was ready to consider all options that may be answers to this problem.

By the time she had made her way through section two, an answer which had been a mere seedling at the start of this mass of swirling lines began taking shape. She trusted that when she reached the center of the maze, the answer would be clear.

Chapter Fifty-Five

Father Talmano watched the figure in black weave its way around the circular maze. She ambled, pausing after each step. He hesitated to go closer. He was on a mission, but she must be too, he reasoned. *Why else would she move so deliberately? Let her finish or suffer her wrath?* Whether he interrupted her walk now or in an hour wouldn't matter, would it? The men who wanted to question her would not leave until they had done so. He could practice patience, he decided.

Father Talmano, like everyone else on these grounds, lived in fear of her. Even the deceased Bishop Newman shrunk in size around her. Talmano had brawled with some tough men in his youth, but not even they could put fear into people like this nun. She was the most intimidating person he knew.

When her pace picked up, his insides nudged him. He had to get her to the bishop's office. Postponing it any longer wouldn't help, it could harm. The longer the officers waited, the more irritable they may become. Lengthy waiting would justify their actions. Someone attacked a young man, one of theirs, on holy grounds while working on a problem for the church. Now he may not walk again. When he could no longer handle the nagging thoughts in his head, he made his way to where the woman in black walked.

He made it to the labyrinth entrance unobserved. She must have sensed his presence as she spoke before he did. "You've come to take me to the bishop."

"Yes." He took an involuntary step back. The temperature felt like it had risen twenty degrees inside the circle.

"I don't suppose I can finish first?"

"It's best to go now. He is waiting and has been for a while."

She let go of her cross and nodded. "You are right." She stepped over the rows until she arrived back at the start. The air, Talmano noticed, seemed cooler, much cooler, and that she looked old and withered.

"Are you okay, Mother?" He was worried. Not a sentiment he had ever had for her.

"I am fine." She patted his hand. "Come, I must face my demons."

One of his eyebrows raised at her odd choice of words. *Samyn was right. She knows something.* He looked at his hand where hers had touched him. He wasn't sure if he would see a mark or not. She had never patted his hand before. He couldn't recall her patting anyone. He had witnessed her using a ruler on a palm but not a gentle hand pat.

Sister Mary Angelina drew herself up to her full height of 5 foot 2 inches. Father Talmano looked down. *Has she always been that short?* Why I haven't noticed that before? He wondered. *Could I have been so terrified of her that my mind made her taller, more imposing?* Other thoughts similar to this played inside his mental home.

"Is there a problem, Father? Are you not coming with me? I assume you were sent to bring me to the bishop." Her eyes bored into his soul, weeding out his excuses.

"Yes, yes."

The mother superior whom they all feared was back. He swore she had gotten taller with that last exchange.

They walked in silence back to the parish building. Each lost in thoughts. Both aware things would change today by sunset. Tomorrow the abbey, the monastery, would be a different place for everyone. Whether the change would be good or bad was something they would find out in time.

Chapter Fifty-Six

Monsignor Talmano knocked on Bishop O'Malley's door. He stepped back and waited for an invitation to enter before opening the door. When the invite came, he gestured to the mother superior to enter first. His father had taught him men always give women respect by acting with courtly manners. Some ingrained habits never die. The mother superior gave a nodded her head in acquiesce to him. She entered, bowed, acknowledged the officers with a nod, and stood in front of the bishop's desk. Monsignor closed the door, bowed, then leaned against it.

Bishop O'Malley stood. "Perhaps we would be all be more comfortable if we sat over there." He pointed to the area by the windows.

Monsignor Talmano walked to the file cabinet where the electric kettle stood. He prepared a pot for tea. The others rose to make their way to the sitting area. A little unspoken discussion took place as they each eyed the chairs and considered where they should sit.

O'Malley helped them decide. He chose a wing chair placed by the wall and in between two windows. The others arranged themselves abstractly. Lt. Samyn sat to the left of the bishop with one place separating them. Sargent Moore sat in the center of the group. The mother superior opted for the chair next to the bishop on his right side. Father Talmano, when he came with the tea tray, settled himself between the officers after offering cups to everyone.

"Mother Superior, you've seen us here often and have wondered why we were around. I'm certain you suspected the story they told you was not exactly true, and you were right." Lt. Samyn stopped long enough for her to acknowledge this. "Do you have any idea why we have been here?"

"No, I guessed there to be more to the ruse than donation seeking, but I never figured out for what other reason you would be on these grounds."

"We were called here to investigate tampering with a grave in the crypt."

"Tampering… with a crypt… whose?" She tripped over the words, but her tone and the lost color from her face suggested she had the answer already.

Right then, Samyn and Moore looked at each other. They had been right to suspect her.

"We found out during our investigation of the opened crypt, Bishop Newman's ring had been removed from his finger, and he died not from natural causes, but from poisoning," Samyn shrugged his shoulders and spread his hands out.

"Whether accidental or deliberate, we're clueless."

"Poison?" She gasped. Her left hand sought her crucifix. She crossed herself after kissing it. "Jesus, have mercy on his soul."

He hoped she would give some sign of her guilt, but his hopes got dashed. From her reaction, it was obvious she hadn't been the one to help him enter another realm. He still suspected she knew who the guilty party may be though.

Samyn opened his mouth, but Bishop O'Malley spoke instead. He muttered sorry to Samyn before he turned to the mother superior.

"Sister, would you be kind enough to tell these officers how you became acquainted with Bishop Newman."

Shock showed on her face. "Your Grace, I told you that in confidence."

"Which is why you are being asked to tell them. They need to be told." His voice sounded kind but it firmly suggested he would not take a refusal.

Sister Mary Angelina steeled herself. She opened her mouth, but nothing came out. "Sister, we're aware you were at the orphanage in Ireland the same time Newman and Bishop O'Malley. We also understand someone sent you away abruptly." Samyn said.

"Aye, but you don't suspect the reason why." She looked him in the eye.

Samyn admitted they did not.

Moore knew Samyn and even if he didn't get why Samyn had a dislike for nuns and priests, he sensed from Samyn's vocal inflection and body language a battle was about to start.

"Mother, if it's not relevant to us finding who killed Bishop O'Malley or attacked Officer Blake, then you need not tell us," Moore spoke to the nun before looking at Samyn. "Isn't that right, Lieutenant?"

"I'm afraid it is relevant." Bishop O'Malley said.

The bishop laid his left hand on her shoulder. She patted it. Something, not quite a smile, but not a grimace either, attempted to express her feelings.

"You are right. The church assigned me to the orphanage as a teacher hours after taking my final vows. I was young, excited, eager to do the work I felt called to." A smile of joy flitted on her face from remembering this time of youth. She paused. Time inched away while she relived those first months.

"Bishop O'Malley and Bishop Newman were still lowly fathers then." She questioned O'Malley, "You had been in the priesthood a short time when you arrived, a few years perhaps?"

"It was my third placement in the church but my first after receiving my masters in theological education."

Samyn was tired of the cat-and-mouse game. "So why did you leave, sister?"

"I got pregnant."

Stunned silence. Neither Moore nor Samyn had a response. This was not what they expected to hear. Bishop O'Malley had mentioned his on-going search for the pregnant nun, but they never suspected the mother superior would be guilty of being an actual mother.

Chapter Fifty-Seven

The clock hands moved several times before anyone spoke.

"But.. you…" Samyn's right arm raised to scratch his head. "You were a nun." The words finally came out.

"Still am." She nodded.

"Excuse me sister, but I supposed nuns took some kind of vow of chastity?" Moore, still in shock, stumbled on his words.

"We do."

"You broke your vow," Samyn said. He kept trying to get his head around this news still.

"Well, in hindsight, I saw that yes, I had done wrong."

Samyn looked at the Mother Superior with new respect. A person he had disliked for many reasons had become an actual human to him. He put the investigation aside for the moment. The urge to find out what would make a person break their promise to the church overcame him.

"How?"

"How did I get pregnant?"

He nodded.

"The same way other women do." Her words sounded hollow, but her eyes showed mirth.

Samyn grew red. Once again, a nun had made him feel ignorant.

"Who…? No, that's none of my business." Samyn held up his hand.

"It wouldn't be if it had no bearing on this mess."

All eyes watched her, waiting in anticipation of the big reveal. What other surprises would she give them?

"Bishop, well father then, Newman, put me in the family way, as we used to say in Ireland."

Audible gasps and clock ticks made the only sounds heard now. Samyn leaned back in his seat. He crossed his hands over his chest and looked at the ceiling. Moore squirmed in his chair. This news made it a very uncomfortable place to be. Father Talmano's mouth hung open. Bishop O'Malley appeared to be the only man unfazed by this news. Moore noticed that.

"Did you know this?" Talmano said to O'Malley.

"When I arrived here, her name sounded familiar, but I couldn't place why. When I saw her, I suspected our mother superior to be the nun who had left, but if she had been carrying a child, why was she still a nun? I thought maybe I'm wrong because the pieces didn't fit together neatly, but when I checked the orphanage records, I was right she was most likely the nun. I had no way to be sure until she confessed to me earlier, and even though she did not say who the father was, I'm not surprised it was Newman. Remember, I told you how he tried to force himself upon my sister."

"When did that happen?" Sister Mary Angelina's took her turn to be surprised.

"In Ireland, at the orphanage. She told me you looked pregnant. The Vatican sent me here to investigate him for some other reasons."

"Did he rape you?" Samyn said.

"No, I wouldn't say that I was raped in a literal way, but you can say I had been in a figurative sense."

"What do you mean, Mother?" Father Talmano spoke for the first time.

"I was young, naïve, and believed that everyone who wore a habit or cassock must be pure and good." Her eyes grew wet. "Father Newman noticed me. He paid me compliments, and as I said, I was young. It flattered my ego he noticed the good work I did. He encouraged me to come to his office whenever I had any ideas on what would improve the lives of the children. I thought he truly cared about them." She twisted the chain which held her crucifix. The pain she carried for so many years released itself in her admission. "I learned his only concern dealt with building his reputation with the Vatican. That no one mattered to him. People were only things for him to use then discard when they served his purpose."

The mother superior sat erect in her chair. She wore no pride, no sense of lost remorse, no veil of secrecy, only a hint of shame at what she called her stupidity. She placed her naked, truthful confession at their feet.

"I sought him out one day. I mentioned I had read about this alternative teaching method and I wanted to discuss it. I told him it may be good for some of our children since everyone learns in distinct ways. He invited to come to his room after the last office."

She huffed out a long-held breath, then began again. "When I got there, he had discarded his vestments. He placed two glasses on a table by his divan. He told me to sit there and offered me one. I couldn't say no, he was over me in the church hierarchy. I took it. It was whiskey, something I didn't drink often. He left his glass on the table. While I talked he stroked my veil and inched closer. The whole time he kept saying drink. He told me how lovely I was. How God had created a most beautiful person in me. He talked about how blessed he was to have some-one like me married to the church like him." Her tears flowed freely.

"He convinced me with logical arguments that when I married the church, I wedded him too. Since we were united in celestial matrimony, it was necessary for us to be joined as one in God's eyes."

Bishop O'Malley offered her a tissue. She took it and smiled her thanks. "It makes no sense, I know, but aided by the whiskey, it sounded rea-sonable." She wiped her nose.

"So we had carnal knowledge of each other. Even though I had doubts about this being right, I told myself it must be or he wouldn't have been able to justify his actions with biblical knowledge and reason. But it was only because of my stupid-ity, naivety, and youth, not that he spoke the truth."

"What a bastard," Samyn said. Moore cleared his throat.

"Well put." Father Talmano said.

"Go on. Continue your story." O'Malley pushed her gently with his words.

"On nights he wanted sex, he would send me a note saying I must perform my wifely duties after the last office. I went." She lowered her head. "I didn't understand I could tell him he was wrong, but it never seemed right to me."   She took a breath and raised her head again.   "Every time I tried to refute one of his reasons why this was what God called good, or why it was the way adults expressed love to each other, he shut me down by saying I understood nothing, I had not been educated as he and that he was teaching me to love the way Christ said to." She blew her nose.

"What a lying, manipulative piece of...."

O'Malley stopped Samyn's rant. "Let her finish, then you can ridicule the church if you need to."

O'Malley gestured for the mother superior to continue. "The last night we came together, I again tried to tell him it was wrong, that this act wasn't what being married to the church meant, and we were committing sin. No, he said. It was only a sin to have sex out of wedlock, and we were married in God's eyes. Then he told me it agreed with me as my breast appeared fuller now. I said my monthlies had stopped, and I kept getting sick in the mornings. He asked how long this had been going on and I told him four almost five months."

"What did he say to that?" Samyn said.

"Apparently I was not the only wife he had. He stepped into his private bathroom and returned with a box, which he handed me. It was a pregnancy test. He told me to take it in the morning. If it showed I was with child to place a pink slip of paper on my classroom door. If I wasn't, then leave the door empty."

She stopped talking and breathed hard. "I did as he asked and put a paper on the door. That night he sent for me." Her breathing and distress grew noticeable.

"Please, does she need to tell all?" Father Talmano begged for this to end.

"Yes." Sister Mary Angelina said. She looked at the officers. "I need to unbury this secret. I have harbored it for too long. He asked me when did I have my last period and got angry when I said four months. He told me I was too far along for an abortion now. I would have to leave the orphanage. He would arrange for me to go a Magdalene Laundry and if I told anyone who the father was, he would deny it and say I was lying. I ran out of his room crying."

Samyn showed his temper by controlling his remarks. "So O'Malley, not only popes can father children. How long has the church let priests have that privilege?"

"His actions angered me too, lieutenant. That is why I made it my mission to investigate him years ago and eagerly accepted the church assigning me here to investigate accusations made against him. It is why I came to you when his tomb got opened." Bishop O'Malley's Irish lilt became very pronounced now. He too struggled to keep his temper in check.

"What's a Magdalene Laundry?" Moore said.

"Places, run by the Irish Catholic Church, where fallen women were sent until they had their babies. They paid for their sin and upkeep by cleaning, washing, scrubbing, ironing, and folding the items sent to them by wealthy families mostly, but also businesses. The public assumed them to be respectable, loving places because the church ran them. The girls forced into one knew differently. They were constantly reminded what worthless, unpure, sinners they had become by the nuns who ran them." Her voice sounded empty. Yet her face showed the pain, rage, and disgust she carried inside.

"The Catholic church supported these places? I've never heard of this before." Father Talmano, disturbed by this information, looked at his robe with pained eyes.

"Aye. It is a black moment in Irish history." Bishop O'Malley said.

"Whose? The churches or Ireland's?" Samyn spit the words out.

"Both."

"When it was my time to birth, I begged the nuns not to kill the child or give it away."

"They killed babies there?" Moore turned to Samyn. "I thought Baptist churches had problems with unwed mothers. You guys make us look like saints."

"I can't say for sure if they did. The girls kept there said so and said the multitude of unmarked graves gave evidence of a high infant and birth mother mortality rate." She stopped to breathe, blow her nose, and wipe her tears.

"I begged to keep it. I wanted my baby. I wasn't sure if I would be in a habit again." She paused and looked only at Samyn. "After I told them who fathered my baby, I grew angry, hateful. Why should I be considered the sinner, a whore, when he put me in this position? Shouldn't he be considered as guilty as I? If I had to spend my life trying to atone, then shouldn't he as well?"

Samyn nodded.

"I convinced the mother superior to let me return to my order and bring my child too. She pronounced it a just punishment, for me to be in his sight with the product of our sin growing up before his eyes. So she arranged that I would always be assigned to where he was serving." She wiped the area under her nose and sniffed a little. A small, tight smile formed but didn't last long on her face.

"I guess she had a tremendous pull in the church or was an excellent blackmailer."

Samyn looked at Moore. "You wondered why I hate the church. Now you see. It's the evil, self-serving behaviors they justify for their own, but condemn in others. It's happened since the foundations of the church. It's ingrained in the hierarchy, it will not change."

"Philip, yes the church has done much wrong and yes it has a dark history. None darker I think than in Ireland where it held sway for so long. It was too deeply entrenched in their society. They held the belief the church's actions were always right. That was a mistake and one they are rectifying. The Magdalene Laundries became a lucrative business. More so with the adoptions they did after washing machines became affordable and the chore less labor intensive."

O'Malley looked at Sister Mary Angelina. "I always pondered would the Irish church had been better off if Oswiu had stayed aligned with Celtic Christianity instead of committing to the Roman church."

Samyn leaned forward. "Your baby, you kept it, you raised it somehow in a convent, so is it here now?"

"The story everyone heard was I am the aunt and the last member of the family and had promised my dying sister I would raise her child. Whether it was accepted, I didn't care. Fortunately, I had a baby girl, so raising it amongst other women proved easy. Bishop Newman grew to hate the sight of me, and rightly so, I suppose. I rubbed it in his face every chance I got how we were married in God's eyes and if he took another wife, he would be committing adultery." Her last words overflowed with bitterness.

"Whenever I caught him cozying up to a young woman, nun or not, I reminded him I had proof of his broken vow. If necessary, I would leave my order, insist publicly he take a paternity test, and have him arrested for rape. If I did, then his days of climbing the church's ladder would be over."

"Sister, I admire your guts," Samyn said. To Moore, he said, "I have found someone to like in the Catholic world."

"It wasn't guts. I had decided while in that awful hell run by the church, I would do everything within my power to keep this from happening to another young woman. I promised God if he let me stay in the habit, I would honor my word. And I have tried to do so."

She picked up her cold cup of tea and sipped it while the men reacted to her story.

347

Chapter Fifty-Eight

"Is your daughter here?" Samyn said.

"She is."

"Is she aware of the truth?"

The mother superior put her cup down. She chose her words before she answered.

"No, I considered it best to keep that secret with me. Like everyone else, I told her she was my niece."

"She never suspected you were lying?"

"She's a simple girl. She has a pure heart, tender spirit, is very obedient, but she's not," she struggled to find the next words. "She's not, shall we say, an ardent study?"

The men looked puzzled. "Let me put it like this, she's not the sharpest crayon in a new box or the brightest candle shining in the window."

Their collective responses meant they got her meaning.

"Nothing personal, sister. I get it. You had a hard life in the church and terrible things happened to you, but…" He addressed the bishop now. "Why did you say this applies to my case?"

"Finish, please." O'Malley gestured to the Sister.

"I suspected Bishop Newman to be up to his old tricks again. Only this time it was with my, correction, our daughter."

"What? Didn't he recognize his kid?" Moores' face showed more than his tone said.

"You would have thought he would have noticed how they shared the same nose, but he had never acknowledged her, had never seen her at more than a distance until recently."

The bells chimed, signaling the office of None was to begin. O'Malley looked at his clock. "We should…"

"No, this needs to be finished. I'll go and make a cover story for you both." Father Talmano left before anyone could agree to his proposal.

"You were saying sister he didn't know his daughter." Samyn prompted her to keep talking.

"No, he didn't. To admit to he had a child would have ruined his career, so he agreed to and promoted the farcical story. He stipulated he wanted nothing to do with her and I agreed. I thought it would protect her. He noticed her because she was still a novice, when others had entered into service. But he had no idea she was his."

"I still don't see how…" Samyn started the sentence. Moore finished it. "How he couldn't know he fathered her?"

"Remember, I kept her away from him, and besides his narcissistic side would not see he was less than perfect. Certainly, he never admitted to himself he broke a vow, fathered a child." She stopped and regained control of her emotions.

"He asked me why she had not taken her vows. All I could think was why could he not see the resemblance to him. Instead of pointing out the similarities between them, I explained she had learning difficulties and we were taking this slowly with her."

"I thought he accepted what I said. Then I heard he told another sister he would help teach her how to become a nun." Despite all the tears she shed, her water well had not run dry. Again, rivers of water fell down her face.

"He didn't?" Moore said.

"He tried. I suspected nothing until recently. She wasn't eating well. My mother instinct said something was wrong, but even then, I didn't think he would use his own daughter." Her pain was clear to all in the room. "I followed her the other morning. She went to the cathedral. When she entered into a confession box, I headed upstairs to the walkway over the apse. I eavesdropped on her confession."

"Did she poison the priest? Did she say that?"

"Not exactly. She is not smart. She wouldn't have any clue where to get a toxin or how to poison someone." She pleaded for understanding from the officers.

" She was upset over what had occurred between them before his death. She said she worried about his going to sleep before she could do as she promised. She was afraid she would not be forgiven by God for not doing her wifely duty. Either someone told her it was wrong or maybe she figured it out, I don't know. In the box, she said she may have sinned because she promised him she would marry him if he did something for her first. He did what she asked him and then he died." She took in a breath, held it, released it, and repeated the process before continuing her story.

" She doesn't know he was her father. She only knew him as a man in holy orders." She switched from pleading to begging.

"What did she ask him to do, Sister?" Samyn said without emotion.

The mother superior ignored his question.

"He had told her the same lies he used on me and others. They were married to the church, so they were married to each other and must consummate their union."

She sucked in a long draft of air and reached for her tea. Her hands were shaking so much she couldn't grasp the handle. The teacup tumbled to the floor. "I'm sorry. I'm sorry."

Bishop O'Malley rose. "I'll clean it up." He smiled at her "It's okay, sister. It's only tea. I've made bigger messes for others to deal with. Wiping up tea, I can handle with ease."

She placed a pat of gratitude on his sleeve before he moved away. He glanced down at where she had patted. She noticed his action and cut her eyes to his face. "That's twice today that I've patted an arm. Forgive me, I'm not myself."

His mouth stretched itself. "No need to apologize sister. Excuse me, I need to get towels."

She drew her cheeks in, then let out a quiet chuckle.

When Bishop O'Malley returned, he placed the paper towels on the rug and extracted from his robe a flask. "Here sister. This may calm your nerves better than Irish tea."

She grabbed it; grateful he understood how sometimes whiskey for medicinal purposes was necessary, even if it meant the partaking of it inside a church. She tilted it up and swallowed a very generous amount before she handed it back. "Thank you."

"Better now?"

She nodded.

"Then continue please."

"I'm sorry. I'm still shaken from what I heard her say." She took a few minutes to compose herself. "She worried it may be wrong, what he said she must do. So she asked another young nun if she too had married the priest, and if it was right for her to do so when she hadn't worn her wedding gown and veil and married the church yet?" The nun breathed in again.

"I don't know if the other nun told anyone about that conversation or not. My daughter asked him if he was sure it was the right thing to do and her beloved father said to trust him. He would never lead her astray." Her face had been pointing towards the floor. She raised it to see their expressions.

Another pause so she could breathe. "She said she felt better and agreed she would do her duty. She trusted him to guide her on her journey. What troubles her now is what happens since she can't keep her promise and was it her fault he died? She's worried she made the tea she asked him to drink too strong, worried that more was wrong than an upset stomach and she didn't help him, worried about what happens when a person dies and a promise is not kept to them?"

"That sounds like a semi-confession to guilt, not just a guilty conscience. Sounds like she knew she poisoned the tea she gave him."

"Please, she wouldn't do that. She's not hateful enough to do that." The mother tiger came out of her now. "She couldn't have killed him."

"But she has a motive. She had an opportunity. That's all we need to arrest her." Samyn said. His voice said he wasn't convinced it was this novice nun, though. Something wasn't adding up to him.

"We will need to talk to her." This time he spoke firmly.

"Yes, yes, I figured you would. I sent her to her room and told her to wait there."

Samyn's finger tapped against his leg. He and Moore faced each other. Again they held a mental conversation. Their facial expressions were the only clue to what they were saying. Samyn hung his head when it had ended.

"Sister, thank you for telling us this. You did not have too, you know." Samyn's words did not offer the compassion he had for her.

"I know."

"Were you informed of this?" Samyn said to the bishop.

"Not everything. I sensed there wasn't something she wasn't telling me when she requested the nun be sent to a new home."

Samyn waited, but O'Malley said nothing else. Neither did the mother superior.

"What is the name of this novice who's done justice without meaning too?" Samyn raised his eyebrows.

"My daughter, Sister Julian."

Chapter Fifty-Nine

The officers, mother superior, and Bishop O'Malley left the building. They walked silently to the convent. The mother superior opened the door and invited them in.

"Quiet please, It is our time of silence ." She paused. "Also it is not customary for men to be in our house."

She pointed to the center hall and gestured for them to follow. She took them up the back stairwell since it was closet to Sister Julian's room.

Samyn noticed the sparseness of the house. Every piece of furniture had a purpose. No extra tables, no empty bookcase, and no decorative what- nots or knick-knacks taking up space. It was a house that reflected the order's vow of simplicity, of having only what you need only in your life, nothing more.

Necessary wooden furniture in various design styles decorated the spaces. The mostly bare walls, painted a soft gray, added to the simpleness of the house's atmosphere. Samyn spotted many candles sitting on the tables and in wall scones. As the house was an older one, he looked for and spied no overhead light fixtures, only a few floor lamps. Near the end of the hall was a staircase painted matte black. Sister Mary Angelina pointed up. They followed obediently as she climbed the stairs at a pace slower than one normally would.

When she got to the top, she hung her head. Samyn could have rushed her, but he tried putting himself in her shoes. *Would he want to hand his kid over for questioning to a couple of detectives?* He decided he would not.

He had no idea how long they stood there. It seemed like an infinite amount of time had passed when in reality it was barely three minutes. He was pulling his sleeve down over his watch when she moved again, quicker now, determined to finish this.

At the second door on the right, she tapped lightly. A young girl, dressed in novice attire minus the hair piece, opened the door. Her large blue eyes grew bigger when she saw more than the mother superior.

She stepped back, not sure if she should gesture them in or bow. She couldn't ask as it was silent time. Her lovely face scrunched up in confusion. The mother superior gave her a half-smile and nodded that it was okay. Sister Julian bid them to enter with her hands.

The bishop was last in, so he closed the door. The mother superior approached Sister Julian and whispered in her ear.

"These gentlemen are here for your help. It is all right to answer their questions."

Lieutenant Samyn introduced himself and Sargent Moore.

"We need to ask you about Bishop Newman." He squatted down in front of her.

"Is it because you can't ask him?" Her blue eyes showed her innocence.

"No, It's because you have the answers we need."

She nodded. Her eyes stayed enormous, whether from fright, worry, or innocence, Samyn wasn't sure.

"Why did he die? Did I make the tea too strong? I was trying to make him better."

"Why do you think he wasn't well?"

"He told me."

Samyn forced himself to be patient and gentle, but her answers were not informative. It feltlike he was pulling teeth. He had this same sensation when guilty suspects dodged his questions. Only he grasped she wasn't trying to withhold any-thing. *This kid's a complete simpleton.* He under-stood why the mother superior insisted she couldn't have knowingly poisoned Bishop Newman.

"When did he tell you that?"

"The last time I was in his room."

She's the type of witness a defense attorney loves. One that gives vague, concise answers. He bit the inside of his jaw before he asked the next question.

"Can you tell me about that? Was it daytime or at night?"

"It was at night. At lunch, he told me to come to his room after Compline. I did, and he asked if I was still poorly. I told him a little still."

"Had you been ill?"

"No. I just didn't feel good. Father Brien said I was not sick. He said I was just tired because I wasn't sleeping well, and that my tummy hurt because I wasn't eating. He said it was because I was upset about not being made a bride yet, but I shouldn't worry."

"Did you tell Bishop Newman what Father Brien said?"

"I did, and he patted my hand and said then that's what was wrong."

"Did he say anything else, do anything?" Samyn wanted this to end soon. He was antsy. His gut was saying she was guilty, but he knew they could never charge her with a crime that would not be exposed.

"He asked me if I told Sister Mary Katherine about our talks and me becoming a wife. I told him I asked her if it was okay to be a wife before becoming a bride. He said why did I do that? And I told him it was because she was always so kind and patient and helpful to me, I trust her because she's my friend." She looked at the mother superior, who was trying hard not to cry.

"Oh no, Did I get Mary Kat in trouble? Was I not supposed to ask her? Should I have asked you?" Sister Julien's face rolled with despairing emotions.

"No child, she's not in trouble and it's okay to talk with someone you trust. It doesn't always have to just be me you confide in." The mother superior gave the saddest smile to the innocent girl. "Now finish your story for these gentlemen, please. They need to hear everything from you."

The novice nodded and stood straight, like a student giving a speech. "He gave me some tea leaves to take with me. He said it would make me well. Then he sent me back to my room. He said he wasn't feeling good. He had a tummy ache. He told me to make a cup of tea before I went to bed and drink it all and in the morning I would be better."

"Did you make a cup of tea when you got back to the convent."

"I did, but I took it to him. I thought if his tummy hurts, then this would help him too."

Samyn had kept his focus on sister Julien. He now switched it. He leaned back on his heels, released the air he had been unintentionally holding, and looked at Moore, then sister Mary Angelina. "Did he drink the tea?" He shifted his gaze to Sister Julian as he spoke the last word.

"Yes sir, after I said I wouldn't leave until he had drank it. He told me to go, but I wanted him to drink the tea and get better, so I promised him I would do my wifely duty tomorrow if he drank it in front of me. He didn't want to, but when he sniffed it he said it was ok."

"What did it smell like?" Sister Mary Angelina asked.

"Mint. I put fresh mint in it. I thought that was the herb you used to make your tummy better. Did I do wrong?"

"No child. You did right." She smiled at Sister Julian, who beamed because of the praise.

"Will you show me the tea he gave you?" The mother superior asked.

Sister Julian pulled a box out from under her bed. She took a small paper bag out and dutifully handed it to the mother superior, who opened it and sniffed. She handed it to the bishop, who smelled the contents.

"Smells like Anise to me." He said.

O'Malley passed the package to Moore, who read the label. He pulled out his phone and typed the name into google. He scrolled down the list that popped up on his screen and picked one. Samyn watched Moore's head make the brief movements it always made when he was reading to himself. When finished, he handed the phone to Samyn.

Samyn read through it twice. He asked Moore if he remembered the name of the toxin listed on the ME's report.

"Anisatin."

"Can I take this tea with me Sister?" Samyn looked at the novice.

"Is it not good for me?" Her big eyes got larger, bluer.

"No," Samyn said the single word as gentle as it was possible for him to do.

Sister Julian looked at the ground. She twisted her fingers. Her head dropped so that her short, bobbed hair fell forward. "Is it what made the other bishop die?" Before she finished her question, her shoulders started twitching, and her breath grew ragged.

Samyn hated crying females. He had never handled emotional female scenes well. How to deal with a crying nun was too far out of his normal uncomfortable zone. He stood there, unsure whether to pat her shoulder or ignore the tears. Hugs were rarely given by him and one wouldn't be offered now. He learned as a child; you don't hug nuns, even if they were only penguins in training.

"Maybe. I need to test it to find out."

"Take it then." She pushed her hands out. "I didn't want him to die. I only wanted him to get better." Water kept falling down her cheeks. She looked at the mother superior. "I messed up again, didn't I?" Her tears flowed forcefully now. She looked at the bishop. "Did I break a commandment? I didn't mean to."

"Don't fret, child. We'll talk about this later but I don't think you did, To break a commandment you need intent, and you had no intent this time."

"Hey sister, I agree with the bishop about the intent thing. Don't you cry about that, all right?" Moore said. He fished a tissue out of his pocket and held it out to her. She uttered thank you and wiped her face. The serenity on his face expressed she was welcome.

"I told him I was sorry. I didn't mean to hurt him. I keep telling him. Do you think he forgives me?"

Before anyone could answer, the mother superior spoke. "We can talk about that later. Why don't you go to the middle school now? It's time for the choir to rehearse. Brother Tim needs you to play the piano." The mother superior clamped her hand over her mouth. "I forgot to have someone finish your task today. The music didn't get changed, I'm sorry. I'll talk to him later and explain."

"Wait a minute, I have one more question. Where are you when you ask him to forgive you? Are you in the chapel? Your room?"

"I go every night to his coffin. I take off the cover, say I'm sorry. The first time, I was so upset, I fell against the lid and it moved. That's how I found out I could open it." She smiled like a proud child who had figured out a difficult problem.

"Sister Sustina told me I should cut his hair and take his ring and bring them to her. She said if I wanted to be forgiven, I needed to make a doll with his things, and stop going to his grave. She said the dead can't talk anymore, but a…" She wrinkled her face then shook her head. 'I forgot what she called it but she said it would be better to ask it to forgive me than a smelly old corpse."

Samyn looked at O'Malley then the mother. "Who is Sister Sustina?"

"The oldest nun in our home. She was born in Jamaica and came to us from New Orleans. She suffers from mental lapses, confusion, because of age. She'll be 102 her next birthday."

"Sounds like she's combined voodoo with Catholicism," Samyn said.

"Sounds like she's a Creole." Moore's eyes twinkled. He had family in New Orleans who practiced both. The lights in his eyes went out with his next sentence. "Be thankful she didn't combine your faith with Santeria. That's some bad juju."

"Did you see anyone else down there?" Samyn looked at Sister Julian.

"I saw a two ghosts last night. They tried to grab me. I think they were angry at me for taking his ring, but I wasn't stealing it." She rubbed her arm.

" I only wanted to know he forgave me if it was my fault he died. I kept the ring safe." She reached under her pillow. In her palm was a ring. It was Bishop Newman's standard, the ring Father Talmano pointed out as missing from his hand, the first time the officers came to church.

"What did you do when you saw these ghosts?" Moore said.

"I got scared. The first one grabbed me when I was trying to cut more hair. I didn't get enough the last time."

"Did you have a knife or scissors?" Samyn said.

"A small knife, a student gave me. He taught me to whittle. I like whittling. I couldn't find my sewing scissors, so I took my knife, but I lost it when the ghosts came after me."

No one spoke. Samyn tapped his leg. He watched O'Malley who was rubbing his face with his right hand while mouthing the words, "Jesus, Mary and Joseph."

"I told Bishop Newman I wasn't finished with his ring yet but it was safe and I was just getting more hair." She smiled at the Bishop. "I felt better after I did that. I didn't like taking his hair without permission."

"Let's talk about the ghosts. What did you do after one grabbed you?" Samyn prompted.

"I was scared, so I hit it and then ran to the steps, but that's where another one grabbed me. He hit me on my arm and my wrist. It hurt me. I struggled but got away. I haven't been back since."

She offered the ring to Bishop O'Malley. "Can you please take this back? I think Sister Sustina told me a story because I don't think it worked. I didn't feel forgiven after I made the doll," She took the bishop's sleeve and leaned in close to his ear. "I felt forgiven after I did confession."

He took the ring from her. Then he suggested she do as the mother superior had asked and help at school.

Sister Julien obediently left the room. Samyn stared at the bag of tea. He could use Blake right now. That kid would have already found out everything about this item. He shook some out onto his palm. "Does this look like tea to you?"

"It could pass for loose leaf tea if the person looking at it wasn't a tea connoisseur," O'Malley said.

"Would fresh mint overpower the anise scent?" Moore said.

"Maybe, probably since mint when freshly ground is strong," O'Malley said.

"Which would explain why he smelled it first and then agreed to drink it," Samyn said. He stretched. This intense session made his muscles cramped and tight. They got this same way when he was in a squatting position for too long or had done too many chest presses at the gym. He looked at Moore. "We have something to do." He turned his palms up in submission.

Moore rose up. He had been sitting on the bed while he took notes. "True dat."

They headed to the door. The mother superior laid her hand on Samyn's arm.   "Are you going to arrest her?"

"For what?"

"Some kind of murder charge."

Samyn shrugged. "I can I guess."

"Will you?"

"Why would I do that? Like the bishop said, she needed intent, and she had none and like you said, she's an innocent. Besides, she's a hero in my book for taking care of a church problem."

"What about for the attack on your officer?"

"I don't think so. Again intent and I'm not sure the district attorney could make a case nor would they want to go up against the church's attorneys. The eventual answer though lies with the person who was injured. He'll have to decide whether he wants to press charges."

The mother superior nodded. "Thank you. I always blamed the months I spent in the laundry around toxic chemicals, and the sparse food they feed us for her mental disabilities."

"You should see them more a savior. Your former bishop wanted her dead." He stopped for her to grasp what the real intent of that was.

"I'm guessing he thought the nun Sister Julien talked too would tell you, mother, or the bishop, about his plan to deflower another virgin. If his intended victim was sacrificed, then anything this other nun said would only be heresy, which doesn't go far in your legal system or ours. He purposely gave Sister Julien a toxin found in dried Japanese Star Anise leaves and told her it was tea." Samyn's words were heavy with disgust and anger. His bitterness towards the church was not held back.

"Do you realize he would have killed her to keep anyone from finding out how he abuses nuns? He may have come for you next, mother. You knew he had fathered a child, your child. What if you found out he manipulated another young girl into having sex with him and it was with his daughter? A childish girl who would have spoken in innocence to anyone about what he did to her?" He let the implications of what could have happened sink in.

He spat the next words towards the bishop. "Just what the church needs, isn't it? One more priest who's not so holy."

He turned to the mother. This time his words had less bitterness, more sorrow." One more kid stuck in an orphanage. One more girl sent to one of your laundries."

Bishop O'Malley defended his faith.

"That would not happen now. The last of the laundries closed in 1996. If she had gotten pregnant, I would have followed the guidelines set up by the Irish Catholic church in 2017 for taking care of any child fathered by a priest."

"Are you saying you guys are in the habit of breaking your vows? Or is it just you Catholic Irishmen that are randy? Are Roman Catholics better at keeping their word or are Irish Protestants?" Samyn let all his bottled up hatred out.

"You need not be such a jackass," O'Malley said. His lilt was in full mode. "The Vatican established its guidelines this year. We Irish admitted we were human and make mistakes first."

"Then if there were this plan to take care of any child, he fathered, why did he try to kill this kid?"

"You don't know that he did. He may have had an allergic reaction to it."

O'Malley's Jesuit training was showing. He used logic to refute Samyn's statements.

"No, he's right." The mother superior's voice interrupted their debate. "Newman trained to be a chemist before he became a priest. He would have known the difference between Chinese Star Anise which is non-toxic and the poisonous Japanese Anise which is used as a natural pesticide. I know that because of my scientific studies. As a holy man, he had knowledge its used by Buddhists who consider it a sacred incense and would ask where they get it."

She faced Moore and Samyn. "He wanted to kill her because she spoke to another nun about his wanting wifely duties from her. I find joy in that Julien used his weapon against him and did so without malice. May his soul rot in hell forever." She emphasized her last words.

"Mother, I think we agree on that." Samyn said.

He and Moore left. They had one more thing to do today.

Chapter Sixty

At the station, they walked in together. "Ready to do this?" Samyn asked Moore.

"If you are," Moore said.

The captain was in his office staring at a pack of cigarettes. "Look at who it is, Golden Boy and his sidekick who can walk. What did you find out about Blake's attacker?"

"Nothing yet. No witnesses." Samyn said.

"Then why are you here, not out working this case?"

"It's Friday, remember."

"So it is. But it doesn't matter. Blake can't do this job now and may never be able to, so he'll be given to the cybercrime division. Nothing wrong with his head or hands, and they need help. So Moore gets to keep his. Congratulations, sidekick."

Samyn and Moore looked at each other. They grinned. Both would enjoy this. Simultaneously, they reached into their inner pockets and withdrew their badges. They laid them down on Martin's desk. Next they pulled their weapons from their holsters and placed them next to the badges. In unison, they slide everything towards him.

"What's this? Get your junk off my desk."

"Do it yourself," Samyn said.

"You can't talk to me like that."

"I think we can, captain," Moore said. He grinned. "Go ahead golden boy and tell him why."

Samyn said no. "We're a team. We do things together."

"True dat."

"Shall we?"

Moore affirmed with a headshake. "We put in papers this morning."

"Golden boy and sidekick are retiring," Samyn added salt to Martins's wound.

Martin threw the cigarettes across the room. "You can't do that."

"All ready did it," Samyn said. He opened the office door.

"After you sidekick."

"You first golden boy."

They walked out of the office. Others in the department had heard part of the conversation. Not all of it, but enough to piece together what had happened. Several came up and shook their hands.

"We'll be back later to collect our personal items," Moore said. They left the building with no regrets.

"Damn, that felt better than I thought it would," Samyn said.

"Where to now, boss?"

They opted to go see Blake. He was in sitting up in bed looking tired and pale.   "Are you ok?" Samyn said.

He shrugged. "I had an intense therapy session. I'm a little tired."

"Any good news?" Moore asked.

Blake looked sheepish. "If you mean have I done the research you wanted, then not really. I'm sorry. This PT is a killer. I keep pushing to do more."

"No problem, rookie. I meant about you though." Moore grinned.

"They'll do another test tomorrow and see if any healing is happening. My PT person said I may not see a change for a few weeks, but I need to keep working on getting my legs moving again. She doesn't think I'll be walking in a month. She's hoping in two, though."

"We found out a few things today." Samyn changed the subject.

Moore and Samyn alternated telling the story they had heard.

"Are you going to arrest her?" Blake asked.

"That's a good question, rookie," Moore said.

"It may be hard to do," Samyn said.

"Is it because of the church and it's reach? I can see the DA not wanting to fight their attorneys forever." Blake said.

"No, but you make a valid point. They have the money to tie it up in court for years."

"Did Martin say you can't charge her?"

"Nope. We told him we had no idea of who the attacker could be." Samyn said.

"Is that why aren't you going to make an arrest?"

"He'll find out, so might as well spill it, boss," Moore said.

"It's no longer within our power to arrest people." They fist-bumped.

Blake looked at both men. They grinned over his puzzlement.

"I was told the headcount needed to be reduced within the department. So we retired today." Samyn said.

"Don't worry about your job. Cybercrime needs some help. Martin said you'll be placed there if nothing changes."

Blake nodded. "I guess that's good. I wouldn't want to stay in investigations without you. Office wouldn't be the same." He didn't sound convincing. "What are you going to do now?"

"I don't know about this old man, but I'm going fishing," Moore said.

"What am I going to do now?" Samyn said more to himself than to the others. He thought about it. It had never occurred to him he should some plan for what would be the next phase of his life? Did he want to still work? Did he want to become some old guy that hung out all day at a waffle house? *What do I want to do?*

"I think right now what I will do is get a piece of pie. Want to join me?"

"Only if you're buying," Moore said.

"Me? Why should I buy? I did a noble thing today. You should treat me."

"What did you do that justifies me spending my now limited money on you?"

Samyn smirked. "I could have arrest Sister Julian and charged her with second degree murder, assault on an officer, but I decided not to, For the first time in my career, I chose not to close a case."

Blake looked baffled. "What do you mean? You said a case against her would drag out in a court so don't you consider that closed?"

Only partially. I told the captain; I had no idea who attacked you and as there weren't any witnesses coming forth..." He shrugged. "Since I am now retired, well I won't be trying to find your attacker, and as I didn't make a case report..." This time a shrug and head shake.

"Oh yeah, I see." Blake didn't sound like he accepted this.

"Look kid, you're still a cop and you're the victim. You have knowledge about your attacker. You can press charges against her. You can decide if she should be turned over to the court system. I'm leaving this in your hands, kid. I know you'll do what's right."

Blake thought this over. "You've given me something to think about while I recover."

"Focus on making a recovery first. Then you can decide has she already been punished by life or not. It's your choice. Just remember she didn't intend to hurt a person, only the ghost that scared her." He slapped Blake's leg.

Samyn looked at Moore. "I hear a piece of pie calling my name. Are you coming or not?"

"I'm in."

"I'll check on you tomorrow, kid."

"Call if you need anything," Moore added as they made their way to the door.

Blake slumped back on his pillow.

"Are you all right?" Moore noticed Blake's weary face.

All this talk on top of his PT had worn him out. "Eat a piece of pie for me, ok. I'd go with you, but sleep sounds better right now." He was snoring before Moore or Samyn could respond.

Moore cocked his head towards the bed. "You gotta admit, the kid's got spunk or you influenced him more than we knew."

Samyn shook his head no. "He had it in him." He hit the light switch on his way out. "He'll need it to survive if he stays with the department. The world has changed a lot since we were rookies."

"True dat. Let's get us some pie." Moore pulled out his phone. "'Lo Tess, it's cousin Mel. What kinda pie are you serving today? Sounds good. Save a couple of slices of the blueberry, peach, and that coconut one. Samyn and I are on our way to get them."

He put away his phone and started whistling "Blueberry Hill".

Samyn chuckled and kept walking. After nearly thirty years of being a cop, his pie was waiting and he was hungry.

Chapter Sixty-One

"So, what about Sister Julian? Do you still want her reassigned?" Father Seamus O'Malley and Sister Mary Angelina were sharing a pot of tea in his private office. They had left their titles outside in the hall.

"I'm not sure, perhaps not." Mary Angelina took a sip and sighed. "When I first heard her confession, it threw me. All I could think was he was up to his old ways again and this time with his daughter. I could see her making the same mistake I had. I was aware what happened between Newman and myself was wrong, Julian would have been like a lamb going to slaughter." She cringed hard enough to shake the cup in her hand. She waited for a few minutes before she spoke again.

"Seamus, was it a mistake not to let her be adopted as an infant? Was I wrong not to let the church sell her to an American family?" She leaned forward and looked at him with pleading eyes. She desperately needed reassurance that she hadn't compounded her mistake so many years ago.

"I don't know." It was the only answer he could give. "I do know it was wrong of the church not to have dealt with him when you named him as the father. The church isn't aware of this, but for years I had been gathering information on Newman. All those young girls who were sent from the orphanage left impregnated by him. The three nuns who were assigned elsewhere had complained to the mother about his predatory behavior. One lodged an abuse claim against him, but nothing happened." He sipped his tea and adjusted in his seat. "I guess it was easier to move the nuns somewhere else than to take on the hierarchy regarding a rising star. But it was wrong."

Despite their inner turmoil's, the room breathed peace. Each sat drinking from their cups in silence. The clock ticked like a metronome, keeping the pace while reflections played in their heads. Seamus broke the calm.

"Will you tell Julian you are her mother, birth mother I mean?"

"Should I?" Mary Angelina placed her cup on the table holding the teapot. She crossed her legs. Her body swayed in time to the clock ticks. Her clapping hands made no sound. She gave Seamus a small, sad smile.

"What good would it do? I'm positive it would confuse her, scare her even. Definitely, it would make her question are any of us what we claim to be?" She poured more tea in her cup. "May I?" She held the pot toward him.

"Please." He offered his cup. "I think you have made a wise decision. Prepare yourself, however."

"For?" She gave him her direct intimidating gaze that scared others.

The woman in front of him had weathered much. She was strong, a force that wore resilience as a shield, but he was ready for battle. He stood so she would have to look up to him.

"You need to know there will be some trying times to come."

She smirked. "As if there had been none before?"

Seamus walked over to his desk and picked up a paper. "You should read this." He put it in her outstretched hand.

Mary Angelina skimmed the page. She looked at him and then read it again. This time when she finished, her body was shaking with rage. She slammed her cup on the table and leaped up.

"Jesus, Joseph, and Mary." Her Irish lilt was unfettered. "In the name of all that is Holy, what were they thinking? Aye, don't tell me they weren't thinking, the bloody stupid Catholic church."

She paced and ranted. Seamus did what any wise Irishman would; He kept his tongue still.

When she noticed he hadn't responded, she got in front of him. "Seamus, what are you going to do? Ya canna let this happen."

He looked down on her face. "I know." Although he was over six feet in height with broad muscular shoulders leftover from his athletic days, the five-foot two-inch woman in front of him diminished his size.

"Well, glory be you know, you say, but that hasn't answered my question. What are you," she pointed at his face, "going to do to stop this blatant act of lunacy?" There was no denying the rage and hurt rolling inside her at this moment.

"I emailed to the archbishop, the abbot, and those above me at the Vatican several days ago summarizing what had happened here and at other places where Newman had been assigned. I suggested every effort be made to find the victims and see to their needs. That was their response."

"This is not right. Once again, they are covering up the sins of their princes. And you telling them to pay blood money to his found victims isn't exactly the act of a brave man." She glared. "You're guilty of helping them believe money makes things better."

"I understand money, even theirs, doesn't make things better, and I never said pay the victims to keep quiet. I said for the church to pay for any counseling these ladies need, to show their remorse in letting him stay in a robe, to do what was right, admit the sin, and ask for forgiveness." His voice which started off soft grew louder and more forceful with each uttered syllable.

Mary Angelina shrank a little now. "I see."

Each fighter retreated to the corners. They regained their composure and met in the center again.

"Have they really convinced themselves that setting him on the road to sainthood will keep his deeds from becoming known?"

"Yes, I suppose they did It takes years to become beatified. By then the victims may be dead or too old to come forward." Seamus walked to the window. He looked out onto the grounds of the church garden. "Usually they have a priest go into retirement. The out of sight, out of mind trick. It looks like they decided to sweep away their wrongs in a different way now. One that people aren't expecting and will accept without question, I suppose."

"So what are you going to do with the truth?"

"I'm holding a press conference tomorrow and releasing the evidence I have against Bishop

Newman. Did I tell you I found he had nicked money from parishes? Not much, still…" He turned away from the window. "I may be defrocked for my actions, but it's the right thing to do."

He went to retrieve the paper still in Mary Angelina's hands. "Not all priests are bad, only a few have tarnished the coat of trust and faith the church wears. When I took this position, I promised myself I would all I could to right wrongs within the walls. Priests and nuns are only human, and all humans fall sometimes in their spiritual walk. They need to be picked up and guided back to the path, not have their falls ignored." He took the paper and placed it on his desk.

"You can't believe Newman had any good in him, can you?"

O'Malley turned around. "No. He was a classic narcissist, and possibly an abuse survivor himself or someone who felt love only comes from sex. He convinced himself he had no flaws, and all he did was right. I met in him our early days. He was haughty, scheming, and thought the church was his oyster and he could enjoy it any way he wanted. Like all schemers and connivers, he kissed every butt he could to keep from working hard, but still get the praise."

"Are you going to tell how he died?"

"The Almighty took care of the problem. Newman learned he was not the one in charge. Why should that be told? No, I will only state the evidence that shows he seduced several women and even though he cannot be brought up on charges, the church will make Penance for him. This time it will not hide wrongs behind robes."

Mary Angelina walked to the door. "I will stand with you if you wish. I've carried my dirty laundry for too long. It's time to leave it in the hamper or clean it."

O'Malley opened the door for her. "Thank you sister, but I will fight tomorrow alone. After that, you may have to tell your story. For now, tell the nuns what is coming and let them know whoever needs to may come to you with no fear of judgment."

She assented. "I will speak with my charges tonight and wash my laundry with them." She took a step out and stopped. "When the dust settles from this, and there will be dust since the media loves a good story, I suspect there will be ones in Rome who will wish they had never meddled with an Irishman, and more so should an Irish woman have to battle with him." She shot him an impish look and left.

Seamus laughed at her comment and began tidying the area where they had their tea. When finished, he sat at his desk, read from the book, *Hebridean Altars*, and meditated. When done, he opened his laptop and began preparing his notes for the press conference. Tomorrow, things would change in the church, and possibly with his priesthood. Recently he had been reminded, confession was good for the soul. He hoped his confession tomorrow would start the long overdue healing needed by all.

Chapter Sixty-Two

Samyn and Moore were in Blake's hospital room when the breaking news signal sounded on their phones and the television. Blake picked up his phone. Samyn ignored his and turned to the tv screen. Moore glanced at the television while he fumbled for his phone.

"Why that son of a gun... He did it. He really did it."

Moore shifted his gaze to Samyn. He had never heard him sound this excited before.

"Hey kid, are you watching this? Turn it up." Samyn tapped Blake's leg.

"I'm reading it on my phone." He tossed the remote to Moore.

Moore caught it, hit the volume up button, all while shaking his head in surprise.

"Well boss, he said he wouldn't let this get shoved under a desk."

On the screen was Bishop Seamus O'Malley standing in front of St. Stephens Cathedral with microphones positioned in near his mouth. Scrolling across the bottom were the words, *Another priest accused. Bishop Seamus O'Malley claims he has proof deceased Bishop Newman abused nuns and adolescent girls during his priesthood.*

"Oh, yeah." Samyn clapped his hands and fist-bumped Moore. "Yes!" Samyn continued exclaiming his exuberance. "It will cost him, but man, oh man,…" He kept shaking his head.

"It might cost you, too." Moore looked at Blake.

Blake scrunched up his face. "What do you mean?"

"If you file charges against the young nun who injured you, well, lawyers and reporters may want to tie it to this fresh scandal. If they do, then it could be revealed Newman was her father."

Blake let his head bob up and down in a slow, controlled motion. "I can see that happening."

"She's a good girl. Simple, innocent in nature, and one who has no idea who her parents are. He had planned to make her his next victim. When he found out she asked another nun about his marriage idea, he decided to kill her. Instead, she used his poison against him, never knowing it would end his life." Moore let Blake dwell on that for a minute.

"Do you want that kid to find out her father wanted to kill her to keep his secret lifestyle going?" He paused and waited for Blake to respond. Blake kept quiet.

"Is bringing her up on charges worth the emotional and mental harm it will do to her?"

"A month ago my answer would have been yes. Now, I'm not sure, but probably not." Blake patted his leg. "This incident has made me realize how something can be taken so easily from you. I've gotten to experience life in a wheelchair and how much hard work goes into therapy." He grinned.

"My upper body strength is improving, and I have gotten some feeling in my toes." His grin retreated.

"I've also learned that being right all the time and showing your right isn't so important."

"Excellent lesson. O'Malley learned too apparently. Never thought I'd see the day someone in the church confess it had sinners in robes," Samyn said. Most of his attention was still on the TV screen and what was happening with Seamus O'Malley at the church. "Kid, that's a miracle happening." He pointed to the TV. "Way to go O'Malley."

"As long as you learn rookie when to do right, which is always. When to be right, which is never with your significant other, unless you're agreeing with her. Always let your better half have the last word. Happy spouse, happy house. So what's going on with Clarissa?"

"Did I hear my name?" The smiling face of the young lady Blake was interested in peeked in the room.

"That answers my question." Moore tapped Samyn's shoulder. "Hey boss, we need to get out of here. Rookie's got better company to keep now."

Moore shifted his eyes towards the door. Samyn sneaked a look and saw Clarissa standing in the doorway holding a pizza box. "Yeah, we need to go, and do something. How about lunch?"

Moore turned Samyn towards the door. "As long as you're buying." He winked at Blake. "Later Rookie."

"After seeing Seamus live up to his word and renewing my faith in mankind, I'll happily treat you. See you around, kid."

Samyn tipped his head at Clarissa as he walked out. Moore pointed his thumb at the bed and pushed her in the room with his head. He whistled, "Always and Forever," on his way out. It was the song he and his Shirley danced to the night they met. He smiled, remembering that night. It got bigger as he thought about the life ahead of them.

"What are you grinning about?" Samyn said.

"Hey, I say we grab some sandwiches, and go fishing."

Samyn punched the elevator button. "Sounds like a plan."

The doors opened. Samyn and Moore stepped into the next phase of their lives.

Author Notes

Throughout Christian history, there have been times of darkness. The Magdalene Laundries, run by four religious orders (The Sisters of Mercy, The Sisters of Our Lady of Charity, The Sisters of Charity, and The Good Shepherd Sisters) and the Mother and Baby homes are apart of the Irish church's dark past.

Survivors have come forward with their stories, and excavations at the properties, such as the one in Tuam, have opened secrets. Steps have been taken to right the wrongs that occurred behind the doors of these institutions.

The movie Penelope, starring Dame Judy Dench, made me aware of what happened to a young unwed mother or fallen woman in the country where my maternal grandmother came from. Dame Judy's performance moved me to think about crafting a story about these places. My personal history made me thankful I did not live there in my youth.

The story grew when I researched more into the Irish Church's past and present. I read several interviews, listened to testimonies from women, both nuns and parishioners, who had been in sexual relationships with priests. I also heard the stories of a few women who had been in the laundries and some who were in the Mother and Baby homes. So while this book is fiction, it is rooted in history.

Abuses have happened in every religious denominations, not just the Catholic faith. Only the Catholic Church's male victims have been talked about in the media.

Bad things happen, but beauty can be painted from the ashes left behind if a victim chooses to become a survivor and forgives instead of seeking to destroy.

I want to say a special thank you to author A.J, McCarthy who gave me her thoughts on the very rough first draft. It was her critique that inspired me to work through the flaws and reshape the book. She showed me how to paint beauty from those ashes.

My friend and beta reader, Coreen, confirmed A.J.'s comments without saying a word. Her lack of response said, "make me want to read it." So Thank you, Coreen. I hope I have fulfilled your unspoken request.

Actions always speak louder than words, not only on a page but in life as well.

www.ingramcontent.com/pod-product-compliance
Lightning Source LLC
Chambersburg PA
CBHW051156190726

48288CB00006B/1681

BE THE FIRST TO KNOW...

Want more heat, heart,
and bad boys who know what they're doing?
Join my list and I'll send the steam straight to your inbox,
starting with a deliciously naughty story: